Accrual Way To Die

An Audrey Wilson Mystery

Accrual Way To Die

An Audrey Wilson Mystery

C.M. Miller

Writers Club Press
San Jose New York Lincoln Shanghai

Accrual Way To Die
An Audrey Wilson Mystery

Writers Club Press
an imprint of iUniverse, Inc.

For information address:
iUniverse, Inc.
5220 S. 16th St., Suite 200
Lincoln, NE 68512
www.iuniverse.com

Cover art by El Jones © 2001
Artofel@AOL.com

ISBN: 0-595-19165-7

Printed in the United States of America

I dedicate this book to you. Your support is deeply appreciated. Contact me at corasbks@compaq.net with feedback.

Epigraph

God save me from my friends. I can protect myself from my enemies—Marshal de Villars

Acknowledgements

For as long as I can remember I've started and ended each day by thanking God. HE never fails.

Publishing **Taxes, Death, & Trouble** was the fulfillment of a lifelong dream. I've received encouragement and support in so many ways from so many people. Please forgive me if you are not mentioned here by name.

My husband, Prentice "put down that magazine and pick up this book" Miller for selling my book to people who can't even read. To my brothers, sisters, nieces, nephews and my son, Brian for helping to spread the word. To list them all would take another book. To Count and Cora Collins who believe in family above all else.

Michelle Curney Willis for hosting the most beautiful Southeastern book party for the release of **TD&T**. To Jan Toler for the classiest book launch party in all of Ohio. Special thanks to Tom Carroll.

To Benita Price and WAIF Radio, Jim Knippenburg at the Cincinnati Enquirer, The Literary Police and RAWSISTAZ bookclubs. Alan Caruba (check out Bookviews.com!), Blackbookshelf.com, The Detroit Writer's Guild, and Pam Walker-Williams.

Last but not least, Karen White-Owens, Barbara Vinegar, and most notably, Donnetta Armstrong. I could have written this book without you, but it wouldn't have been nearly as good.

I thank you all from the bottom of my heart.

I

"Ugh!" Audrey groaned. She was determined to work through the discomfort, though the sweat pouring from her face and her pounding heart didn't make it any easier. The television was turned up nearly full blast, filling the air with the sounds of the exercise video. The soundtrack was terrible. It twanged like something rejected from a 70's Blacksploitation flick. She wanted to turn it down and put in some upbeat CD's, but if she did that she couldn't hear the aerobics instructor.

A large wet 'V' darkened the middle front and back of her gray tee shirt. Only ten minutes into her workout, and already she felt like quitting. But the cellulite peeked out from beneath her red shorts, rippling her outer thighs like a sea of chocolate cottage cheese. If she planned on continuing to wear those size twelve suits, she'd better keep on moving.

Today was Friday, her late day. Fridays were usually spent taking a little time for herself. She let herself sleep later than her usual 6:30 wake-up. She'd begin her morning exercise routine whenever the urge hit. If the spirit didn't move her by mid-morning, a hard look at her soft thighs worked every time.

"Ugh!" she groaned again, verbalizing the discomfort as she struggled to do the repetitive leg lifts, the most dreaded part of the workout. With each passing year it was becoming increasingly difficult to maintain a weight that she felt good about. She grudgingly admitted to herself that she was losing the battle of the bulge.

The light exercise that she was accustomed to doing when she was younger just wasn't keeping the fat at bay. Her size six days were long gone. Now it was a struggle to squeeze into tens and twelve's. With her forty-second birthday looming, it was time to get serious or give up. The choice was simple: maintain a serious workout routine or start shopping for her clothing at the same places that supplied circus tents.

She half-heartedly followed the repetitive instructions from the video. Billy Blanks was usually good at motivating her into attempting all those roundhouse kicks, but this morning, her heart just wasn't into it. She'd been letting the machine screen her calls all morning. This time when the telephone rang, she took it as a sign from God that she wasn't meant to suffer like this. At least, not today. She hit the mute button on the remote and picked up the phone.

"Hello." She huffed into the mouthpiece, lifting the end of her shirt to wipe away sweat. The rank odor that escaped when her shirt was lifted caused her to wrinkle her nose.

"Hey, I'm glad I caught you. You got a minute to help me solve a puzzle?"

"No, not really." Audrey's tone reflected her annoyance. She could have given herself a roundhouse kick for not letting the machine pick up the call. It was just after 10:00 a.m. and Norma Jean Strange was calling her for the third time that day wanting more direction on the work she was doing for city government. Audrey hated being rude, but the woman was making her head hurt.

Earlier that year Norma Jean had been appointed Finance Director of Rosemont, the only black township in Ohio. She'd gotten the position through connections made at her former government job with the Tax Assessor's Office. An experienced accountant, Norma Jean was having difficulty dealing with the pressures that come with managing the finances of a small city. She seemed more unsure of herself with each passing day and called Audrey constantly for support. When Audrey told her sister Renita about this, she was able to sum up Norma Jean's behavior as an example of someone who lied herself into a job. She thought it was time for Audrey to cut the cord. Push Jean from the cushy nest of her support.

But the funny thing was Norma Jean had never been like this before. Audrey had known her since they were children and she'd always exuded a level of confidence that Audrey admired. Suddenly she couldn't figure two plus two without double-checking the results with Audrey.

"Damn Audrey, you don't have to sound so cold." Norma Jean was saying. "When I told you about the job you said to let you know if you could help, but whenever I call you lately you act like you got some kind of attitude." Norma Jean painted on the guilt with an industrial sized roller.

Audrey grabbed a towel from the arm of the sofa and dabbed at her neck.

"I'm sorry, Jean." The response came out as a guilty whine. Never one to miss an opportunity, Jean seized this one and ran with it.

"Audrey don't make me remind you how far back we go." She paused for effect, long enough for Audrey's insides to do a quick flop. "You know you my girl. That's why I came to you before anyone else with this opportunity to make some of dis' good gubment money." Norma Jean laughed.

The street vernacular came naturally to the Ridgeview Housing Projects native. She was smart as a whip and had been granted a full scholarship to the Academy when she was just twelve years old. This was quite a feat considering that Rosemont Academy was one of the nations most prestigious private schools where students weren't even considered unless they had a history of excellent marks. But that wasn't the only history that increased chances of gaining entry. Candidates were generally selected from families that were already a part of the Academy tradition. Besides Norma Jean and her sister Carolyn, Audrey knew of no other

Rosemont Academy students who lived in the projects. The girls had passed their entrance exams with flying colors and made the trek each day on a student shuttle. While Carolyn was tall, quiet and reserved, tiny Norma Jean walked the halls of the Academy like she owned them.

They'd become friends when she happened by one day after school had let out. Audrey had the misfortune of being on the losing side of a fight with the school troublemaker, Sandra Green. Sandra was a big, yellow, pimple-faced girl with a bad attitude who liked to keep stuff going. Sandra had Audrey around the neck so tight she nearly passed out. Norma Jean attacked the bully like a tiny tornado. She was as quick as a cat and all over Sandra like a bad rash. From that day on she and Audrey were virtually inseparable all through school.

Norma Jean stood four feet eleven inches and was still no more than a hundred pounds. Ninety percent of that was chutzpah. Her laugh was full-bodied, incongruous for someone so compact. The howling from the other side of the phone had stopped. Norma Jean was serious now, determined to get her way.

"But enough about the contract that we have. I wouldn't call you if I didn't trust your judgment."

Shit, Audrey thought, the contract. A headache pounded through her right temple.

"Your expertise and insight goes far beyond what I could ever hope to aspire to." Norma Jean continued. "That's why I'm so glad that you agreed to work with me."

Audrey plopped down on the sofa in defeat. That blasted contract. The seemingly innocuous document that indentured her to Jean. What the hell was she thinking making Jean an offer like that? But who would've thought the child couldn't make an independent decision about the simplest things? She didn't think that her offer of help would lead to her friend's total dependence on her.

After the first few months, enough time for anyone to be over new job jitters, Norma Jean was as insecure as ever. Audrey decided the best way to nip the situation in the bud was to start nipping at the Township's coffers. She told Norma Jean that she would have to start charging for her time.

She then gave Norma Jean a ridiculously high rate, figuring 'That's the end of that.' A week later Norma Jean called her back. Not only did she accept her proposal, but offered her a hefty signing bonus. The Board had agreed to everything that she asked and approved using her as the Township's financial consultant. Without missing a beat, she produced a whole list of questions and arranged a meeting so that the members of the Board could meet the newest addition to the Rosemont Township government team.

Feeling like a steer being roped and branded for the rodeo audience, Audrey was too shocked to say no. She gulped out a 'yes', ignoring the queasy feel in the pit of her stomach. She attended a meeting the following day where the Rosemont Township Board of Trustees responded to her enthusiastically from their expensive leather chairs as they reviewed her credentials. Her queasy stomach curdled as she accepted the limp hands they extended along with their mealy-mouthed platitudes. But when the main course is money, one tends to scarf down a lot of bad tasting appetizers. Audrey knew she was selling herself short. But she really needed the substantial check she would be getting each week. The downside was Norma Jean taking opportunities like this to remind Audrey of their agreement.

In the end, she agreed to work with Norma Jean three days a week. Though Friday wasn't one of them, Audrey received a bonus for any work she did on her days off. She'd set a mental timer when the call began. Norma Jean would be billed accordingly.

"I'm having problems getting these damned numbers to jibe. Do you think you could pop over sometime this morning and have a look-see?" The amount of pressure she applied today was excessive, even for her.

"Jean, this is really a busy time for me..."

"Come on, Audrey. What *you* got to do that's so important?" Though Audrey was getting noticed since she'd taken the position with the Township, Norma Jean knew she had no other clients.

"Well, if you must know, I'm working on a proposal for B.A. Wilson. I was on my way to an appointment." She lied. "As a matter of fact, I have meetings scheduled all day." Audrey mouthed a silent prayer of forgiveness, hoping God wouldn't strike her down. B.A. Wilson was the company she'd formed with her brother Bobby. Audrey wished the hell she did have a prospective donor for the company. The truth of the matter was she'd been using the money Jean had been paying her to bolster the fledgling company's weak cash flow.

"Come on. Help a sister out." Norma Jean had gotten her second wind. She was determined to be the first to cross the finish line of wills. "We're preparing for the state audit and you know how those people are."

"You used to be one of 'those people' yourself. You know every number in there forward and back. You're probably just tired. Try stepping away from it for a minute. You'll find the problem."

"What I think I've found here is not just another misapplied entry."

"What do you mean?" Though Audrey was intrigued by the thought of a discrepancy, she refused to be baited. She just wasn't in the mood today.

"There are some questionable, no, downright suspicious items that I've found. It involves members on the Board of Directors. I want a second set of skilled eyes that I can trust to look at these numbers before I start accusing people of stealing."

"You think someone on the Board is stealing?" Audrey was hooked. She could almost hear the reel whirring. She'd soon be flopping on the bank helplessly at Norma Jean's feet.

"It looks that way. Can you meet me sometime today?"

Audrey was determined that she wasn't going to work today. Period. Norma Jean was determined to get her way. Audrey shook her head in defeat, agreeing to meet her friend that next day for brunch at Jean's new home in Clairmont Hills. Audrey hadn't seen the place since the week of the closing, so she was interested in seeing it fully furnished. She also admitted to herself that the thought of getting inside information about a scandal involving those stuck-up board members was a temptation she couldn't resist.

* * *

Later that evening, Audrey sat in Let Them Eat Cake, her favorite coffee bar in Rookwood Commons, waiting for Dennis. She hadn't seen her ex-lover in over a month. When he called that afternoon wanting to see her, her initial inclination was to refuse his invitation to coffee. But it was Friday night, she had no plans, and she was as tight as a spring from dealing with Norma Jean and all of her drama. It wasn't all bad. Her connection with Rosemont Township was giving her a good income and plenty of exposure. She stayed so busy it was difficult to make time for herself.

She sat at a tiny orange Formica topped table, ignoring the tempting aroma of freshly baked sweets. Audrey decided to make good on the lie she'd told Norma Jean earlier and follow-up on a few contacts she'd made that might be interested in contributing to B.A. Wilson.

Sitting near the florescent lighting, as far away from the goodies as she could, she pecked away at her laptop, outlining a financial proposal for a potential client. When she looked at her watch and it was nearly eight o'clock, Audrey's brow furrowed in annoyance. Dennis should have been there an hour ago.

"I can't believe this is happening again." Audrey said to herself, dismayed at the level of vulnerability she still had to him. It was her own fault for letting her lust be her guide. The only reason she was being bothered with Dennis at all was because he was GQ fine and had the stamina of a stallion. But now he'd pissed her off and she wasn't in the mood. She'd started putting away her laptop when she felt the wet kiss on the cheek and smelled the rich woodsy scent that told her Dennis had arrived.

"Hey Angel-girl! You look fantastic. How was your day?" Dennis stood before her as inviting as a Caribbean sunset, all smooth-skinned and groomed. He flashed the smile that made women swoon. It wasn't working on Audrey. She continued collecting her things. Walking over to the trashcan, she dumped the cold cup of coffee inside and reached for her valise. Her anger overshadowed the tingle that stirred between her legs as she drank in his dark, athletic beauty. How could anybody that damn fine be such a jerk?

"Did I miss something here?" The perplexed query raised his thick eyebrows. His dark eyes pierced hers beseechingly.

"Yeah, you missed our date." She replied sharply. "But don't worry about it Dennis, that was the last one you'll have with me."

She was sick of him anyway. The sex was good but he didn't have anything else to offer. It just wasn't worth the aggravation. Dennis was shallow, and as dull as a butter knife. She would have forced herself to put up with his banal chatter for two hours or more before they made it to the bedroom and then made an excuse at the appropriate time to end the date. But now she was too irritated to even think about sleeping with him.

She hated it when someone set up a meeting and then was late. And with Dennis, this was a chronic situation. She was reminded of the other reason that she had stopped seeing him. Not only was he boring, but he had no regard for other people's time. It showed a total lack of respect.

"But Angel-eyes, it's eight o'clock. I'm not late this time. We said 'eight at Cake'. Remember?"

"Dennis, our date was for seven. I don't know who the hell you made a date at eight o'clock with, but it wasn't me."

He opened his mouth to reply but she held up her hand.

"Don't even bother with whatever excuse you've cooked up. I'm not hungry for it, okay."

"Oh, Angel-pie! Come on, don't be like that..." He stamped his foot and poked out his full lips. He reminded Audrey of a big, black, sexy-ass brat. She imagined giving him a good spanking, and then sucking the juice out of those pouty lips and feeling so satisfied. But that wouldn't be happening tonight. She had drawn a line in the sand. She was through with him.

Audrey walked towards the door, then turned and came back towards the table. Dennis held his arms wide, waiting to enfold her.

"I knew you couldn't stay mad at me. Come give me a taste of those sweet...hey!"

She walked past Dennis. The room had become crowded and several people looked in their direction and snickered. Embarrassed, he looked away from their inquiring eyes as Audrey brushed by him, making her way to the pastry counter.

"I'll have a slice of the double espresso chocolate cake to go, please." She'd be damned if she'd spend another Friday night without getting some kind of pleasure. A light brown portly fellow, dressed like a chef, wrapped a huge slice of the sinful confection and exchanged it with Audrey for five dollars. She walked past Dennis again on her way out. Now he was cussing.

"Ain't this 'bout a bitch! You'll see the next time I ask your black ass out!" He jumped up and down, his fingers curled into tight fists. "You'll regret this shit!" He flung the angry words at her. Hateful daggers darted from his eyes in her direction.

Audrey ignored him and the snickers from nearby tables. She walked through the heavy glass door, feeling his dark eyes burn into her back as she headed to the lot and her waiting car.

* * *

Since the most interesting part of her evening thus far had been the proposal she'd created, Audrey decided to return to work. The building housing her office was located on Plum Street in an area of downtown Rosemont that was in the process of a renaissance. The owners took advantage of the situation, giving the small building a facelift recently. No sooner had the new light gray with plum trim paint job dried than the tenants were informed of a rent increase effective at the beginning of their new leases. Some renters who'd reached the end of their contracts moved out. Their slots were quickly filled by other small businesses, predominantly in the areas of medicine and law.

Audrey hadn't been in the building very long herself, and fortunately, her lease wasn't up for another year. That would give her ample time to prepare for the mental and financial jolt of shelling out the extra cash if she decided to stay.

There were only three offices on the ground floor. The chiropractor had moved out in April. The dentist's office, which was vacated in August, had recently been rented to an attorney. Audrey's office was at the end of the hall past the other two.

She unlocked the door, pushing it with her foot as she balanced the laptop and the boxes of food, easing them onto an end table before tapping the light switch. She closed and locked the door, then carried the food past the reception area to her small office.

Clicking on the light, she sat the carton onto her desk, feeling the bottom first to make sure there was no liquid dripping through it.

Audrey turned the computer on before going to collect the laptop. She started a pot of coffee so that she could have a cup with her cake later. First, she would have dinner. The dusty bottle of wine in the wet bar would be just the right touch for the shrimp and vegetables she'd picked up at Wang Pao's, the Chinese restaurant next door to her office.

Audrey clicked opened the file and ate while she calculated the numbers a final time before e-mailing the spreadsheets and instructions to her assistant, Carrey, on the transparencies needed for the presentation. The phone rang.

"What the hell are you doing at the office?"

"Hey, Ren." She crunched on an egg roll, turning the mouthpiece of the phone away in hopes that the action muted her chewing.

"I thought you had a date with Dennis."

Audrey gulped down the food and sipped some wine before pushing the speaker button and sitting the receiver in the cradle.

"So did I." She sipped some more wine and when her mouth was clear, continued. "He was late and I got pissed and left."

"I guess it's easy to lose track of time when you're trafficking commodities; so many rock stars, so little time." Renita sighed dramatically. "Where do you find these people, Auddie?" Renita reverted to her childhood nickname for her big sister. "You always gravitate towards men with that loser profile."

"What are you talking about Renita?" Audrey no longer cared if Renita heard her chewing. She opened her mouth and took in a heaping forkful of low mien.

"You know what I'm talking about. I'm talking about you and all those losers you attract." Renita paused. "What you eatin'?"

"None of your business and I do not attract losers." Audrey frowned into the box of take-out. Renita was making her lose her appetite.

"You are a loser magnet." She rushed ahead before Audrey could defend herself.

"Tonight it's Drug Running Dennis."

"He does not sell drugs!" Audrey was incredulous. "He has his own import/export business. He's very successful, too."

"Uhm hum, whatever. What about the dentist with that rotten-ass tooth in the front of his mouth? That trifling bastard was pulling more tail than teeth. I say, 'Physician, stop thy drilling and heal thyself'."

Audrey looked at the ceiling and rolled her eyes. Her food was getting cold and she wished she had let the answering machine intercept the call from her younger sister. She pushed the mute button, dove into her plate and tried her best to ignore Renita's diatribe.

"And what about the funeral parlor director that picked you up for a date in the damn hearse? That brother was definitely a minus. And don't get me started on Jerry Hollingsworth and Emory Kimborough. The only one that was worth a quarter was Jules Dreyfus and you were scared of him."

Audrey reactivated the sound on her end of the phone.

"All right. Enough already. Jerry and Emory were not losers. We were incompatible. And I'll have you know, I was not afraid of Jules, he was just too young."

"Too young and too white."

"Just because you like getting dogged by white boys doesn't mean I have to."

Renita's silence gave Audrey a tiny feeling of retribution. "Take that!" she said to herself, masticating the tiny conquest and swallowing it with the pasta.

It was mean of her to dredge up what she knew was a painful memory for her sister, but she was sick of Renita making sport of her past relationships. Maybe now she'd change the subject. Audrey didn't need to see her pitiful love life flash before her. She was depressed enough. Though it was true that she didn't seem to have much success in matters of the heart.

She had called off her engagement to Jerry Hollingsworth after finding him with another woman. Without giving herself time to get over that pain, she dove feet first into a marriage with prominent attorney Emory Kimborough. That was a disaster from the start. The divorce was as unceremonious as the marriage had been. She'd started seeing Jules, a white attorney she'd met in her old office building. Jules Dreyfus hadn't dogged her. She never gave him the chance. The relationship didn't feel right to her so she didn't see any point in dragging out the inevitable.

They'd gone out a few times. She liked him well enough. But she couldn't get used to being out with him in public. Renita told her she was being silly when she mentioned the looks they'd get from people in the street.

"If you stop seeing him to please them, how's that helping you?" Renita was right of course. But Audrey still couldn't relax. She tried to dismiss it, but she knew it wasn't just in her head. She noticed white guys eyeing her like she was a hooker and she could have sworn one of them gave Jules the good ole boy thumbs up. And that wasn't all. Black men looked at them hatefully while mumbling under their breaths. White women flirted openly with him like she was a non-entity. One black woman gave her a high five; another said she was sleeping with the enemy. It got to be too much. She had to stop seeing him before she went off on somebody. So she broke it off. Jules begged her to reconsider, but she couldn't. It just didn't fit.

Determined to make the relationship work, Jules called her repeatedly. But she never returned his calls and eventually, they stopped coming. Since that break up, her relationships with men were totally surface in nature. That works for a while, but the lack of commitment felt like being on a liquid diet. It might get results, but it left one feeling kind of empty inside.

Renita's one and only heart break was at the hands of a French flutist who's abusive treatment had left her wallowing in the gutter like anyone's thrown out trash. It was wrong for Audrey to resort to her trump card, but she was tired of Renita berating her sad love life. The mere hint at picking at the scab that was Franchot Arnaud was enough to cause Renita's acerbic tongue to recoil.

"So that sorry muthafucka didn't show up, huh?" Renita's tone had warmed considerably. She almost sounded sympathetic.

"His sorry ass came, but he was over an hour late." Audrey scraped the bottom of the cardboard box with her fork.

"Shit Audrey, you were stupid for waiting for him that long."

So much for sympathy.

"I brought my laptop and worked the whole time. I didn't even realize it was that late until he showed up."

The defending response came out like a whiny excuse. Pitiful. Her embarrassment was undeniable. She wished she had lied and told her sister that she took Dennis to her place, fucked his head off and felt so energized, she had returned to work. But who would believe that shit? Certainly not Renita. Between sensing her big sister's pain and not wanting to relive her own tender memories, Renita sensibly changed the subject.

"You work too much, girl. The fact that you took a friggin' computer on your date speaks volumes about where the evening was headed anyway."

"Speaking of working, why aren't *you* working on a Friday night?"

"I'm at work. I'm in Jack Offs' office."

"You better quit calling him that before he hears you."

"Hell, everybody calls him that. He's probably the one that started it with his filthy ass. If his hands ain't on the table, they workin' out. He's one nasty piece of work. He'll be playing with hisself, then wanna shake somebody's hand."

"Eeegh!" The two of them said and laughed.

Renita was a jazz singer who had a contract at a local club. The club owner, Jackson Waller, was a less than scrupulous character who'd been everything from pimp to pusher before, in his words, "settlin' down and becoming a legitamite binness man". Renita hadn't recorded or toured in years, but she'd missed singing. When Waller called her to sing at The Spice Rack, a nightclub he'd opened, it didn't take long for her to agree. The very generous offer he extended made her decision that much easier. Though he claimed to be out of "the life", he was still well connected. He paid Renita top dollar for performing at the club three nights a week. The Spice Rack was definitely on the map and was considered a must stop for anyone visiting Southwest Ohio.

"I'm going out for the first set in a minute" Renita told her. "I just thought I'd call and see if you wanted to come down tonight or tomorrow."

"Thanks, but no." Audrey said. "I think I'm going to wrap it up here shortly and head for home. I got a meeting in the morning with Jean so I don't want to stay up too late."

"Oh, let me guess. She needs you to do some more of her work for her, right? That heifer is just trifling. I can't believe they payin' her all that money and she don't know left from right."

"That's not true, Renita. Norma Jean is very bright. She's just being conscientious."

"My ass!" Renita spat. "That bitch don't give a damn about shit but herself. She's using you Auddie."

"How can you say that? I thought you guys were friends."

"That's *your* friend. I mean, she's all right, but I wouldn't exactly call her a friend."

"She's not only my friend, but she's paying me very good money to consult on all financial matters regarding the Township."

"Well, I hope it's *real* good money." Doubt and suspicion threaded Renita's words.

"What do you mean?"

"Just watch out for her, Auddie."

2

Audrey pulled the Saab to a stop in front of the row of condominiums and killed the engine. It had been an unseasonably hot afternoon, leaving behind humid, sticky air that did little to cool the night. She felt the energy drain from her pores, depleting any desire she had to do her evening walk. She looked into the starlit sky, turned the key and opened the door. Freedom pounced from a neighboring ledge, startling her as he pushed his way into the house.

"Rude bastard!" She said, shaking her head and smiling. After her marriage to Emory Kimborough dissolved, Audrey visited the Humane Society. She came home with the orange Tabby she'd named in honor of her new independence.

Audrey kicked off her shoes and sat the bag containing her laptop and various files next to her desk. Just in case her mood changed, she went to the bedroom and put on her smoke gray sweats.

Freedom called to her from the kitchen. Audrey followed the loud meowing and found him in the center of the Mexican tiled floor sniffing around for his dinner. She filled his dish with the chicken gizzards she had picked up from the butcher and accepted the purr of thanks by tickling him underneath his chin. He happily wolfed down the dark, slimy meat while Audrey heated a bowl of spicy, red salsa and cheese in the microwave.

She fished around in the cupboard for a bag of tortilla chips. Before she opened the bag and poured them onto a plate, the aroma of heated peppery sauce and cheese attacked her senses. She placed the steamy snack on a tray with a glass of ice tea and carried it to the living room.

She punched the speaker button on the phone and listened to her messages while she got situated in front of the television. Several hang-ups, two sales pitches, and a heavy breather later, she turned her attention to her plate. Touching the power button on the remote, Audrey sorted through her mail while Nona LaRhone of Channel Five began reading the eleven o'clock news.

"To update News at Eleven's exclusive story of a grisly murder at the Rosemont Township government building, here's Tonya Elling. Tonya, what's the latest?"

"Nona, as reported exclusively on Channel Five just moments ago, the woman who was found murdered in one of the city government buildings has been identified as Norma Jean Strange, the Finance Director for Rosemont City Government. The body of Ms. Strange was found in the Southwest wing of the campus. The details of this homicide have not been officially confirmed, but this reporter has learned, in this Channel Five News exclusive, that the victim's death was due to acute head trauma.

"This section of the campus is directly across the street from where the students of the Academy attend classes. Apparently, it was late this afternoon or in the early evening when the murder occurred. The students had left the area at the approximate time that the crime was committed. The school and the general and administrative offices of Rosemont City Government are housed here.

"Ms. Strange was appointed Director of Finance earlier this year. She was single, in her late thirties and a native of the Rosemont area. We still have no information on surviving family and the killer is still at large. A member of the custodial staff, who contacted the police, found the body. He was questioned by police and released. An anonymous tip to News Five led to this exclusive report. The police are releasing few details other than confirming that it was Ms. Strange who was brutally murdered. We'll have more on this story as it develops...back to you in the studio, Nona."

"Tonya, do the police have any ideas who might have committed this crime?"

"The police are releasing few details other than the victim's identity and that an investigation is underway in this heinous crime. Detective Rob Hollingsworth of the Rosemont Police Department will be completing his initial investigation tonight. Police Chief Hyram Phillips will hold a press conference, tentatively scheduled for 12:00 Monday. Any further discussion on the case is being reserved until then."

"Thank you, Tonya. In other news..."

Audrey could not believe what she had just heard. She stared in disbelief at the TV screen as figures came into view, mouths moving in slow motion. The audio suddenly slowed to a dragging slur. Her friend has been murdered? Who would do such a thing and why?

The realization of the news report tore into her brain and ravaged it like a knife with a serrated edge. Audrey flung herself onto the couch and burst into tears. Sobs racked her until her face was swollen and her throat was sore.

Why would anyone want to kill Norma Jean? Then she thought about how pushy her friend could be and how she often got on her nerves. Perhaps others were not as patient with her overbearing demeanor as Audrey had been. She struggled to understand what had happened and why, and also, felt bad about their last conversation. Audrey felt guilty for putting Jean off when she'd called that morning. Their last discussion replayed itself in her mind, filling her with dread. Norma Jean said she had proof that one of the Board Members had been embezzling funds. Could there be a connection between the information she'd uncovered and her death? If Audrey had answered the call for assistance, would Norma Jean still be alive? It would not have taken but a minute to verify her findings. That was all Jean had asked of her.

But Audrey had turned her down. Together, they would have notified the authorities and Norma Jean Strange would still be alive. She had failed her friend in life. The least she could do was help figure out who had caused her death.

Audrey grabbed a handful of tissues. She blew her nose and cleaned her face. Without further thought, Audrey jumped up from her place on the sofa, slipped on a pair of tennis shoes and drove down to City Hall.

The street leading to the Administration Building was in a state of utter chaos. Two rival news stations had tangles of cables, cameras, lights and other equipment set up in front of City Hall. Camera crews scurried around the scene, taping their versions of the breaking story and trying to stop Channel Five from gaining any more ground.

The police had the periphery of the city offices cordoned off with wooden barricades making it necessary for Audrey to drive several blocks away from the throng. Parking near a streetlight, she headed towards the turmoil, pushing her way to the front.

As she drew closer to the Administration Building, the sight of the yellow tape affixed to the entrance sent a sharp pain deep into her heart. CRIME SCENE. Norma Jean Strange, the little girl who had spent half her childhood sleeping on a bundle of blankets at the foot of Audrey's bed, had been killed.

Wet-hot tears chilled her face as memories of her friend flooded her heart and mind. Through blurry eyes she spotted Rob Hollingsworth talking to several uniformed officers. Tall, chestnut brown and muscular, Rob was the kind of man who stood out in a crowd. Audrey watched him giving his staff directives. He looked over at her and smiled. The smile was a comfort to her as was his presence. He walked over to her. She welcomed his embrace.

"Audrey Wilson." Rob squinted at her questioningly, like her being there was as out of place as anything he could imagine. He arched his eyebrow in concern, studying her face. "What are you doing here?"

"I heard about what happened on the news. I was just talking to her this morning, Rob. I can't believe this. We were colleagues...friends." The emotions came rushing forth again with the reality of the situation. Rob wrapped his athletic frame around her as her tears flowed. After a moment, he pulled her away, holding her at arms length. He searched her eyes intently before speaking.

"You shouldn't be here Audrey. Why don't you go home?"

"But, you don't understand." She dug her fingers into his arm. She needed to touch him, touch anything that would remind her that she wasn't dreaming.

"I was to meet with her tomorrow morning. Did she leave a note or anything?"

"Anything like what?" The strong arms that held her in comfort moments before had pulled away from her. They were now crossed defensively in front of his chest.

"Anything! Like a clue as to who would have wanted to hurt her?" Audrey searched his face, trying to read something in it that would explain the unexplainable.

"I can't discuss any evidence related to this case with you, Audrey."

"So you did find something! What was it?"

"Hold on Audrey. I told you nothing of the sort. What's up with all the questions, anyway?" He eyed her suspiciously, trying to ferret out clues as to why she would be there.

"I told you, we were friends, Rob. We both went to school at the Academy. Over the years we stayed in touch and recently began working together. We had a meeting scheduled for tomorrow morning."

Audrey wondered if she should share with the detective the last conversation she'd had with her friend. He eyed her as he would a suspect and she was beginning to feel like one. She and Rob Hollingsworth had a relationship that moved beyond the bounds of business. He had almost been her brother-in-law. Her relationship with his brother Jerry had ended badly, but she and Rob had maintained a distant, but very real friendship.

"I find it strange that you would appear at a crime scene like this Audrey. What were the two of you meeting about?" He wasn't acting like a friend but like a detective on a case. It made Audrey a little nervous.

"It was just routine accounting stuff." She shrugged. "You know how folks get when it's tax time. She just wanted me to bless the quarterly reports that were due."

She wasn't sure why she was skirting the truth with Rob. She could see that she was only making herself look more suspicious by the way he was checking her out.

"And that prompted you to drive all the way over here in the middle of the night? I think you need to go home Audrey." He said again. She didn't like the change in his tone. He wasn't making a request.

"If you want to follow the case," he made a sweeping motion towards the pandemonium, "you'll have to watch it on the news like the rest of Southwest Ohio."

"This is all so shocking, Rob. I just talked to her this morning." The crowd continued to swell. Audrey felt her air supply diminish as the throng thickened around them. She looked out at all of the commotion and trembled. Her face was warm and she felt like she was going to be sick. When she turned back to Rob, he had stepped away and was addressing a reporter who had pulled up along side them.

Audrey felt worse now than before she'd talked to him. She wished she *had* stayed at home. But, what about Norma Jean's report? She had to find it. But how? She crossed over Elmwood Road and opened her car door and sat for a moment before starting up the engine. She couldn't go home now. She was too wound up. The dashboard clock read 12:30. She decided to go over to the Spice Rack and talk to Renita.

* * *

The club was packed. It had been a while since she'd been to the Rack on a Friday night and Audrey hadn't counted on there being so many people there. She could barely hear the music beneath all the noise. She wedged herself between the swell of partiers, squinting back the acrid cigarette smoke. When a waitress approached, Audrey ordered Absolut and tonic with a twist of lime. The drink arrived relatively fast, considering the size of the crowd. Audrey sipped from a glass of what tasted more like absolutely tonic. Even the slice of lime was dull. But the drink relaxed her just the same.

She sipped the watered-down concoction while tapping her foot to the music that the DJ played. The band was on break. Audrey spoke to a few of the guys as they circulated amongst the crowd. Lloyd Eckstine, the bandleader, with his usual smooth self, pulled Audrey to him, kissing her cheek.

"You Wilson girls look so much like chocolate, you can give a man diabetes."

"How you livin' Silver Fox?" Audrey cast a toothy grin at her favorite pianist.

"Cain't complain. If I do it won't solve a thing." Lloyd's mouth opened to display long, cigarette and coffee stained teeth. His smile deepened the dimples in his cheeks that even the dim club lighting couldn't hide.

"Now I know you family and all but you could at least put on some clothes and street shoes when you come to see us."

"What?"

He pointed at the white Reeboks and the baggy sweat suit.

"We don't have a casual Friday policy here young lady." Lloyd smiled down at her; the silvery waves of his hair cast a halo-like glow in the club lighting.

"Oh, I'd completely forgotten that I'd changed my clothes and shoes. I was on my way somewhere else and just stopped in to see Ren. Where is she?" Audrey looked past Lloyd into the bulge of people beyond him.

"She in here somewhere, flitting around, being the diva." He craned his neck, searching the room for a second before turning his attention once more to Audrey. "She might be in the back with Waller. Why don't you find a table while I track her down."

"Thanks Lloyd." Lloyd Eckstine had been carrying a torch for Renita for more years than Audrey could remember. As she did with most men she liked, Renita had sex with Lloyd once or twice, then treated him just special enough for him to think maybe she'd give him some again one day. It wasn't likely to happen. But as long as Lloyd followed that dream, Renita was able to get anything she wanted from him.

Audrey snagged a table that had just been cleared nearby and sat checking out the festive crowd. The DJ was good, in spite of the fact that no one seemed to be listening. Noah Webb's sexy violin was wasted on this crowd. But for Audrey, the music was relaxing.

After more than thirty minutes, she still hadn't seen Renita and it was almost time for the next set. She debated whether to buy another weak drink or go on home when she saw her sister pushing her way through the crowded room in her direction.

"I had a feeling you'd be here tonight." Renita pulled her locked hair behind one ear. "Lloyd told me to hurry up and get you out of here makin' the place look bad. I must agree—you do look like you just left the hoop court. Whassup with the get up? Coming in here dressed like the rappin' accountant."

"Shhh!" Audrey whispered and motioned for her to sit down. "Have you seen the news tonight?"

"No. What happened?" Renita lowered her voice conspiratorially.

"Somebody killed Norma Jean." Audrey's words came out thick and faltering, like she was forcing out a terrible lie.

"What?" Renita drew back in disbelief.

Audrey wanted to take back the words; like that act alone would change the events that lead to her being there. Suddenly the crowd was a boisterous mob. The room seemed to be spinning. Was she going crazy? She grabbed her sister's hand and squeezed it. The tactile move helped confirm for Audrey that this wasn't a crazy dream, or a horrible nightmare.

"Norma Jean Strange. Somebody killed her. She was working late in the Admin Building and somebody killed her." Audrey's words tumbled out like jagged ice, cold and abrupt.

"What? I can't believe it." Renita sat in shocked disbelief. Then she smiled nervously. "You're not kidding. Are you sure it was *our* Jean?"

"I'm sure, Ren. I even went down to City Hall. It was a mess. Police and news people everywhere. Rob Hollingsworth was there. I tried to get some information from him but he was playing Joe Cop and wouldn't get up off of nothing." Audrey leaned closer, lowering her voice. "The meeting we scheduled for tomorrow morning was to verify her suspicion that someone was stealing. She had some kind of report."

"You don't think she was killed because the thief discovered she had the report, do you?" Renita wondered out loud.

"That's exactly what I think. What other reason would somebody have for wanting her dead?" Audrey shuddered. She still couldn't believe that any of this was true.

"Who knows? I mean, how well did we really know her?" Renita asked. "She and her family lived in the projects for years before she her sister Carolyn started attending the Academy. We didn't meet them until then. She told us about the things that happened to them. It's a wonder they survived it."

"Yeah, I know. I guess that's part of the reason why I put up with her. I felt kind of guilty that they didn't have the same firm foundation that Mom and Dad gave us. That could very well have been us." Audrey reflected. "When Daddy died, Mom could have married someone who did the same horrible things that bastard Peters did to his stepdaughters. But then by the time Daddy died, we were teenagers."

"Yeah. Bobby would have kicked any muthafucka's ass that tried some foul shit like that with us." Renita stiffened defensively. Bobby Wilson, a professional basketball player, was the girls' rowdy brother.

"Jean must have run away over a dozen times, and poor Carolyn, slashing her wrists like that." Audrey said in a small sad voice, remembering the hell the two girls had gone through.

"She was only fifteen." Renita stared off into the distance. Audrey knew that she too was once again in 1975, remembering the Strange sisters sleeping over at their house. They would drink Barq's orange or lemon-lime and eat Grippo's tangy barbecue chips like there was no tomorrow, dancing to 45's all night in the room that Audrey and Renita shared. What was merely a tiny bedroom for the Wilson sisters was for the two girls from the projects a sanctuary from the madness of home.

Arthur Peters married the girls' mother when they were seven and nine. He started sexually abusing them soon after he'd moved into the home. They met the Wilson sisters when they all attended Rosemont Academy. Carolyn and Norma Jean started coming over to the Wilson's house nearly every day. It didn't matter that their stepfather would beat them for not coming straight home. Audrey and Renita looked on with sorrowful expressions when they'd see the sister's days later. Norma Jean and Carolyn displayed the fresh scars they'd gotten like badges of honor. The Wilson sisters didn't know about the invisible scars. Those were deeper, bled heavier and hurt far more than anything they could fathom.

Audrey couldn't remember when Carolyn changed from drinking orange and green pop, and smacking on potato chips to swilling Wiedemann beer and dragging Kool cigarettes. It was around the same time Audrey had accompanied the Strange sisters to Twelfth Street Clinic. Which was around the same time Carolyn told them about her pregnancy and that there was no way she was going to bring that sin into the world. None of them ever thought that she would take her own life.

"Jean had done everything to distance herself from all that. She had accomplished so much. What a tragic way to end up after all that fighting." A tear spilled over and rolled down Audrey's face.

The two sat in silence for a moment. Renita looked over at her sister who had taken out a small notebook and was fishing around in her purse for a pen.

"What are you doing?"

"Well, I don't know who killed Jean or why, but I do know one thing."

"What's that?" Renita asked, her eyebrow rose suspiciously.

"It's got something to do with that report she was working on and the embezzlement she'd uncovered at the school. I'm going to get that report that she wanted me to see. I'm going to make sure that the bastard who killed her pays for what he did."

"What? Are you out of your fucking mind?" Renita's voice had risen to such a degree that patrons at nearby tables looked over at them curiously. Audrey shot Renita a stern glare.

"Ren, she was counting on me." Audrey replied softly. "Her last request was a cry for help. For all I know, nobody else even knows about what she'd found. Then again, maybe her death had nothing at all to do with what she'd found."

"Well, that's why God made policemen." Renita picked up her glass. Finding it empty, she set it back on the table forcefully. She snapped her fingers at a passing waitress, and pointed to their glasses before continuing. "You ain't a cop. Let them figure this shit out. What did Rob say when you told him your theory?"

Audrey looked away from her sister's intense gaze.

"You didn't tell him? Are you crazy, or what?"

The band was taking their places center stage. Audrey was glad that Renita couldn't stay and finish making her case for what an idiot she was for not dropping this thing. Renita rose from the table, but leaned down and whispered in her ear before she left.

"Don't get involved in this mess, Audrey. You go around snooping and poking in stuff that doesn't concern you and you may get hurt. Think about what they did to Norma Jean."

* * *

Audrey pulled onto the cobblestone street. She moved to open the car door and once again, fell apart. Sadness and guilt overwhelmed her. If she had come into the office as Norma Jean had asked, her friend may still be alive. Or perhaps the killer would have gotten a two for. That sobering thought forced her from the car.

It was still too early for most sane people to be up. The street was deserted. She slammed the car door shut. It met the doorframe loudly, cracking open the morning silence like country fresh eggs. During the drive home she had attempted to design a plan on how she was going to get her hands on Norma Jean's report. But the mental dictation was repeatedly interrupted by her sister's arguments as to why she shouldn't pursue this thing.

What if Renita was right? What if there is some crazed killer out there, so desperate not to have his thievery brought to light, that he would kill again? Or maybe it was something more personal that led to her demise. Norma Jean knew plenty of people. Who knew what types of characters she was involved with? Renita made a strong point. Although they had all grown up together and kept in touch even when they had gone away to different colleges, there had been a distance. How well did they really know each other? Speaking for herself, Audrey knew that there were things about her own past that she had never shared with Norma Jean. It would not be much of a stretch to find her friend had secrets of her own. "Audrey Wilson," she chided herself, "You've been reading too many mystery novels. Sometimes you have to suppress your fears and go with your gut." Her instincts told her that the report was the key to Jean's death. If the situation were reversed, she knew that Norma Jean would do right by her.

Through her work with Norma Jean, she was at least casually acquainted with most every member of the Board. First thing Monday morning, she would meet with the key members to see if it would lead her to the report. She knew that she had to be careful in her approach. The last thing she needed to do was let them think that she had been tipped off that something was amiss with the financials, especially if the thief and the killer were one and the same.

3

At 10:30 a.m. Monday morning, Audrey stood before the desk, shifting her weight from one foot to the other, in the Township's business office. The thin, gray haired woman at the reception desk transcribed notes into a computer. She answered incoming calls, one of them personal, and conversed with other people who came into the office. But each time Audrey approached her, the action was met by a frosty coldness that was typical for the woman who put the 'R' in rude. She'd had limited dealings with the Executive Administrative Assistant during her work with the Township and she'd always been kind of nasty. But Audrey didn't work directly with her so the woman's behavior didn't bother her then.

Audrey approached the desk half a dozen times during her forty-minute wait. She had been 'shushed' several times and ignored several more. Audrey's anger was replaced by a nervous energy as the minutes ticked by. She knew she was being handled but what could she do? She couldn't let this inconsequential idiot derail her mission. Once Audrey's anger was in check, the woman's behavior amused her. It was funny how small-minded people often exerted self-manufactured authority in the insignificant areas they felt they controlled; no matter how ridiculous it made them look.

The nameplate read Sarah Collins. In another life she'd probably been a Doberman, German Shepherd, or some other type of attack dog. But in this life she was just Theolonius Griffin's secretary.

Audrey watched in silence as the woman continued about her tasks. Upon continued inspection, Audrey determined that the woman behind the desk was young. Although she had a full head of silver hair in the crown and a roan 'V' near the nape, she was scarcely older than Audrey was. Audrey guessed her age to be early to mid forties.

After having fully established her position of dominance, Sentry Collins shoved her keyboard underneath her desk and addressed the peasant who stood before her.

"Yes?" Her glare reflected a mixture of irritation and disinterest.

"I have an appointment with Mr. Griffin." Audrey stood tall and spoke confidently. This didn't win any points with Ms. Collins. She seemed to get off on intimidating her victims. Audrey wasn't having it.

"Your name?" Her cold eyes peered over wire-framed glasses, burning into Audrey.

"Audrey Wilson, Sarah."

"Who are you with?" Sarah Collins asked as detached as if she'd never seen Audrey. Sarah's face drew an almost convincing blank. Oh, bitch, please! Audrey thought. What the hell is wrong with this fool?

"I used to work with Norma Jean Strange, Sarah." She couldn't believe this woman was acting like they'd never met. The Doberman bent down and barked into the module on her desk.

"An Audrey Wilson is here to see you." She said after an exaggerated sigh.

Asshole. Audrey couldn't believe this chick. Having already dismissed Audrey, she returned to her work. Despite the fact that it was totally ineffectual, Audrey cast her best evil glare at Miss Collins who tapped away perfunctorily at the computer like there was no one else in the room. What was this woman's problem? Wasn't it part of the receptionist's job to make visitors feel welcome? For the life of her Audrey couldn't understand how Sarah Collins kept her job.

Before Audrey had time to further ponder the duties of Miss Collins and the level of her job security, the heavy oak door opened suddenly, propelling Theolonius Griffin into the room like a top. He was tall, slender, late forties to early fifties, with neat white teeth that spent most of their time poised to reveal the rehearsed smile that he extended to Audrey as he reached for her hand. His tailored suit flattered his athletic build. He strutted like a rooster, an overseer of the biggest hen house in the county.

"Audrey! Come on in and have a seat." The large door opened onto a deceptively small, but elegantly furnished office. Audrey sat down in a chair that was so comfortable it made her remember the sleep she had missed over the weekend.

"What can I do for you today?" Griffin maneuvered his lanky frame behind a beautiful desk whose wood matched the door and chair rail. He sat with the fingers of each hand threaded together. His gold wedding band caught the rays of the morning sun and cast the brilliant shards around the room.

"It's so good of you to see me on such short notice, Mr. Griffin. I know how busy you must be."

"Please, call me Theo." He smiled. "And remember that Theo Griffin is never too busy to set aside a few moments for a beautiful woman."

Audrey bristled at the comment, remembering her distaste for this man when she met him the first time at one of Norma Jean's CRUTCH mixers. These horrible get togethers, held the first Friday of every month, were gatherings of pseudo intellectuals who spent the evening trying to impress one another.

This night it was held at the Stork Petite, a posh banquet hall in a historic hotel in downtown Cincinnati. The less than courteous wait staff, that obviously didn't know when the reservation was made that CRUTCH was a black organization, overshadowed the beautiful art deco appointments and breathtaking view of the riverfront. Though never verbalizing it, the cold stares and chilly responses to queries made it clear they didn't appreciate the decendance of hundreds of blacks encroaching on their establishment.

CRUTCH, (Commitment, Relief, & Upliftment Toward Community Healing) was formed in 1968 by concerned community leaders in the wake of the riots. Audrey's parents had been charter members so it was a natural progression for the Wilson's to maintain a level of involvement. CRUTCH's mission was to pull together the commitment of time, money, property, training, or any other resources, from the haves and distribute these gifts to those in need. CRUTCH provided everything from small business loans to lunch money. The concept was successful because it was based on exchange. The small business that was given help, had to hire a certain number of employees who might not find work elsewhere. The kid who got lunch money had to visit a senior center or pick up litter at a playground. The premise was simple: shared resources empowered everyone. And everyone has a stake in the community.

An offshoot of the organization, Jean's CRUTCH mixers were responsible for fundraising and corporate solicitations. Sadly, many of the participants attended the monthly functions to advance their personal agendas, using CRUTCH as a vehicle to gain entrée into circles that might not have included them otherwise. As beneficial as the structure was, sharp distinctions in class existed. Though the word equality was woven throughout the organization's mission statement, the caste system was alive and fully functioning within the invisible bounds of its constitution.

Norma Jean Strange had never been a part of that set when they were growing up. But one would never know it by the way she glided around with the same pretentious air as the others. In recent years, she'd banded with the social climbing faction of the community, who were staunch supporters of the foundation. They used it as a platform for any and every crusade currently en vogue.

The alliance had been extremely beneficial for Norma Jean Strange. She was on the short list of invitees of every socialite in the tri-state area.

This particular evening, Theo Griffin had openly flirted with a pretty young woman who was considering membership. Griffin's wife, Juanda, sat in a corner of the room all evening drinking while her husband shamelessly pursued this woman. Audrey remembered feeling her pain on the one hand, and on the other, thanking her stars it wasn't happening to her.

"Well, Mr.…Theo, as you know, Norma Jean Strange and I were working on the financial records for Rosemont when she was, when she passed away."

"It's a shock what happened to poor Jean." He leaned closer, emitting a sigh that was heavy with sadness. "And the way that it happened, gruesome. What kind of animal could do a thing like that to someone as beautiful as Jean? I'm sure that I speak for everyone here when I say we loved her and she will be sorely missed."

"I still can't believe that she's gone." Audrey replied. They were both silent for a few seconds before she continued.

"That's the reason that I'm here." Audrey crossed her legs, and repositioned her hands on her lap. "Jean was so dedicated. She felt honored to hold the position and prided herself in the good work that she did. We had a meeting scheduled last Saturday morning, but then…"

"Look. This has been hard on all of us." Griffin rose, walked around to Audrey and handed her a box of tissues. Audrey wiped away tears then blew into the soft paper before continuing.

"Did you see Jean that day?" She had to be careful in how she questioned Griffin. If she made any enemies in questioning the Board, she didn't want Theolonius Griffin to be one of them.

"Of course."

This wasn't going to be easy for her.

"How was she...I mean, when you saw her last?"

"What are you implying?" He backed away from her, and then went back behind his desk. The look he was giving Audrey now was decidedly less cordial than when the visit began.

"I'm not trying to imply anything Mr. Griffin. This has been so upsetting. I don't know what to do."

"I can see you're upset over this. It's painful, but we must go on. I'm sure Norma Jean would have wanted it that way." Griffin's attempt at being conciliatory rang hollow. Audrey wondered what kind of relationship her friend and this man had.

"I agree. As I said earlier, that's why I'm here." The tears were gone. She spoke with a cool authority that seemed to unsettle him.

"Beg pardon?" He stiffened. The words sliced through tight lips. Though he tried to maintain a controlled façade, she could tell she was upsetting him by the elevation in the volume of his words.

"As you know, Norma Jean hired me as a consultant." Audrey pressed on. "We were working to put together the quarterly reports. I feel that I owe it to her to complete the job."

"That's really not necessary, Audrey." His cold eyes held hers.

She could tell that he no longer wanted to talk to her. But she wasn't sure why. It was hard for Audrey to read him, especially now that the words were being filtered through the stone wall Theo Griffin was erecting.

"You remember my wife Juanda?"

Audrey nodded.

"Well, Juanda is tying up any remaining loose ends. She will review Jean's work and make the final government submissions." He shifted a stack of papers from one side of his desk to the other. "We plan on hiring a new director as soon as a respectable amount of time has passed. So you see, there's really no need for you to worry about any of that."

"Well, I'm very glad to hear that. But I'd feel terrible if I'd left any unfinished business. You know how efficient Jean was. It would be no trouble for me to complete anything that she hadn't finished. I could come in a few hours a day..."

"That won't be necessary." He replied curtly. "If you will submit an invoice for any unpaid services rendered, I will personally see to it that you are fully compensated for that and for the term of the contract."

"Thank you, that's very generous." Audrey offered her warmest smile. "But please extend my offer of assistance to Juanda. I'm familiar with all of the reporting systems that Jean established and I might be able to save her some unnecessary time and headaches."

"I will tell Juanda that you are available to assist. She'll call you if she needs you." He continued the shell game with the papers on his desk and making gestures that signaled an end to the meeting. Audrey had to find a way to gain access to Norma Jean's office.

"Do you think it would be okay if I went to the Finance Office and collected my files?"

"What files are those?" He stopped playing with the forms on his desk, no longer trying to mask his irritation. She had overstayed her welcome.

"I had some private files that I really need to have back. They're just spreadsheet templates and business profile outlines that I use whenever I work with a client. This all happened so sudden. We were planning to work last weekend so I left my things there. I really need to have them back if that's okay."

She pulled herself up taller in her seat. Audrey hadn't worked with Norma Jean all those months without learning something about persistence. It must have impressed Griffin. Her cool, authoritative countenance seemed to thaw the icy wall he'd erected.

"Of course it's okay." Theo Griffin the wolf was back, devilish grin and all.

"I'm on my way to a meeting. I'll have Miss Collins give you the key on the way out." Griffin picked up the telephone and gave the order to the matron guarding his door.

"Thank you so much, Theo." Griffin shook Audrey's hand in a way that was strangely seductive. He held it just a breath too long. Instinct told her that he was watching the movement of her butt girdled inside the tight black skirt as she exited his office.

The Doberman extended her paw, giving Audrey the key and instructions to the office. She started to tell her that she knew where it was, but she just let her drone on before thanking her and leaving the room.

On the door were remnants of the yellow crime tape, flapping like ghoulish hands beckoning her into the horror that had occurred there. Audrey touched the switch, flooding the room with florescent light. Except for the closed blinds, Norma Jean's office looked the way it always had. A large Oriental rug underneath the heavy wooden desk, rich brocade upholstered furniture, lots of shiny green potted plants throughout. And the étagère displaying Norma Jean's pride and joy, the colorful faux Faberge eggs. Norma Jean had an enviable collection of the beautiful, intricately patterned eggs in varying sizes. From the miniature ovals, inlaid with tiny swirls of color that rested daintily on a rich bed of red velvet, to heavy, flat-bottomed eggs the size of coconuts, it was a magnificent display. Short, smooth wood pedestals supported amazing three-foot tall ellipsoids encrusted with gold, mother-of-pearl, and enamel accessorized the corners of the room. It was a dazzling grouping that always elicited responses and opinions ranging from glorious to garish.

Though she had an impressive collection in her office, the expensive eggs were kept in her home. These were amassed in her travels and through antique catalogues. She expanded her collection further by ordering from TV. Audrey remembered a call once from an excited Norma Jean when the last of her Joan Rivers' *Imperial Collection* had been received. She reported proudly to Audrey that she had a whole room designated for treasures from television and magazines. At the time Audrey remembered thinking, "Yeah Jean, whatever."

Audrey looked at the five shelved wall unit again. Some of the larger eggs were missing, or had been moved around. Strange, Audrey thought, but then Norma Jean liked to give the ornate baubles to friends and associates. Perhaps she had recently given some away.

She ran her fingers down the warm wood, examining its contents carefully. There were usually more than a dozen of the vibrant eggs on the third tier; each perched on its own gold-plated gilded stand. Audrey's favorite, an egg painted with a delicate lace and pearl design, was in its usual position as was the *Nautical Nocturne* with its lighthouse piercing the night sky. The delicately brilliant *Blue Glacier* with its wonderful winter scene stood as proudly as ever. The lovely blue and white *Cameo Madonna* was perched on the shelf above the others.

She'd half listened as Norma Jean told her the story of the original eggs and the royal Russian family who had commissioned their creation then smuggled the bejeweled ovals out during some war or other. Norma Jean was all into it; knew the names of the parents, the children and all their relations. Audrey remembered one of those times. She had smiled and nodded as her friend prattled on, all the while wishing Norma Jean would shut up and sign the check she'd promised so she could get the hell out of there.

Her reverie evaporated as she looked around the room. It seemed empty without Norma Jean to fill its space. The emptiness was not only due to her physical absence, but the nonexistence of her spirit.

A chill worked its way down her spine as she stepped around dried splatters of blood on her way behind the desk. The gritty crunch beneath her feet as she stepped in remnants of broken glass, made her pause. Audrey drew a belabored breath. Had she not seen these vivid reminders of her friend's death, she could have pretended Norma Jean was out for lunch, or away on vacation. But there was no denying the telltale droplets. Someone had met his or her fate in this room. That someone had been Norma Jean Strange.

She released the breath with a little relief seeing that the police hadn't taken the computer. But they were investigating a murder, not theft. Of course they wouldn't take the machine.

Norma Jean didn't believe in clutter. She would have frowned at the bits of finger print powder residue left by the investigators. As was her custom, the desk was stripped of everything but a gaudy, blue egg shaped paperweight and the computer. Audrey ran her fingers over Norma Jean's chair and shivered. Sitting in her friend's seat gave her an eerie feeling.

She extracted the box of floppy disks from her bag and hurriedly booted the computer, searching through file drawers while she waited for the screen to come up. She knew that she wouldn't have time to get too much snooping done today. She grabbed the vendor files and shoved them into her briefcase. She had brought along a key ring containing all the homeless keys that she had collected over the years and kept in her kitchen junk drawer. She searched the ring until she spotted one similar in appearance to the gold key she had gotten from the secretary. Audrey marked Norma Jean's key with a black dot and exchanged it for her key from home, slipping it off the ring and putting the office key on in its place just as she heard someone coming. It was Lady Doberman.

The frosty personality and icy gray hair were totally incongruent on the slender statuesque woman who stood before her, hand extended.

"I've come for the key."

Audrey handed it over to her with thanks and a smile.

"How much longer do you think you'll be?" Sarah Collins eyed her suspiciously.

"It shouldn't be but about thirty more minutes. I just got the PC to boot up and now I have to find..."

"Just pull the door shut when you leave to lock it." Sarah Collins cut Audrey off abruptly; obviously not interested in anything else she had to tell her. She pulled the door shut and walked away, her heels clicking smartly on the polished tile floor. Disney could have cast this witch in its animated version of Cinderella as the wicked stepmother. The clock was ticking. She'd better get finished quickly before she turned into a pumpkin.

Sweat dotted her forehead and upper lip. She released a relieved sigh when the system was finally up and ready. High-strung and flustered, Audrey dropped the box of floppies. Black plastic squares splattered over the plush rug like playing cards. She scrambled to collected them, fumbling to put one into the slot.

It took nearly thirty minutes to copy the files. Audrey was so nervous during the operation, she hoped she hadn't screwed anything up or destroyed information in the process. She'd have to check the files from home or at her office. She shut the system down and turned out the lights. Another sharp pang of sorrow pierced her heart as she closed the door on the way out of Norma Jean's office.

* * *

It was nearly noon when Audrey got home. She kicked off her pumps and sat down on the sofa, rubbing her sore, swollen feet. She clicked on the TV and waited for the 12:00 News.

As promised, there was Police Chief Hyram Phillips issuing the official statement regarding Norma Jean's death. The custodian found the body, was questioned and released. The cause of death was acute trauma to the head. Phillips made no comment on possible suspects. He talked to the media for about ten minutes more. Then it was over.

Whenever the cameraman pulled back, Audrey could see Rob Hollingsworth. He stood behind Phillips, stoic, looking straight ahead at nothing.

Audrey spent the rest of the day looking over the files. There was a coversheet and a flowchart with footnotes. Theolonius Griffin was listed as President and Chief Operating Officer of Rosemont Township. A sharp black line linked Griffin's name and title to Sarah Collins, his Executive Administrative Assistant. Fancy name, Audrey thought, for a secretary. The Treasurer was Griffin's wife, Juanda. Laughton Glen was listed as the Chief Information Officer and Sylvester Alstead held the title of Director of City Planning. The name of the bank was included in the footnotes, and Price Brothers Incorporated and GAS Diversified was listed among the selection of creditors.

Though Price was well known, Audrey had never heard of GAS. She'd known Griffin's wife Juanda for years. She remembered Alstead from one of the CRUTCH mixers and decided that the two men would be easier to talk to than Juanda would. They probably could give her little more than periphery information, but she could use that to bolster herself for the real challenge of the three, Juanda Griffin.

When they were growing up in Rosemont, the former Juanda Long was one in the cluster of girls that everyone called Dark Diva. Audrey didn't know where the name came from since none of its members were darker than a paper bag.

Their biggest claims to fame were shopping, hair and make-up, taking other girls' boyfriends, then reminding those girls at every opportunity how inferior they were to them. Audrey laughed, thinking about it now. But she could still remember how she felt, how the teasing hurt. Those trivialities had shaken their teenaged world.

She blinked away the painful memory of the tears shed when being constantly told you were not good enough because you didn't have the right look. Many little girls had been like Audrey, burning scalp and skin with straighteners and lighteners. Audrey always wanted to have a little chocolate skinned girl of her own. She wouldn't let a day go by when she wouldn't tell her how beautiful and special she was. Audrey had been too ashamed to tell her own mother. Esther Wilson would have been surprised to know that her daughter was guided by such nonsense. The sad truth was that many blacks felt it was better to have fair skin and silky hair. Dark Diva used this as their primary weapon to cut at the other girl's insecurities. To Juanda and her clan, appearance was everything. It seemed rather poetic that she should end up married to a man like Theolonius Griffin, who took every chance he could to embarrass her and make her look bad in public.

As a result, Mrs. Griffin was cold, embittered, and even nastier than she had been in her youth. Audrey was certain that she could take the frosty Sarah Collins, who guarded her husband's office, and melt her into vapor. She wondered how the two evil women managed to work together.

She took out the pen and note pad that was still blank after her visit with Renita on Friday night. She jotted down everything she could remember about her conversation with Norma Jean. Then she wrote down the names of the Board of Directors of Rosemont Township. At the bottom of the list she added the name of Sarah Collins. On the page designated for Theo Griffin she jotted down information from their brief meeting and made a mental note to call Juanda, Laughton Glen and Sylvester Alstead in the morning.

Opening one folder, she produced a thick, spiral bound book, which was the last five years financial reporting. Everything appeared to be in order for 1994 through 1999. She began to comb through all of the quarterly and year-end reporting. The reports for 2000 showed that there was a hefty increase in revenue, which was offset almost to the dollar by costs. That struck her as strange, but the corresponding highlight letters fully supported the expenses shown.

The letter spelled out the construction of the new wing, which included heavy overruns due to an increase in overall building costs. The contractor, Price Brothers, was widely known and, Audrey assumed, reputable. Harrison Worldwide was responsible for drawing up the plans. The architectural and engineering firm was recognized as one of the best in the world. But there had been dozens of subcontractors used on the construction. It would be necessary to do background checks on any who were unfamiliar to her, or at least review Jean's accounts payable records and invoice files to verify the validity of their work. She'd need to check the incoming and outgoing checks as well. How was she going to get all of this done?

"Carrey!" she said out loud.

Carrey Pensky was the best administrative assistant she could have ever hoped for. A college friend, Sydney Lawson, who was now the owner and Chief Editor of a gay/lesbian newspaper, recommended him to her. The Lawson family, owners of newspapers and breweries since the early ninetieth century, was one of the wealthiest in Ohio. Audrey met Syd at Ohio State. Syd had chosen to attend OSU against her family's wishes, but with her brilliant mind she had no problem garnering a full scholarship. Humiliated at having his daughter attend school on the public dole, her father supplied her with a hefty stipend. She and Audrey became good friends despite their different backgrounds.

Sydney Lawson was so down-to-earth; Audrey couldn't believe she was one of the publishing, beer baron Lawsons. She had the Lawson name, but not their stodgy exclusionary views. It nearly killed her parents when she began publicly expressing her opinions on race and sexuality. Her fiery speech and flaming red hair was a constant, vivid symbol of their college experience.

Syd was still the same firebrand she had been during college. She remembered Syd telling her that the maid had to get the smelling salts for her mother when she saw Syd on TV during the Florida Recount mess. She stood in the center of an inflamed mob of demonstrators waving a royal blue Gore/ Liberman sign and giving a Bush supporter her middle finger.

Her newspaper ran candid, unbiased editorials during the senseless slaying of Timothy Thomas, and the weeks of civil unrest that followed. She even met with the mayor of Cincinnati to participate in forming a committee that would facilitate the healing process. Sydney Lawson was quite a character.

Carrey Pensky had done a summer internship at Syd's newspaper as an office manager. He turned down the staff writer position Syd offered him when the stint was over. She was so impressed with him that she kept an eye out, alerting him to employment opportunities flexible enough to work around his schedule. He didn't want to be bound to traditional office rules or to a rigid nine to five workday. In spite of that, he was punctual, had a great understanding of accounting and excellent bookkeeping skills. He was extremely quick and had he the desire, could easily pass the CPA exam and make a good living in accounting. But being a part-time financial administrator was all the day job he wanted. His real passion was rock music. He played lead guitar with his band, *Stain*, at one of the college area coffeehouses four or five nights a week. Even when he'd come into the office after working into the wee hours, his hair still damp from shampooing out the previous night's color or gel, he always kept everything together. He dressed impeccably, looking more like a business partner than her administrative assistant. Audrey would turn the research over to Carrey.

This decision made her feel so relieved that she decided to take a walk. She pulled on her blue sweat suit and walking shoes. When she opened the door, Freedom barged in crying loud enough to wake the dead. Apparently the day's hunting had netted slim results. He ran to the kitchen and his waiting bowl of fresh chicken parts.

* * *

It was a mild evening. A cool, welcoming breeze combed through Audrey's hair and caressed her skin. She walked at a brisk pace from her birch-lined street with its neat brownstones, all the way to Solstice Lane, several blocks from where she lived, before heading back home.

As she approached her block, she had the strangest feeling that someone was watching her. Glancing to her left and right, and finally turning completely around, she saw nothing that seemed out of place, until she turned the corner to her street.

The whine of the car alarm met her as she approached her house. Glass covered the ground on the passenger side of her car; the glimmering shards jabbed at the twilight, daring the night to consume the waning light.

Her first thought was to run to the car and see if anything had been taken, but then she remembered something she had heard or read about break-ins and hesitated. Her heart pounded with the adrenaline of anger and fear. She noticed the moving curtains at the house next door and wondered if anyone had seen who did this. She'd seen the elderly lady occasionally go in and out of the house next door. Though Audrey had never approached her, she had gotten Ruth Etta Mashburn's mail delivered to her mailbox by mistake. Audrey had just put the letters where they should have gone without knocking. Now she wished she had been more neighborly. Even if the woman did see what happened to her car, she may not tell her.

Looking around the deserted street, she was alone except for the loud wail of the car alarm. She turned it off and cautiously went into the house, grabbed the cordless phone and called the police.

4

Rob Hollingsworth appeared at her door, it seemed, before she'd had a chance to hang up the phone good. Audrey didn't know why a senior detective would have been dispatched to investigate a case of vandalism. When he arrived, she led him to the place where she'd parked her car. He waited while she did a thorough inventory. There was nothing missing. Rob told her it was most likely kids fooling around who got scared off by her alarm. He'd do a bit of canvassing in the neighborhood if she wanted.

"The best defense against this sort of thing is the formation of a block watch. Get together with your neighbors and see if they're receptive to the idea. The precinct conducts classes on the subject and will give you any assistance that you need."

He spoke in the detached manner of someone who's seen so much crime that he did not personalize it. But Audrey detected something else as well. It may have been her imagination, but it seemed that whatever had made him keep his distance the other night was still present. What would make him distrust her?

When they returned from surveying the damage to the car, she busied herself making coffee and cleaning up imaginary water spots from the kitchen counter. Rob's behavior was irritating the hell out of her.

"What time did you leave for your walk?" He was looking at her like she had broken into her own car.

"It must have been about six thirty." Audrey absently checked her watch. "I've been here working most of the afternoon and I wanted to get outside before it got too dark." He eyed her suspiciously as she spoke. She couldn't hold back any longer.

"What's up with you, Rob? Did I say or do something to piss you off?" She set a cup of coffee before him with enough force for it to spill over the cup, beyond the saucer's edge and onto the table.

"Why do you ask that?" He evaded her gaze. Picking up a hand towel, he started wiping up the spill. She snatched the cloth from him and finished cleaning up the mess herself.

"Don't do that to me, Rob. We go back a long way." She shook the towel in his direction. "I can tell you're not being straight with me."

"I'm sorry if I haven't been myself. But to tell you the truth, this case and Norma Jean's death has really gotten to me." He seemed suddenly unsure of what to do with his hands. He finally rested them on the cup, looking into it for a moment before taking a sip. Audrey regarded him curiously. The rock-hard façade softened. His shoulders slumped with the release of the weight of his pending confession.

"I can't believe what that monster did to her. She was beaten, punished. She loved Faberge eggs and had a collection of reproductions in her office. The killer used one of the larger ones as the murder weapon."

Audrey swallowed audibly, remembering the colorful collection of eggs that her old friend kept in her office étagère. The vivid picture of the obvious gaps in the arrangement when she had visited the office haunted her now. Norma Jean's favorite knock-off was the coconut sized, white marble *Blue Swan*. The long-necked bird floated on a beautiful blue lake, with a wintry scene behind it. It was nearly ten times the size of the other eggs and quite a bit heavier. That was the missing egg. How terrible for someone to take something that you love and use it like that against you. It's like the ultimate slap, twisting the knife, rubbing in salt.

But until the murder, Rob hadn't known Norma Jean. How did he know that the eggs were her prize possessions? Since she had them everywhere, maybe he'd just put two and two together. She had them everywhere like many people who collect things. But only a few collectors are as overzealous as Jean was about those eggs.

"The person who did this knew her. He took his time." A ragged breath ripped through him before he continued. "She was beaten savagely."

Rob put his head in his hands, and then rubbed them through his hair. He mumbled something that Audrey couldn't make out. His voice trembled, then trailed off. She'd never seen him cry. It shocked Audrey when Rob suddenly broke down. They'd known each other for years and there was only one other time when she had seen him lose his cool. His friend and partner, Jake Hurley, had been hit by a truck and killed. If that wasn't bad enough, Rob had been there, but had seen nothing that would help catch the killer. He'd gone through a terrible ordeal before the truth was known. It had been awful for him. Audrey put her hand on his quivering shoulder. The act seemed to comfort him.

"He wanted her to feel every blow." He continued. "Nearly every bone in her face was fractured. Her face was so cut and swollen you wouldn't have recognized her. She'd been pummeled all over. I've never seen anything like it." He looked up at Audrey. The sight of his puffy red eyes broke her heart.

"Her fingers were broken and bloody from her efforts to ward off the attack." He looked away, embarrassed by the unrestrained show of emotion. Audrey reached over and hugged him.

"Why would anybody want to make her suffer like that?" Her face was pressed into his chest, muffling the words that stirred up Rob's anger.

"I don't know." He ripped himself from her embrace. "It was mean-spirited, vicious and cruel. A cruel way to die. Whoever did this to her wanted her to suffer. He knew he was not only hurting her physically but damaging her prized possession in the process." Rob sniffed, looking up at Audrey with hurt, angry, red eyes.

"Audrey, Norma and I were seeing each other." The fragile words were whispered through trembling lips.

"What! I had no idea..."

"Nobody did. That's the way she wanted it. This is such a small town and she didn't like the idea of being caught up in the rumor mill. So we kept our relationship on the down low."

"I can definitely relate to that." Audrey raised her brow knowingly. Rosemont was a small town and many of its inhabitants had small minds that they liked to fill with gossip. That had been a contributing factor to her break-up with Emory Kimborough. Everyone knew him. Everything they did together hit the papers. It was pretty overwhelming at times. She could understand Rob wanting to keep his thing with Jean on the DL.

"You must have cared for her a great deal," she shrugged, and then looked at him quizzically. "Isn't it a conflict for you to be involved in this case? Won't you get in trouble at work?"

"Fuck 'em." He snorted, then waved the air with his hand, shooing away self-concern. "They wouldn't like it if they knew we were involved but at this point, I don't care. I mean, I ain't trying to broadcast it or nothing, but if they find out, they find out."

Rob's protruding lips pulled into a frown. After being passed over for the position of Chief of Police, Rob was on the outs with the Rosemont Police Department. He had acted as Interim Chief for a number of months following the suicide of his former boss, Chief Buc Buchannon. When it came time to permanently fill the vacancy, the department went outside and brought in Hyram Phillips.

Audrey knew that this was still a source of irritation for Rob. It had been made even more painful as it had come during the same time that his partner and friend had been murdered.

"I had no idea you were going through so much. Don't keep this bottled up inside, Rob." She touched his hand gently. "If you ever need to talk, call me or come over." She gave his hand a squeeze. "She was my friend, too."

"Thanks, Audrey."

"I was surprised to see you here tonight." She changed the subject hoping to take him beyond his grief. "Why do they have you answering calls for car break-ins?"

"I was close by and knew this was your street. I responded out of curiosity." Audrey's diversionary tactic seemed to work. Rob was back to himself. "I'm sorry this happened to you, but I'm glad that we got a chance to talk."

He touched his head like he had just remembered something.

"Did you call somebody to fix your window?"

"Uh hum. A guy from Dr. Glass is on the way."

"Good." He tore off one of the carbonized sheets that he had been writing on when he'd first come.

"Call this number and they'll tell you how to get a copy of the official police report for your insurance company."

"Thanks, Rob." She reached for the paper. "I'll take care of that first thing in the morning."

"Call your insurance company tonight." He ordered, pointing a stern finger at her. "They should have a check in your hands before the week's out."

"All right." She gave him a hug at the door. He was such a nice guy, she thought as she turned the double deadbolt. Thinking of the detective and her friend as a couple made her smile. What a perfect pair she thought, swallowing the sadness that rose up at the thought that Norma Jean was dead. Poor Rob.

5

Tuesday morning started out bad and became worse with each minute. First, Audrey woke up late. With everything that had happened recently, she'd forgotten to set her alarm clock. The meeting with the Norton Group law firm was at nine. It was seven forty-five when she woke and there was no way she could get dressed and make it across town before nine o'clock.

She rose from the bed, stumbling to her desk to get her Rolodex. She stubbed her toe on the door jam and crashed to the floor. Her knees ached from the fall and burned from the rub of the carpet. Water sprang to her eyes. She grabbed her throbbing toe and noticed the acrylic nail on her thumb had popped off, leaving a ragged stub in its wake.

"Shit! Why today?" She reached for the phone, calling every number that she had for Mr. Norton. She was able to leave messages, but she wanted to talk to J.C. Norton live. As she hung up the phone, she could see the very lucrative account of Norton, Holmes, and Ford slipping right through her fingers.

"I can't believe this." She mumbled to herself as she dialed the number for Minn's Salon. She slammed the phone down when she heard the recording. Of course they're not open, it's only eight o'clock. Being late because you overslept was the worse excuse that she could have, especially with so much on the line. This contract could firmly establish her as a serious player in her field. It wouldn't look good if she wasn't there for the initial presentation. She had to pull a rabbit out of her hat or kiss the account good-bye before she even got it. She called her office.

"Good morning, Wilson Associates."

"Carrey! Thank God you're there." Audrey pushed the speaker button so her hands were free to glue on the wayward nail and buff it while she spoke.

"Where else would I be girlfriend? How's the big meeting going?"

"It's not. I desperately need your help." She recited the morning's highlights while she retrieved a fresh suit and under garments and told him what she wanted him to do.

"Calm down, Miss Thang, nothing is as bad as it seems. I'll take care of everything."

A nearby cathedral's bells chimed ten o'clock just as she reached Twin Towers. It was the most exclusive business address in Rosemont. Brass, stone and glass adorned every visible part of the Towers. Between the two buildings, a beautiful waterfall rolled softly down a craggy formation that was surrounded by mounds of colorful flowers.

Audrey pushed through the tall, smoked glass revolving doors and headed for the bank of elevators to her left. She pressed her knees together to keep them from knocking as she waited for the mirrored elevator car to take her to the twenty-eighth floor.

The receptionist showed her to a glass-enclosed meeting room where Carrey Pensky stood before the projected image of the transparencies he had put together, explaining how WA could trim the law firm's bottom line.

Audrey watched through the glass for a moment, catching her breath and mentally preparing herself to take control of the meeting. Tall, slender and dressed in a tasteful navy blazer and light tan linen slacks, Carrey had the attention of everyone in the room. His blonde hair was combed away from his lightly tanned face, giving him the look of a young corporate mogul just back from a nautical jaunt around the world. Audrey beamed feeling relaxed for the first time that day.

J.C. Norton and the three gentlemen who sat opposite him rose when Audrey entered the room.

"I'm terribly sorry about…"

"Hey, it's not a problem." Norton smiled broadly. "You left us in the very capable hands of your assistant, Mr. Pensky, who not only told us about your unexpected change in plans with your client this morning, but has presented to us your very enticing proposal. If you can produce everything that he's told us thus far, plus be in two places at once, it's going to be hard for us to say no to you, young lady."

"Thank you, J.C.," she said taking his hand. "And thank you Carrey. Carrey is definitely my biggest asset. I have no idea what I'd do without him." Carrey blushed modestly. His blue eyes twinkled as he held the clicker towards Audrey so that she could pick up where he'd left off.

"Before we resume, I'd like you to meet my associates." Norton, a short solid looking man of about sixty, turned toward the man on his left. "Harry Ford, Jr. is one of our senior partners and son of our founding member."

Audrey shook the hand of the thin, sallow faced fellow. Ford seemed mild enough initially, until he locked her into his firm gaze. Killer instinct. Audrey sensed he was quite formidable in the courtroom.

"Clyde Grayson is our accountant. He's been with the firm for almost a decade. You would be dealing directly with Clyde. He has already expressed a great deal of interest and excitement at the prospect of working with you." Grayson pumped her hand heartily, giving her a welcoming smile.

"Marshall Fixx is the newest member of The Group," Norton was saying. "Joining us from Boston. He's consulting with us on a major case involving a messy international thing which will require that whomever we hire to handle financial concerns, is experienced in all aspects of international finance."

Audrey assured Norton that she had expertise in every area of her field. Grayson was still holding her hand. She half listened as he told her how he looked forward to hearing her ideas. Her attention was already on the tall, dark, and gorgeous thing that called himself Marshall Fixx.

He was about six two, maybe taller, with the build of a serious swimmer, cyclist or some sport where zero body fat was a prerequisite. Audrey's attraction to him was immediate. His deep brown skin with red undertones reminded her of a chocolate covered cherry. She was so deep into her culinary fantasy, that she unconsciously smacked her lips.

"Excuse me?" he was holding her hand now, looking down at her. Was that laughter in his eyes?

"Uh, what? Oh, I said it's good to meet you, Mr. Fixx."

His eyes twinkled. It was like he'd bored into her head and was reading her dirty thoughts. Embarrassed, Audrey pulled her hand away from the laughing man and took her position in front at the projector. He distracted her during the remainder of the presentation, an annoying little smirky grin pulled at the corners of his mouth every time their eyes met. It seemed the more professional she tried to be the more his look seemed to mock her. She didn't like him. She imagined he must be one of those pretty boys who had women everywhere. He probably used them like an allergy sufferer uses tissues, leaving them crumpled and wet on the reject pile. Well, she'd show him that she wasn't some hanky to be blown into and discarded. The fact that she was letting him get under her skin bothered her. She didn't even know this guy and after today, it was unlikely she'd ever see him again. Audrey cleared her thoughts and pressed on.

Despite the way the day began, the meeting went very well. Norton promised to get back with her before the week ended to let her know his final decision. While Audrey and Carrey collected their presentation paraphernalia, the men discussed the basketball game that was on TV the previous night.

"Yeah, the Cavs aren't the same without Bobby Wilson."

"Bobby Wilson! Oh, please! You're right about one thing, Cleveland is a much better team without his sorry ass."

Fixx made the comment. Remembering Audrey was in the room, he apologized.

"I'm sorry. I get carried away sometimes talking about the game."

Audrey didn't respond. She gave him a nasty glare that seemed to unsettle him. He probably mistook her reaction as finding his language offensive. Though she thought the foul language was inappropriate, Audrey Wilson was offended by the comment because it was made about her brother.

Bobby Wilson's basketball career had been a succession of highs and lows. After more than a dozen years as their power forward, he'd left the Cleveland Cavaliers two years ago and was struggling to re-invent himself. Basketball had been all he'd known and he was having a difficult time trying to make a living away from the court. The fledgling business Bobby had reluctantly agreed to share a partnership in with her to help athletes with investments was just beginning to show a profit.

There was no way this idiot Fixx knew that they were related. Figuring he had corrected his discretion, he continued expounding on his knowledge of the game. Audrey bit the inside of her mouth until she drew blood. Carrey just gave her that 'let it go' look while they finished gathering their things and headed for the elevators after saying goodbye to their hosts.

"Did you hear that jerk?" Audrey was fuming as the elevator descended. "Who is he to talk about Bobby like that? He doesn't even know the deal. See that's what's wrong with people. They think that sports figures are not human. How would he like it if the whole world could see him at work and constantly scrutinized everything that he did? I'll tell you how he'd like it, he wouldn't! I hate people like him."

Carrey had become more than just someone who ran Audrey's office. They had developed a friendship that allowed her to vent and authorized him to tell her just what he thought. Carrey knew her brother and sister, and he told Audrey about his bed-ridden mother. They even discussed their relationships. Sometimes talking to Carrey was the same as talking to one of her girlfriends.

"Audrey, honey, he's a corporate litigation attorney." Carrey responded. "The whole world *does* watch him at work."

"Humph! He's a hick-town lawyer trying to impress."

"He's from Boston."

"Whatever!" Audrey punched the L button furiously, it's hot amber glow reflecting her mood.

"Don't you think you're pouring it on a bit thick?" Carrey looked at her and shook his head.

"What? You heard him in there saying those mean things about Bobby. And all through my presentation, he was laughing at me."

"Excuse me for saying this, but don't you think you're being just a bit self-absorbed?" Carrey shook his head at her pitifully then smacked his lips at her for affect. "That man was *not* laughing at you."

"You didn't see him?" She stared at Carrey in disbelief. "It was so blatant I felt like slapping his face."

"Audrey, I know you had a really bad morning, but you've had bad mornings before. What's up girlfriend? That damned Dennis fucking with your head again? Or is it Norma Jean?" Carrey looked into her eyes, and then looked down at the floor. He wiped at an unexpected tear. "I'm still feeling that loss too. You know Jean was my girl."

Audrey's friend and her office manager had liked each other. Being so wrapped up in her own feelings about this whole thing, she hadn't even considered that her assistant might be grieving over the loss of Norma Jean too.

Apparently, he had admired her a lot. They would talk for hours about fashion, hair and make-up. They'd talk non-stop about the Style Channel and every new line of every new thing and how "boss" or "baaad" it was. She had never seen a man and woman have such a level of superficiality in common. Carrey's admiration of Jean's looks was more than surface. He had even confided to Audrey that if he ever decided to have plastic surgery and a sex change operation, he would have wanted to look exactly like Norma Jean. Audrey didn't know if Jean would have taken that as a compliment, so she never told her of Carrey's ambition.

She didn't want to share her theory on the reason for Norma Jean's fate, that she had uncovered a theft ring and had been silenced because of it. She still had to come up with a way to get Carrey involved in researching the construction vendors without making him suspicious.

"You're right, Carrey. I just need to chill a minute. Are you okay? Do you want to take a few days off?"

"Oh honey, I'm fine." He shifted the boxes from the meeting on the dolly, making sure that the straps were secure. "I'd go nuts at home; sitting, thinking. I'm much better being at work, trust me."

"When we get back to the office and check the messages, I think I'm going to spend the rest of the afternoon at Minn's." She looked down at the makeshift nail repair she'd done earlier. "I could use a good massage and I need to get my nails fixed. You want to come along?"

"Naw. I got a ton of stuff to do and you know I need to leave early Friday to help get the concert coordinated."

"Oh, that's right. Are you excited?"

"You bet I am." Carrey's eyes danced at the thought of his passion. "We have so much fun at our gigs. You should come."

"I've got plans this weekend, but thanks for the invite." It wasn't the truth, but the last thing she wanted to do was spend an evening bouncing around with a bunch of people half her age. Carrey understood.

"I know you're not into the young, white rock jam, but we do rock girlfriend."

"I know. Renita and I saw you at Sawyer Point in Cincinnati ...remember?"

"That was bitchin'!" He leaned into Audrey, smiling at the memory of the event. "But the club is better. We have to put a little water in our act when we play in the 'Nati."

"I can dig it."

They headed in opposite directions to their cars. When Audrey reached the office parking lot, Carrey was already rolling the dolly towards the entrance. He stood at the doorway until Audrey parked and caught up with him.

"Well, I'm going to make a few calls and I'm out." She said.

Once behind her office door, Audrey compiled a list of all the companies that were used for the construction on Rosemont Township. She included addresses, telephone numbers and columns for dates and contact names. She e-mailed the list to Carrey with instructions to find out who the principals were, each company's date of inception and a history of any activity with Rosemont Township.

On her way out she told her assistant that she was still tying up loose ends on projects that she was working on with Jean.

"Bless your heart." Carrey clucked matronly. "Jean was so lucky to have a friend like you."

6

Audrey spent a relaxing afternoon at Minn's Day Spa getting pulled and primped and exorcised of all the poisonous stress that was building up over everything that she had been dealing with lately.

At five o'clock, she went back to the office. With Carrey gone for the day, she could take some time to pull together her thoughts on this morning's meeting and come up with her next plan of action on how she could get her hands on that report.

She stepped into the lobby of the 710 Plum building, making her usual long strides toward her office, when the door to the first office opened abruptly. A man barged right into Audrey, knocking the wind out of her. She landed on her bottom, blinking to regain focus. When her vision became clear, she looked up and cussed.

"Oh shit!" she looked into the face of Marshall Fixx, squinting at him evilly. Refusing the manicured hand that he offered to assist her from her place on the floor, Audrey leaped to her feet as though propelled by jets. She glowered at the man before her as she brushed imaginary dirt from her the back of her skirt.

"Please, let me help you with that," Marshall said. He was tall, dark, and fine. His magnificent, blinding white smile held her in its power. He was as charming as Billy Dee Williams in *Lady Sings The Blues*. She was still absent-mindedly brushing at non-existent dirt. He moved closer, attempting to assist her in the unnecessary exercise.

Audrey stopped brushing at her skirt and glared at him. Humiliation heated her face and neck. No he wasn't going to touch...There it was again, that mocking tilt to his lips, that teasing gleam in his eyes.

"You get out of my way!" she warned. "What are you doing, following me? I'll call the police if you don't get out of here now!" Marshall laughed out loud at this.

"We're a bit full of ourselves aren't we? For your information, I happen to be a tenant in this building. My office is right here." He pointed to the gold plated lettering on the door, which read MARSHALL FIXX, ATTORNEY AT LAW. Audrey knew that a lawyer had moved into what had been the dentist's office. When she met Marshall Fixx this morning she had no idea that he was her new neighbor.

"Great." She said, and then mumbled half-heartedly. "Welcome to the building."

"Thank you, Miss Wilson." He said, ignoring her sarcasm. "So, you want to come in and have an office warming drink with me, or would you rather have dinner? You look like a meat and potatoes kind of girl to me."

Audrey's brow furrowed. The nerve of this guy. She didn't appreciate the crack about her weight, or his forward manner. Not responding to his invitation, she pushed past him down the hall to her office. She could have sworn she heard laughter before her door closed.

Audrey picked up the phone and punched in Renita's home number.

"Girl, I'm so mad I could scream!"

"Calm down, big sister. Whatever it is can't be *that* bad."

"Have you ever met someone that you immediately could not stand?"

"You mean hate at first sight? Hell yeah, all the time. You know me—I hate everybody. I can't stand my damn self sometimes."

"I'm serious, Ren. I've had one of the longest, most exasperating days that I've had in a while." She proceeded to tell her sister about how she started out late for the meeting, and how her entire day seemed to swirl into the toilet from that point. She told her about Marshall Fixx and what he said about Bobby.

"Well the man's entitled to his opinion. You know how crazy I am about the Baby Boy, but he did kind of suck his last few years with the Cavs. This guy had no idea Bobby was your brother. If he had, I'm sure he would have used more tact."

"Yeah, maybe. I guess I was on edge with all that had gone wrong this morning. But I still think he acted like a butt hole."

"Audrey?"

"What?"

"Did you get the contract?"

"I don't know." Audrey scratched her head, and then looked down at her neat pink nails. "I mean it went pretty well. Carrey is a lifesaver. He had them all eating out of his hand by the time I got there."

"Ooooh! A room full of men, licking out of his hand; just what every gay man wants!"

"Shut up, fool. I couldn't have dreamed of a more professional assistant than Carrey. He was wearing nice business attire and he didn't have that gel in his hair that he sometimes wears. He's really a good-looking guy. I doubt they even knew he was gay, or cared for that matter."

"You are *so* naïve sometimes, Auddie. I don't care what he was wearing; Stevie Wonder could see that Carrey Pensky is gay. If he can't, Ray Charles can give him the 411."

"What difference does it make, Ren? The man does a damn good job. I couldn't ask for a better office assistant."

"All right, all right. Don't get all worked up." Renita hesitated pensively for a moment. "Come to think of it, I didn't know Carrey was gay when I first met him."

"See." Audrey smiled. She liked being right.

"But when he invited us to his cookout and the hot-dogs tasted like shit..."

"Shut the hell up Ren so I can finish telling you what happened." A sigh of exhaustion escaped. She shook her head in wonder at Renita before continuing. "I went to Minn's for the afternoon..."

"You still going to Minn's? That place is so tired! I keep telling you, you need to start going to *RAJ* with me. Girrrl, Bridget will hook you up! You won't need to wear them fake ass acrylics once she gets your nails in good condition."

"Renita! Can we stay on point here? Just try it once." Why couldn't she have a sister who could follow a conversation for more than five seconds?

"Okay. I'm just trying to help you, but if you don't care..."

"Anyway," Audrey continued. "I left Minn's and went back to the office. Who comes barreling down the hall crashing right into me? Marshall Fixx! Turns out he's the thing that moved into Dr. Marcuson's office."

"Wow. That's some coincidence. What's he doing with The Norton Group if he's got his own practice?"

"Who knows? I think he's doing contract work for Norton. He mentioned some international something or other. Who cares? Do you know he didn't even apologize after knocking me down? Then he had the nerve to ask me into his office for a drink."

"Were you wearing any drawers?"

"What?"

"Maybe he liked what he saw when you were down there fumbling around like a punch drunk prize fighter."

Audrey pulled the phone away from her ear, tempted to hang up, and then cracked up laughing.

"Renita, you ain't got good damn sense." She laughed.

"So did you go?"

"Hell no, I didn't go!"

"Why not? You're not doing anything else. You definitely ain't doin' *anyone* else."

"That's just not where my head is right now. I need to get some clients to replace the huge void left when my work with the Township fizzled. If I do snag Norton, it'll be a conflict to be screwing one of the partners."

"I thought you said he was some kind of contractor. That doesn't count. Does it?"

"I don't know. I don't like him, so it doesn't matter."

"Well for someone you don't like, you sure are letting him occupy a lot of brain cells. Don't be afraid to take a chance Audrey. Even if he is working directly with Norton. He's a lawyer. They can always find a loophole. Especially if finding that loophole leads to getting some booty."

"You are *too* silly." Audrey laughed. Maybe Renita wasn't so dizzy after all.

"Just make sure you make him wear a condom." Renita instructed. "He's probably riding every piece of tail he meets."

"That's reassuring." Audrey snorted. She already had enough misgivings. "Don't worry, I'm way past making them wear condoms, Ren. I'm into getting hair samples and checking DNA."

"I heard that."

"Hey." Audrey was sorry for the unkind thoughts she'd had about Renita. "Thanks for being my sister."

"You won't be thanking me when you get my bill."

"Bye Ren."

7

The next day Audrey sat at a small table in the Rookwood Cove restaurant waiting for Sylvester Alstead. The Rookwood was a diner tucked high on a hill in Mount Adams. She was glad that he had agreed to meet her there for lunch. Maybe the change in location from the Rosemont Annex, and a couple of the Rookwood's notoriously potent drinks would help loosen his tongue and he would give her some good information on the construction expenditures.

She could see the wisp of a man coming towards her now. Sylvester Alstead was all of five foot four, when he wore his lifts. His polyester, blue-gray suit reminded Audrey of the Easter suits little boys wore when she grew up in the 60's. She half expected him to produce a basket full of multi-colored eggs.

Alstead's thin, salt-and-pepper hair was neatly trimmed and wavy from brushing and a heavy dose of Murray's that held it in place away from his nutmeg-colored face. Tiny, stucco colored teeth peeped at her from behind thin mustachioed lips. Everything about him was diminutive, except his hands, which were so disproportionately large they made him look even more comical.

Audrey accepted his paw, which was surprisingly soft. When Alstead sat down he extended his hands on the table. They were truly beautiful. The fingers were long and manicured, the skin smooth and without a blemish. Audrey stared at them for a moment before she realized that he was talking.

"It's so lovely to see you again, Ms. Wilson." Alstead's voice had a high, almost feminine tone that caught Audrey off guard. She hadn't remembered this from their earlier meeting, but then they hadn't really spoken. There'd been so many people at the mixer that night most introductions had been acknowledged by quick nods of the head or polite smiles. Or maybe he had sucked down a snout full of helium before he entered the restaurant. The falsetto was so ridiculous Audrey bit the inside of her lip to suppress the laughter that bubbled inside her. He smiled from his seat across from her, not trying to disguise the meaning in his gaze as it roamed from her face, down to her breasts. She struggled to position herself so that the fullness was less apparent.

When the waitress came over, Audrey ordered a latte. Alstead ordered coffee, water, and a corned beef sandwich, all the while never taking his eyes off Audrey's breasts.

She averted her gaze as though she had been the voyeur when his eyes finally moved to her face. He looked her straight in the eyes as though he hadn't completely undressed her moments before.

"What is it you wanted to see me about?" Alstead asked.

"I wanted to talk to you about Norma Jean Strange. As you know, she and I worked together."

He stretched his long fingers out in her direction. She had never seen such beautiful hands on a man. She wanted to touch them. It seemed the more she looked, the nearer to her they came. His fingers were almost touching hers now. He looked at her in such a suggestive way, she began to think maybe Ren was right; she had been lonely so long that she was starting to give off desperate vibes. Audrey removed her hands from the table and pressed her back into the seat, moving as far away from him as the worn brown vinyl would let her.

"Yes. She used to mention you quite a bit." Alstead was saying. "She thought quite a lot of your abilities. Knowing she would be under a lot of scrutiny, she wanted to make sure that everything was being handled properly. She was something else. Smart girl, and so pretty. Due to the construction, we got the opportunity to work closely together. I got to know Norma Jean *very* well."

Audrey really had to bite her tongue now. Was he trying to suggest that he and Jean had a thing together? There's no way Jean would have given this ventriloquist's dummy the time of day. People say all kinds of things when you're not there to defend yourself.

"She told me what a whiz you were with financial analysis and that she didn't know what she'd do without you."

"She told you that?"

"Oh, many, many times."

The waitress was standing before them suddenly holding a black tray. She placed the hot, frothy coffee before Audrey and the platter with the heaping sandwich, chips, and a pickle before Alstead. He thanked her, waiting until she left before examining his food. He took the thick, toasted slice of dark rye from the sandwich and moved the meat around so that it was more evenly distributed before putting the bread back where it belonged.

He bit into his sandwich. Alstead chewed slowly, once again enjoying the view across the table. Audrey unfolded her napkin and tucked it into her collar. Alstead seemed visibly disappointed. He swallowed his food and reached for his water glass.

"She really thought very highly of you. I find intelligence in a woman quite an appealing quality. "

Alstead's unrestrained leering coupled by the scary puppet falsetto was unsettling. A chill ran through her as she watched him gazing at her lustfully. He was so obvious it was insulting. He didn't even care. His powerful glare incinerated the paper napkin then worked the buttons loose on her blouse, stripping it away. His laser beams attempted to burn through her forearms as she raised them in an attempt to cover herself even further. She thought about the old ads she'd seen as a child in comic books. *X-ray glasses! See through doors, walls, and clothes!*

"Uh, yeah. Did, uh, Norma Jean tell you about any special projects that she was working on?" She rubbed her arms to warm the chill brought on by her jitters. "She was putting together an extensive packet of documentation for an audit we were anticipating, but I don't seem to be able to find the information that she'd gathered so that I can complete the work."

Alstead suddenly removed his hands from the table. He eyed her suspiciously before he spoke.

"It was my understanding that you were no longer employed by the Township."

"I'm not, uh, officially," she stammered, looking down into her lap.

Audrey hadn't expected resistance from the little man. Apparently, he'd already spoken to Griffin, who'd made it clear that Audrey was no longer doing any work for the Township. She struggled to recompose herself.

"It's just that Norma Jean was so dedicated. I know how thorough she was and there's no way she would leave a job half done."

"You got that right," he said, working around a mouth full of food. "Mmmm! This sandwich is good." He licked one of his long fingers suggestively. "Yeah, Norma Jean was one lady who did not believe in doing something half-way."

"I want to clean up the stuff we were working on. It's my way of honoring her memory." Audrey welled up. She hoped the comment didn't sound like bullshit. She removed the napkin and used it to wipe tears that didn't exist.

Sizing up Alstead, Audrey took a chance. It was the oldest trick in the book but she was confident it would get results. As if on cue, she began to cry. Sure, it was a cheap way to score points, but it usually worked with a certain type of man. It was what she and Renita called going into your douche bag of tricks. When she felt the angular fingers touch her hand, she knew she was in the house.

Alstead scooted around to her side of the booth. She bent forward slightly so that his hand grazed her breasts. He took the liberty of putting the other one on her thigh. She could feel his hot breath on her face and smell the corned beef. His breath quickened at the sight of the soft brown mounds of her cleavage pulling him in for a closer look. She knew that he would open a vein and give her a pint of blood if she asked him to.

"Please, don't cry. You'll mess up that pretty little face." He pulled out a handkerchief, extending it to her. "What can I do to help you?"

"I'm sorry." Audrey abandoned the ragged napkin and took the cloth he offered. She dabbed at her face dramatically. "I hate it when I get like this."

"Don't you worry about a thing. Let me take care of everything for you." His hand inched higher up her mustard colored wool skirt; his long thumb wormed its way between her thighs, too close to the center. She gasped, wiggling away from his grip on her. His hand brushed over her, giving himself more consolation than her. She'd better get this over with before she wretched right there at the table.

"I need answers to a few questions." Audrey said between sobs. "I promise I won't bother you again."

"It's no problem. Ask me anything you like."

Audrey took a few deep breaths. She wiped her eyes with a dramatic flourish. When it seemed an appropriate amount of time had passed, she cleared her throat, took in a breath and continued.

"Can you tell me the process involved in securing vendors for the construction work? I mean, was it the sole responsibility of Price Brothers Construction to garner these companies and what kind of background checks did you do on these firms?"

"Well, the majority of the companies were long time Price subs; but there were others that Mr. Griffin himself recommended. In those cases, I simply approved the vendors to go into the system. Norma Jean was really great at helping me with the accounting end of it. I'm not good at that kind of stuff. She used to say it was a way to keep us both honest."

"What did she mean by that?"

"We would both check into the areas that we were familiar with. I made sure that the jobs being invoiced were relevant to the project and she'd make sure that the bills were paid. It was sort of a double check."

"So it was like you didn't have to worry because you knew somebody always had your back."

"Exactly." Alstead affirmed. He took another bite of his sandwich. The passionate "Mmmm" sounded like he was having sex with the food. Audrey was ready to end this meeting.

"Oh, my goodness!" she said, checking her watch. "I'm supposed to be across town in forty-five minutes." She took a sip from her cup before grabbing her purse.

"Well, can I drive you somewhere?" Alstead appeared to be deeply disappointed.

"Thank you, but my car is right across the street and I'd hate to inconvenience you."

"I'd really like to see you again, Audrey." He touched her arm with those hands. A shiver went through her.

"I'm really busy the rest of this week." She said quickly.

"Give me your number." He volleyed back. "I'll call you."

Audrey fished one of her cards out of her bag and handed it to Sylvester Alstead, all the while praying to God that he would lose it before he left the restaurant.

* * *

Audrey hurried to her car, not quite sure what to make of the meeting with Alstead. Was he suggesting that he and Norma Jean had put their own spin on the team player concept? That perhaps they had even traded sexual favors? As vile as the idea seemed, hadn't she just done the same thing with him herself? She shuddered at the thought of his hand moving up her skirt. Alstead's touch lingered like a bad aftertaste.

It reminded her of a summer when she was a child. Her brother Bobby smashed a cockroach inside her blouse. She would never forget the gooey green, wet, brown crunch, the stiff hairs of its legs clinging to her shirt when it could no longer cling to its own life. She felt that somehow, the bug had gotten the better of the deal. At least its death was swift. The thought of it still made her queasy all these years later.

Audrey practically ran from her car and straight for the bathroom, pulling off her clothing as soon as she was locked inside the sanctuary of her home.

Just as she had felt more than thirty years prior, she wanted to cleanse herself of the nasty feel of the insect. The water in the shower was almost too hot for her to stand.

8

Audrey pulled up in front of the 710 Plum building and was immediately sorry that she had decided to come there. It was nearly eleven o'clock. She was tired and longed to be home in bed. But one of the files had been misplaced and she couldn't rest until she was sure that it was secured with all of the other Township information.

This was a bad way to start. Tighter controls had to be kept on this stuff from now on. If anyone found out she had the township's files or if the wrong people got hold of any of this information, it would not be good for her. She still hadn't decided when she would return to Jean's office. The thought of sneaking around after hours gave her goose bumps. Not only was it illegal, but it just wasn't the kind of thing she felt good doing. The sour taste that bubbled up from the pit of her stomach every time her mind touched on the idea of the felonious behavior kept her reaching for the antacids. She knew her spirit voice was telling her this was wrong. Her lack of nerve was a warning to stay away from there.

When she passed Marshall Fixx's office, Audrey could see a light coming from beneath the door. If her luck held, he would keep his ass in there and leave her alone.

When she opened the door to her office and turned on the light, she saw the file lying on her desk. How could she be that careless? Had Carrey seen the file? If so, would anything inside garner suspicion? Audrey could only blame the haphazard way her life had become on the fact that she was squeezing too much into her days. She made a mental note to schedule a week of beach time as soon as all of this was over.

Audrey grabbed the file, turning out the lights before locking up for the final time that day. On her way to the elevator, she glanced down at Marshall Fixx's door. The lights were out.

The wind had kicked up a little, blowing a warm gust in her face when she opened the door leading onto the street. In the distance, she saw the familiar figure of a tall man with a wisp of a woman, walking together. They stopped alongside a row of cars parked at the curb. Audrey stepped into the shadows and held her breath, watching them. They stopped suddenly, exchanged a few words and embraced. Marshall Fixx pushed her golden hair away from her face. The woman pulled him down towards her waiting kiss.

9

Marshall Fixx sat in front of his PC that evening daydreaming about his encounter with Audrey Wilson. She'd come into the meeting room like a dynamo, taking immediate and complete control. Her smooth dark skin glowed as she pointed out the benefits of a partnership with her company.

She had a beautiful face, framed by long, straight, black hair, which flowed easily over her slender neck. When she turned away from them, Marshall couldn't help but check out her voluptuous round ass, and big legs that went for days. Her smile was warm, with even, white teeth that looked like they had helped put some orthodontist's kid through college. The full lips made him want to go exploring. He longed to discover what kinds of things came from lips like that. And what kinds of things went into them.

He hoped that she didn't notice him staring at her. During the entire meeting, he had been so engrossed in his fantasizing about her that he was sure she must be able to hear his thoughts.

When he saw her in the hall that evening, his heart jolted and his pulse quickened with excitement. As fate would have it, they were sharing the same office building. There must be something at work other than coincidence, which would have let this come about. Perhaps Audrey Wilson was meant to play a significant role in his life.

When was the last time he'd met a woman who pushed him off balance without even trying, and kept him there? Marlena perhaps, in the early years of their relationship. But none of the women he had met since the divorce.

Thinking of Marlena reminded him that he needed to call Toots this evening. Maybe he should fly up for the weekend instead. He knew his son would like that, even if his mother didn't appreciate it too much.

He couldn't blame Marlena for the way she responded to him. He had been wrong. His stupidity had cost him his family. She was a good woman and they had a healthy and talented son. Marshall had thrown it all away.

Maybe with time, she would be a bit more forgiving—for the boy's sake. He pulled the telephone towards him to make the call. If Marlena had no objections, he'd fly up on Friday. Before he finished dialing, there was a knock at the door. He walked to the outer office to open it.

"Happy office warming!" Chloe wrapped herself around him like a cat, giggling when she almost dropped the bottle of champagne and glasses that she held in her hands. The items clinked up against themselves as he caught them, leading her and the libations into his office. Chloe giggled again like she'd already started on the booze without him. From the top of her pastel pink blouse she produced a multi-colored noisemaker with bright pink foil frizzed at the bottom. She blew into it and laughed through giddy, full red lips.

"Are you surprised?"

"I am. When did you get to town?" The words slipped cold and quick through tight lips. What the hell was she doing here?

"Oh, I haven't been here too long." She strutted around the room, bold and full of confidence. It was one of the characteristics Marshall had initially found so attractive.

Compact and petite as a Barbie Doll, Chloe was an attention getter. When she entered a room, everybody knew it. The heels of the pink pumps were more than three inches high, making her a towering five foot two. The highlights in her golden hair shimmered in the florescent lighting. Leaving a trail of sweet heavy fragrance in her wake, she strutted around the office, running her finger along the wainscoting behind the reception desk. Looking down at her fingers, she wiped them on her hot pink suit.

"How did you know where to find me?" He certainly hadn't told her. Chloe was the last person he wanted to deal with right now. Chloe Dillmore had worked as Marshall's paralegal in Boston. They'd had a good working relationship for months. Until a few weeks of spending several long nights working on the case of a major client led to a night of passion on his office divan. That's when everything changed.

The affair lasted long enough to destroy his personal life and chip away at his professional one as well. Chloe was a sweet girl with a psychotic side that surfaced when things didn't go her way.

"Everybody knows Marshall Fixx, the famous litigation attorney. Aren't you going to open the bubbly?" Chloe walked around the office like she was casing it for some crime she would commit at a later time. Knowing her, Marsh thought, that's probably just what she was doing.

"Maybe some other time." Marshall didn't try to mask his irritation.

"No time like the present I always say." Chloe moved towards him, rubbing her firm body against his. He caught her hand, roughly pushing it away before she had a chance to pull down his zipper.

"Let's not start something that we can't finish."

"Come on, baby. You remember how good I make you feel." Chloe purred.

"You really never made me feel that good, Chloe."

She drew back, hurt. Then she was angry. She pushed her porcelain face towards his. Hot words flowed like lava from her pouty mouth

"What the hell is that supposed to mean?" Her skin smoldered red with embarrassment and anger.

"It means just what I said." He spat back. "Look, I'm tired. I've had a long day. I'm finishing up some things I had to get done. Then I plan on going straight home and hitting the sack. Alone. I'm preparing for a new client and with the consulting work I'm doing, I scarcely have time to take care of my base clients. That's why I'm here tonight. If you'd called I could have explained that to you and saved you a trip."

"Hey, keep your explanations." Chloe waved a dismissive hand in his direction. "You didn't have all these excuses when you were trying to get me to fuck you while I was going through my divorce." She folded her arms across her chest and jutted a petite hip out defiantly.

"Let's not rehash all that again." Marsh walked to the other side of the room, then turned to face her angrily. "I just want you to understand that I didn't mean to hurt you. It's just not going to work between us. Can you understand that, Chloe?"

"Oh, I think I can figure it out."

"Can you? Good. Let me call you a taxi or see you to your car."

This is the last thing I need, Marshall thought. He grabbed his keys and turned out the lights. They walked together down the street. She pointed to a red mustang with a white ragtop. He could see the tears in the light of the streetlamp and brushed her hair from her eyes. She pulled away from him. Marsh hated that she was in pain, but he didn't want her to think that he wanted to be with her. He put her key in the lock and opened the door for her. Chloe pulled him down towards her, desperate. She kissed him deeply. He figured if he went along with it, she'd go away and leave him alone. But to the contrary, she mistook his participation in the act as evidence of his desire for her. She smiled hopefully.

"I'll give you the number where I'm staying."

"Why, Chloe? I'm not going to use it."

Chloe glared at him sharply. Looking behind her anger, he saw the pain she was still in over their break-up. He felt bad, but what was he supposed to do? He'd told her it was over between them a long time ago.

"I'm sorry." He couldn't think of anything else to say.

"You *are* one sorry bastard!" She wiped at tears, smearing a dark line of mascara down her cheek. "But you're not as sorry as you're going to be."

"We've got nothing more to say to each other." Marsh tried to lead her to the car. "Why don't you just go on back to Boston?"

"I'm staying right here for as long as I want." She pulled away from him. "You brushed me off before and I'm not going to let you do it again. I let you treat me bad then. You're not going to get away with it this time."

"You're talking crazy Chloe. I'm going home. Don't come here again."

Marshall headed towards the parking garage. Why did this crazy heifer have to re-surface? She'd practically stalked him in Boston. Now she was here, trying to pick up where she left off.

In the distance, he saw the unmistakable stride of Audrey Wilson, going towards the lot across from the office building, walking with such determination and purpose. Seeing her, he totally forgot about Chloe and began moving in Audrey's direction, deciding to gamble that she'd talk to him. He quickened his step.

"Audrey. Hold up a minute."

Audrey hesitated, and then continued on. Stepping up his pace, Marsh wondered if she'd heard him. She stopped in front of a shiny black Saab. Climbing inside she sped away before he could reach her.

"Damn!" He stood at the edge of the lot, dejectedly. She had ignored him. He must be making a nuisance of himself. Perhaps his approach had been wrong. Maybe he'd stop by her office one day this week and invite her to lunch.

"Who the fuck was that?"

He had successfully pushed Chloe out of his mind. But she was still there. She had pulled up beside him in the tiny coupe, her blue eyes turned black by the night sky. Her face twisted in anger as she spoke.

"Is that the reason you didn't have time for me this evening?"

"Why don't you go on home or wherever you're staying? I'm not in the mood for this shit tonight."

"Well, I am! You're not going to brush me off like I'm nothing."

"Chloe, go away."

"Or what are you going to do?" Her face was twisted into an evil grimace.

"I'm not going to do anything Chloe, not with you and not to you. No matter what kind of scene you try to make, it doesn't faze me." He threw his hands up in exasperation. "I'm done."

"We'll just see about that. If you think I'm just going to step aside and let that bitch take my man, you got another thought coming." She poked a threatening finger in his direction.

Marsh looked at her and shook his head in disbelief.

"You need help." Still shaking his head he looked in the direction the Saab had taken. "You have a good night. I'm outta here."

A barrage of obscenities pelted him as he turned and headed once again for the parking deck. He knew what Chloe was capable of and prayed she wouldn't make good on her threat. Audrey didn't deserve this nonsense. But he knew Chloe and knew this wouldn't be the last of her. A hot knot tightened in his stomach as he started up his car and pulled out into the darkened street on the way home.

10

"Girl, guess what? I was leaving the office tonight and I saw that bastard Marshall Fixx slobbering all over some white girl."

Audrey called Renita almost before her front door closed. She couldn't remember the ride home. The fire burning in the pit of her stomach caused her to lose track of time and space. She totally loathed this man. Why did he irritate her so?

"And? Just because you tried to make him out to be a sociopath doesn't mean the man has no social life." Renita's pronounced yawn left no denying her level of interest in the conversation.

"Why would he ask me to dinner when he's got a woman?"

"Maybe he doesn't have a woman. That could have been anything Audrey. Maybe it was a grateful client showing her appreciation."

"Yeah, right. Whatever it was, I'm keeping my distance. The last thing I need is another problem."

"Why's it got to be a problem? If he asks you out, go. What could it hurt?"

Renita had a different take on relationships than Audrey. She was never hesitant in approaching a man that she found attractive. If she felt like screwing him ten minutes after they met, that's exactly what she'd do. Renita found Audrey's vacillation boring. Sometimes Audrey wished she could be as cavalier about relationships as Renita.

After they'd hung up, Audrey considered what they had discussed. Why not go to dinner, and dinner only, with a good-looking man? He *was* attractive and she didn't have to marry him. It was only dinner. He was kind of irritating, but she wouldn't deny that she felt a spark every time he was near. Why not check him out? Renita was right, that woman could have been anybody. As an attorney, he dealt with all sorts of people. She'd just wait and see how it played.

11

An overcast sky was the backdrop to the parking area as Theolonius Griffin stood at his window on Thursday morning. The conversation with Sylvester Alstead had caught him off guard. Not only had Audrey Wilson been issued payment for her services, but she had also been compensated for the term of her contract with the Township. She had no reason for any further association with The Board, yet she was still going around questioning everyone who had worked with Norma Jean Strange. What was she up to? Had she uncovered their plan and was now making some kind of backhanded attempt at extortion? If it was money she was after, she could forget it. This thing had already gotten bigger than the initial intent. Pretty soon every man and his gray haired uncle would be slicing off a piece of the ever-narrowing pie.

Whatever she was after, she seemed pretty determined to get it. She'd talked to everyone but Laughton. Luckily they'd been able to keep that insipid fop in the dark about the entire operation. He cared more about trying to maintain his golf score than keeping up with the inherent problems with the Township's financial software.

Juanda already told him that Audrey Wilson had been calling her to get together. The intent certainly wasn't for a social meeting. Though she and Juanda had known each other since childhood, they could hardly be considered friends.

Griffin told his wife to go ahead and talk to her. It was almost time for their meeting to take place. It bothered him that she was out there snooping around. She was on a hunting expedition of some sort. But what was she looking for? How much did she know? It seemed that if she had evidence of what they had been doing, she would have made her move. But she had approached none of them about money.

He let the curtain fall and walked away from the window. He knew they'd been asking for trouble when they hired her as a so-called consultant. It had been Norma Jean's idea to bring her in as a shield. But they realized all along the potential for that part of the plan to backfire on them.

He walked over to the office door, checking to be sure that his secretary was away from her desk before closing it. Griffin pulled open his bottom desk drawer and moved back a weathered baseball glove to reveal a fifth of J&B. He splashed a small amount into a glass and turned it up.

When he looked out the window again, he was just in time to see Audrey Wilson close the door of a black Saab and head for the door of the building, carrying a leather-bound folder. Griffin hoped that Juanda remained cool during their discussion. No matter what he had taken her through, she had proven herself loyal in the past. He trusted she would not fail him now.

Thirty minutes later, Griffin watched as Audrey Wilson glided down the steps, self-assured, her long, shapely legs accentuated by shiny black pumps. He snickered when she stopped suddenly, stock still in front of the vandalized car.

He laughed out loud watching her gaze dismally at the flattened rear tire. The engine would not respond to her repeated attempts at starting it. He hadn't expected them to do anything beyond letting the air out of the tires, but the look on her face was priceless. He'd have to give them a little something extra for their initiative. She'd most likely spend the rest of the day at the dealership taking care of her car. That would give the two thugs he'd hired even more time to place the recording devices throughout her house.

She paced in front of the car talking on her phone. He detected her agitation even from his distance to the street. This should serve as an indicator of what happens when one delves into areas that don't concern one. If she were as smart as Norma Jean claimed, Audrey Wilson would take this as a warning that she should mind her own business.

Griffin swirled the liquid around in the glass before gulping down the last bit. He checked the window again. She continued the frantic pacing, the cell phone pressed into her face, her mouth moving animatedly. She looked around as if expecting the offender to step forward and confess. Maybe she was looking for a knight to ride up and rescue her from her distress.

"Smart-ass bitch. Look at her." He mumbled under his breath. "She doesn't look so smart now."

He chuckled softly, wiping the inside of the glass with a towel before putting it and his stash back in their hiding place. He headed out of his office and onto the street. Griffin smiled as he approached her, asking if he could be of service. Detecting a nervous irritation as he drew near, he was filled with delight. Perhaps this was enough to give her second thoughts about snooping around. If this this weren't enough, Griffin would have to be a bit more persuasive.

12

Audrey stood by her injured auto waiting for the wrecker. She'd contacted the police as well. To have her car vandalized twice in less that a week was just a little too much coincidence for her to swallow. Could someone be trying to coerce her into dropping her questions related to the Township?

No sooner had the thought entered her mind than she saw the lean frame of Theolonius Griffin bound down the steps.

She wasn't sure which seemed less sincere, his smile or his offer of help. She told him she was waiting for a wrecker and that she'd be okay by herself until the tow truck arrived. The police and the wrecker arrived simultaneously. Audrey talked to the officer who scribbled onto a carbonized pad, while the tow truck driver scooped up her car and waited for his turn to get some information.

Griffin made small talk with the officer a few feet from the tow truck. Audrey was going to thank him but the obvious glint of satisfaction lighting his eyes stopped her cold. The attendant helped her into the cab of the truck and it pulled off.

*　　　*　　　*

An hour later Audrey sat in the waiting area of the SAAB dealership nursing a cup of dark brown sludge that was being passed off as coffee, and flipping through a magazine. She only pretended interest in it while she thought back on her meeting with Juanda Griffin. She could tell from the start that Juanda had little interest in meeting with her and even less in taking her up on her offer to continue helping with the books. She still needed to get hold of that report. If she weren't able to persuade Juanda to let her come back, she'd have to use the key she'd swiped and come back at night. Juanda Griffin wouldn't budge.

"We've got everything under control." She was iceberg cold. "Norma Jean was so organized we had no problem with the ledgers. The tax filings will be a breeze."

"But what about the other government filings?" Audrey hoped that a winning smile and a courteous demeanor would melt the old berg. "Some of the documentation is complicated and requires an experienced eye to ensure there are no problems later."

"If *you* could do it, so can I." The woman stood, signaling an end to the meeting. "Now if you'll excuse me."

What in the world is going on with these people? When she'd worked there as a consultant, the staff, though not the most personable group, was very responsive, welcoming her queries and recommendations. Now they all behaved in a guarded, almost sinister way. When Audrey spoke to Juanda Griffin a couple of days ago, she seemed cordial enough. But this morning she behaved in a manner that was beyond rude.

Even though they had grown up together and attended the same schools, Juanda kept calling her 'Miss Wilson'. Whenever Audrey called her by her given name, Juanda Griffin looked over the rims of her designer frames and wrinkled her lips as though she had just sucked on a lemon. Audrey wasn't always the fastest horse out of the gate, but she realized the implication. Juanda was 'Mrs. Griffin' throughout the rest of the meeting.

Audrey checked her watch to verify the time on the waiting room clock. Eleven fifteen. Rummaging through her bag for her cell phone, she called Renita. No answer. Her sister was probably still sleeping. She returned the phone to the bulging black bag and retrieved the note pad. Audrey turned to a clean sheet and put Sylvester Alstead's name at the top of the page. She wrote down everything that had occurred during their meeting from his appearance to his demeanor when she'd questioned him. On a separate page, Audrey made notes regarding everything she'd discussed with Juanda. She checked to make sure she hadn't left out anything before returning the pad to her bag. Restlessness prevented her from sitting there any longer. Audrey collected her things, snubbed the salesman who'd earlier tried to persuade her it was time to trade in her '94 900 S for a new 2002, and went to customer service.

She stood there, patting her foot impatiently while the clerk pulled her paperwork and called the repair technician.

"Miss Wilson, the rear tire has an inch long gash in it. There was no evidence of glass in or around the hole." He raised his brow. His sidelong glance and expression sought an explanation for the ruptured tire. When none was forthcoming, he continued.

"Seems to have been deliberately caused. The cables to your battery were disconnected. The folks who towed you should have caught that and corrected it. How much did they charge to bring you in here?"

"Never mind that." Audrey snapped. "If you're going to have my car much longer, I'll need to have a loaner." The last thing she needed was to be patronized by this guy.

"We replaced the tire and re-hooked your juice. You're ready to roll Ma'am. Just pay the cashier and she'll give you your keys." He pointed in the direction of a woman behind a counter at the building's entrance. Audrey paid the bill and grabbed her receipt and keys.

Weariness dropped over her like a net as she got inside the car and pulled out into traffic. Up ahead, a colorful row of flowers lined a brick walkway leading to a strip of tiny shops. She pulled the car next to her favorite health food store. A little quiet time feeling the calming effects of herbal tea would help her forget about the trials of the morning.

Audrey turned off the ignition, walked around to the sidewalk and let the blend of rich, spicy fragrances pull her into the store. She selected chamomile and sleepy time teas and a packet of patchouli bath beads. Her shopping done, she left the tiny shop and stood before the car, fumbling with her keys. As she was opening the door, a dark, late model car whizzed by her. If she had moved a millisecond more slowly, she would have been knocked across the street.

Audrey pressed herself against the Saab. Her heart pounded rapidly as she considered what had almost happened. That car had nearly hit her. Could it have been a coincidence or was someone trying to do her harm? If it was just an honest mistake, why didn't the driver stop to see if she were okay? The gray, overcast sky may have reduced the offending drivers visibility. Or maybe not. Everything had happened so quickly, Audrey hadn't been able to get a good look at the car. She didn't know the model or make of the dark sedan. Looking around, she cautiously swung the door open, slid behind the wheel and quickly locked herself in. With trembling hands she put the key in the ignition and let the windows down. Gulping the misty air and the rain showers pelting her face helped to clear her head. She started up the car and slowly headed for home.

It was almost noon when she reached the row of condominiums and parked her car. She ascended the stairs and tried to steady her nervous hands while unlocking the door. Drained of energy and still shaken, she flopped down on the couch and sat there until she felt herself calming. Remembering the tea in the small bag she'd brought inside, Audrey went to the kitchen and turned the burner on under the stainless steel kettle.

The whistling pot jolted her from the dream-like state she had drifted to. She poured hot water over the fragrant square pouch. The herbal steam soothed her, relaxing her senses and easing her mind. She grabbed the cordless phone and called Rob Hollingsworth.

When the doorbell rang for the third time, Audrey went over and peeped through the hole. She opened the door and let Rob inside. After she'd gone into a recital of all the things that happened with her car that morning, he just brushed it off as a schoolyard prank.

"A prank? What about that idiot who tried to run me down?"

"That was *your* fault." He held up his hand and continued before she could object. "You should never open your car door into oncoming traffic. You probably gave that poor driver a heart attack."

"So why'd you come over here, to give me a ticket?" Rob Hollingsworth had canceled out the calming effects of the chamomile tea long ago.

"No. I need to ask you some questions related to a situation we've uncovered. How closely did you say you worked with Norma Jean on the accounting for Rosemont Township?"

"We worked together on nearly everything except cash disbursements. She hired me as a consultant and I signed off on all of the higher-level entries that were made. I also made recommendations on how to file various governmental reports. What's up?"

"We had our own accountants review the books which were confiscated the night of the murder." Rob seemed suddenly as weary as she had been. He plopped down into a chair like a rag doll. Audrey leaned near him, concerned.

"What's wrong? Was there a problem with the books?"

"There is evidence that someone was embezzling funds from the Township." The statement hung in the air like a noose. Audrey wasn't about to step into it.

She didn't know what to do or say next. She hadn't mentioned to Rob what Norma Jean had uncovered. With the questions he had asked her when he came in, did he suspect her of any wrongdoing? Audrey decided to play it innocent. Hell, who's playing? She *was* innocent.

"There's no way. Norma Jean and I reviewed everything together. I never saw any evidence of anything improper."

"Perhaps she didn't want to involve you in her scheme."

"Scheme? What do you mean *her* scheme? Are you saying that Norma Jean was stealing?" Audrey's eyes bucked in disbelief.

"That's what it looks like, Audrey." Rob looked at her curiously. "Did you know someone was stealing?"

"No. I had no knowledge of anything like that." She hoped she sounded convincing. "If someone was stealing, what makes you think it was Norma Jean?"

"We've reviewed her personal accounts. The evidence is all there. It has all the markings of a classic case of embezzlement. You know the deal, sudden extreme change in lifestyle. She recently bought a brand new car and she fully furnished a home in an upscale neighborhood. I knew that she was making a good salary as director so I didn't think anything of it before."

He tried to sound nonchalant, but Audrey heard the tremor in his voice. Lines furrowed his forehead like a newly plowed field. It seemed he had aged considerable in the last few days. His sad eyes moved away. He didn't want them broadcasting his vulnerability. Audrey remembered that he and Norma Jean had been dating. Rob was still in pain.

"Audrey, I thought I knew her." His eyes were a mask of hurt and confusion. "Why would she do such a thing?"

Audrey didn't answer him. She couldn't. This didn't make any sense. Norma Jean wanted her to confirm a suspicion that she had. She must have known that the evidence would lead to her. Why would someone who was stealing do something that stupid?

And she was dating Rob. Didn't she care that he might lose his job if he were connected with someone who committed a felony?

If she told Rob of their last discussion, he'd think she had been lying. He'd wonder why she was just mentioning this so long after Norma Jean's murder. Since she hadn't come forward, he would think she was involved.

"Audrey, I have to ask you something." Rob look at her, away, then back again. "I'm sorry that it's come to this but you're mixed up in this thing no matter how you look at it. The question is to what degree. I need for you to surrender your personal and business financial records."

"What! I've already told you I was a contractor, nothing more."

"Did you have knowledge of any wrongdoing on the part of anyone?" His gaze held hers. She was afraid of what he'd read in her eyes. And afraid to look away.

She should have been prepared for his question, but she wasn't. Once it was said, the whole mess took on a greater meaning. Audrey knew that she was in big trouble. There was no getting around it.

"No. And before you ask, no, I was not stealing myself." She said indignantly.

"Your finances will have to be audited none the less. It took our private audit firm next to no time to find irregularities on the Township's books. Why wouldn't you have found the same things?"

"She was my friend. I was doing her a favor. I was there for moral support more than anything else."

"You just said you were involved in everything." The words splayed in her direction like a shotgun blast.

"What I meant was..."

"The Board of Directors of Rosemont Township hired you to do a job." He cast her a skeptical glance. "I'm sure that their reasoning was to make sure that a system of checks and balances were being adhered to."

"Norma Jean did the real work." Audrey explained. "I signed off on reports she compiled after ensuring their overall reasonableness. I was there in a support capacity only."

"So you were only accepting payments."

"They were not 'payments'." Audrey spat, incensed. "I was an employee being paid for services rendered."

"You know how this looks, don't you? Turn over your records, Audrey."

"What if I refuse?"

"The Feds have already frozen your assets." His voice was firm. His tone, serious.

"How can they..."

"A good portion of the money that was coming in for the construction costs was from government grants." He continued. "So whether you agree to it or not, they've got you."

13

Later that afternoon, Audrey arrived at her sister's place and walked inside the tastefully furnished townhouse like a zombie.

Renita tried talking to her but she just sat there nursing her gin & tonic. She was on her third drink when Renita snatched the glass from the table and dumped its contents down the sink. She moved close to Audrey and sat down.

"Are you going to tell me what's wrong or are you just going to drink yourself into oblivion?"

"I just found out that Norma Jean was the person stealing from the Township." Audrey slurred without looking up.

"You're drunk." Renita searched her sister's face for a hint of temperance.

"You're right. I am drunk. But that doesn't negate the fact that Jean was stealing."

"That doesn't make any sense, Audrey. Who told you that?"

"Rob Hollingsworth." Audrey felt for the glass of liquor that was no longer there. "They were seeing each other, you know."

"Rob and Jean were going together?" Renita curled her lip in disbelief. "Get out!"

"I promised Rob I wouldn't say anything, so don't say anything about it, okay?" Renita shook her head. "Anyway, he was just as stunned as I was, maybe more so."

"If she was the thief, why would she ask you to help her determine if someone else were stealing?" Renita asked.

"That's what I've been trying to figure out. Maybe she was going to use me to hang the theft on somebody else." Audrey looked dejected. Her head hurt from trying to figure this thing out. "I'd been working with her for months. I never saw anything out of line."

"But you weren't looking for embezzlement, you were looking for...what the hell were you looking for?"

"I was assisting with reporting. Period!" Spittle sprinkled the back of her hand and she wiped at it with a napkin. Audrey was getting a little tired of explaining her role with the Township. She was beginning to feel paranoid.

"She was probably very selective in the information she presented you." Renita scratched her head like the revelation was some pesky irritant.

"Yeah, and I didn't ask too many questions. I really didn't want to help her. The stuff she had me review was so trivial. It was almost as if..."

"She was trying to set you up." Renita said the words that Audrey couldn't. "That bitch!" She slammed her palm on the table. "I told you not to trust her ass."

"I should have listened to you, Ren." Audrey said ruefully. "But I never would have thought Norma Jean would set me up like this." Audrey pushed her hair away from her face. "Since I considered Jean a friend, I was careless in my review of the work she put before me. I knew that she was a good accountant so I never dove into the details. I just signed off if the bottom line looked reasonable."

"That's exactly what she was counting on. So they have solid proof she was stealing?"

"Rob told me that her bank records prove it, not to mention the six hundred thousand dollar house in Clairmont Hills. He told me it's fully furnished. "

"I didn't know our little friend was living so large. They had to have suspected something at her bank, or was she sleeping with the bank president so he would look the other way?" Renita asked.

"It wouldn't surprise me. But that's not the worst of it. The Feds have frozen my assets."

"Oh shit!" Renita's eyes bucked in disbelief.

"Oh shit is right. Major portions of the township's revenues were from the federal government. There was a sixty million dollar grant. The funds were not appropriated in the manner contracted by the Feds. They're still following the paper trail. They think I helped to divert the expenditures."

Renita went to the cabinet and returned to the table with two tall glasses, a liter of tonic water and a sealed bottle of Bombay Gin. She filled a dark bucket with ice and sat it in front of Audrey. She cut a lime into eighths and brought the bowl of green wedges to the table. The two sisters sat and sipped their drinks until they turned watery from the melted ice.

Renita touched her sister's hand. Audrey's eyes were tired, but her face possessed a strong determination.

"What you gonna do, Audrey?"

"I'm going to find out exactly how the embezzlement occurred. If I have to turn that office upside down, I'm going to get to the bottom of this." Her index finger sliced the air angrily for effect. "They may have blind-sided me with this bullshit, but I'll be damned if I'm going to roll over without a fight."

"Be careful, Audrey. We still don't know for sure what happened to Norma Jean. Nobody has said how much money we're talking about in total. Judging by her change in lifestyle it must have been a substantial amount. It could be the reason she was killed."

"It could be that someone got tired of her playing games." Audrey countered. "She was secretly seeing Rob and allegedly that weird-ass Alstead. She seemed to be lying to everyone. Anybody could be the killer. I'm so mad right now, I could kill her myself."

"Maybe if you talk to Rob the two of you can form an alliance. I don't think he could possibly suspect you of being involved in this." Renita patted her hand sympathetically.

"Form an alliance? Shit, Rob's about ready to vote my ass off the island."

"He thinks you were involved?"

"You didn't see the way he was looking at me and hear the kinds of questions he was asking." Audrey shook her head, doubting that Rob was prepared to trust her or anyone else. "He's probably afraid to let his guard down, and I can't say I blame him. He's a cop first and a friend second. Look at what happened when he trusted Norma Jean. I just don't feel I could confide in him."

"I think it's a mistake to go snooping around that place when nobody's there. Anything could happen to you."

"Not if you come with me." Renita drew back her hand like Audrey's flesh had gone cold. Audrey didn't look at her sister. She knew what she would see.

"Now I know you're crazy."

"Come on, Ren." Audrey touched her shoulder, trying to encourage her. "You could play look-out."

"This isn't a game, Audrey. This is about murder and prison. Someone has died and it looks like you have a pretty good chance of being set up in an embezzlement scheme."

"Well if you won't help me, I'll have to do it alone. Maybe everything that you're saying is right. But I need to be as prepared as I can be. I don't know who's behind this thing. But I'm not about to just let them play me for a sucker."

"I hear ya' girlfriend. They might beat me, torture me, and kill me. But I pity the fool who tries to play me. I'd better help your mule-headed ass get through this cause I can see there's no talking you out of it."

* * *

That night Renita pulled her gold Toyota Land Cruiser across from the Administration Building. They watched as one of the custodians propped the front door open and went around to the back of the building, presumably to smoke a cigarette. They had to move fast or they would not be able to gain entry. Renita pulled the car across the street. Before she could turn off the ignition, Audrey was fussing.

"Do you think we could be a little bit more conspicuous? Park this big ass thing over there in the shadows, would you?"

"Look, don't start no shit or I'll drive away and leave you here to deal with these criminals by yourself."

Audrey kept quiet as Renita moved the vehicle to a more secluded area on the street. The sound of the car door and their feet hitting the pavement seemed magnified tenfold as they walked toward the building and slipped inside.

They hurried down the hall to the office that used to belong to Norma Jean Strange. Audrey extracted the key she had lifted from the Doberman. It turned easily in the lock. The room was completely empty.

"What do we do now, Sherlock?" Renita cast Audrey a snide gaze.

"Now, we go home."

14

The next day Audrey felt exhausted as she headed towards her office. As soon as she opened the door, Carrey was out of his seat and running towards her, like Butterfly McQueen in *Gone with the Wind*.

"Audrey! Audrey! You remember that tall fine black man who was at the Norton meeting the other day? Well, he was here."

"Marshall Fixx?" She feigned indifference.

"That's him! That's him!" Carrey waved his hands like Audrey had just won a round of charades. "He left his number and said something about wanting to meet with you to review his portfolio. He's the attorney who moved in down the hall into Dr. Marcuson's office. Isn't that a coincidence?"

"Did you schedule an appointment for him?" Her heart flip-flopped, but on the surface, she remained calm.

"Your 2:00 canceled, so I put him in there."

"You gave him the standard list of documentation he should bring?"

"Of course. That and the paperwork for self employed professionals."

"Great." Audrey took the stack of remaining messages back to her office. Most of the notes were from creditors or companies trying to sell her their latest software, or whatever service or industry they were in. There was a message from Sylvester Alstead. He had called her nearly a dozen times since their meeting. The final note in the pile was from Rob Hollingsworth. He left his home number. Audrey sat down and dialed.

"Hey, Audrey. Thanks for returning my call. Listen, I'd like to run a couple of things by you. Can I stop by your place this evening, say…eight o'clock?"

She agreed to meet with him. Rob clicked off before giving her details as to the purpose of the meeting. Since he gave no clue as to what their meeting would be about, different scenarios toyed with her throughout the morning, breaking into her concentration. Did he really suspect her of any involvement with the theft? Did he have more shocking news about Norma Jean? Had they found out who the murderer was?

When her two o'clock appointment arrived, all thoughts of Rob Hollingsworth, Norma Jean Strange, and everything else that wasn't Marshall Fixx, dissolved and washed away.

As soon as he flashed his brilliant smile, Audrey remembered how he had laughed at her on their last two meetings. She was determined to show him that although he might have knocked her on her ass the other day, if anyone was going to be run over today, it was going to be him.

During the interview, she determined his current situation and made recommendations on how he could further maximize the return on his investments. His portfolio was heavily weighted in real estate, stocks and some bonds. Though many of his holdings in tech stocks were under performing, they were solid companies and would soon rebound. He was in great shape financially. Audrey advised that at his age he was safe to shift a greater portion of his investments to stocks and that he keep all of his son's estate accounts in the aggressive growth stocks that would continue to give him the excellent overall returns that he was currently getting. It pleased her that Marshall Fixx seemed impressed with the advice and with her level of expertise in the field. Then she got to the serious stuff.

He was forty-six, she read, born and raised in Boston. No surprise there. The thick accent was a dead giveaway. He was divorced, and had a ten-year old son. She wondered if he was dating anyone. Her mind drifted back to the night she'd seen him kissing that woman.

"Thank you, Ms. Wilson for your very thorough review and for confirming some things that I felt needed addressing. I guess there's just one thing left to discuss."

"What's that?"

"Will you have dinner with me tonight?"

Audrey felt a flutter. She wanted to shout, YES! But she had to stay cool.

"It's not my practice to mix business and professional relationships."

"Our business is over. I've already got an excellent financial advisor, so there's no chance of us getting into anything inappropriate. Unless, of course, you want to."

Though he was becoming more interesting to her, Audrey was irritated. She was losing business everyday and had little time for games. The cash cow she had been milking had gone dry. She was not amused by whatever Marshal Fixx was trying to pull.

"I'm afraid I'll have to decline the invitation Mr. Fixx." She stood. "If you'll excuse me, I'm expecting another client."

"I did it again, didn't I? Look, have dinner with me. I'm not really the moron that I seem. You just make me nervous and when I'm nervous, I act like an idiot. Have dinner with me, Audrey. Pleeeze!" His big, heavy-lidded eyes became dewy.

Audrey laughed in spite of herself. It was obvious that he was a man who was used to getting his way. Despite the fact that she felt her feet teetering on the edge of her comfort zone, she finally acquiesced.

"I have an eight o'clock meeting so it will have to be an early dinner."

"I know the perfect place. I'll pop back down at five."

He stood and walked to the outer office where they shook hands and he said he'd see her later. He smiled at Carrey, opened the door and exited. Carrey started hyperventilating, fanning himself dramatically with his hand.

"He said he'd see you later. Do you have a date?"

Audrey ignored the question and handed Carrey a file.

"Would you file this for me, Carrey?"

Carrey wasn't finished talking about Marshall Fixx and was determined to continue the conversation whether Audrey contributed or not. He prattled on like a schoolgirl.

"Did you see the ass on him?" Carrey said.

Yes, I did. Audrey thought. I sure did.

15

Dinner was at Nichio's Italian American. They had the best pasta in town along with a variety of traditional American fare. With its Old World décor and secluded tables, it was one of the city's most romantic restaurants. Audrey couldn't help but wonder at Marshall's choice of eateries.

Midway through dinner, he had come close to completely redeeming himself. Marshall was witty, well spoken and attractive. The candlelight shone on his face, and danced seductively in his dreamy, mischievous eyes. As she gazed into them, the flame twisted and curled into a beckoning finger, pulling her into his spell.

A spark filled her with a desire that she could no longer deny. He had whisked her away, high on a cloud. It was like a beautiful dream where she was a princess and he, her prince.

"What time is your appointment?" He broke the spell. She crashed onto the ground hard, her coach, again, a pumpkin.

"What?"

"I said, what time is your appointment?"

She looked at her watch. It was six forty-five. She grabbed her bag and he rose as she struggled to stand while digging through her purse.

"I need to make a call. Would you excuse me?"

She felt slightly woozy from the liquor and told herself to slow her pace as she headed for the ladies room. In the cozy mood lighting of the ladies lounge, Audrey felt free to release the breath she had been holding. Could it be that she'd finally met a decent intelligent man who was fine to boot? She used the toilet, pausing to check her make-up as she washed her hands. Then she sat on the circular sofa in the outer lounge area to place a call to Rob telling him she was on her way home. She would make it there in plenty of time if she left now. But she hated to leave.

"Your appointment still on?" She shook her head sorrowfully. She pulled her lips into a downward pout and made them quiver. He laughed, moving over to pull out her chair. His hand touched her back like a warm whisper. She let the tingle it produced vibrate through her, enjoying the thrill of it. She sat across from him, mesmerized by his handsome face and his charming personality. She really didn't want to leave. But he summoned the waiter, paid the check and they left the restaurant.

Audrey had insisted on driving separately. They stood outside, romanced by the pallet of pastels that graced the sky as the sun set, waiting for the valet to bring their cars.

"Well, this is me." Audrey said when her car rolled up. "I really had a nice time. Thank you."

She turned to step inside the car as a young, slick haired man held her door. Marshall grabbed her hand, pulling her close. She thought he would kiss her. She wished he would.

"When can I see you again?" His touch sent a rushing river of lava through her. Her dark brown face grew red with warm excitement. She felt the white hot heat of his hand when it grabbed hers.

"Let's get together this weekend." Audrey said. She wanted to see him again and saw no reason to hide her interest.

"I know a great place where we can ride horses." Marsh replied.

"I love horses. Though I have to admit, I'm not much of a rider." Stars danced in her eyes and butterflies fluttered in her stomach.

"I'll pack a brunch for us." He said.

"Sounds perfect. But let me bring the food. I'll call you at your office."

He was still holding her hand. He lifted it to his mouth and softly kissed the back of it, then turned it over and kissed the inside. He rolled her fingers shut.

"Hold that for me until I see you again."

Audrey smiled and pressed her closed fist to her chest and then to his. She stepped inside the car and drove away.

16

Theolonius Griffin looked cool and relaxed in his paisley smoking jacket and bedroom slippers, sitting across from the man in his study Friday evening. The easy pose masked the hot anger that bubbled beneath the surface. He shouldn't have been surprised by the news, but he was caught off guard none-the-less. He hated this shit. That bitch Audrey Wilson was still snooping around, still asking questions. What on earth was she up to?

Ronnie Steele, the janitor that worked in the Administration Building, was earning his keep. He'd said he was taking a smoke—of crack no doubt, when he saw a gold SUV pull up in front of the school last night. Audrey Wilson and another woman had gotten out and he followed them to Norma Jean's office. It was a good thing he'd had the foresight to have the place cleaned out when he got the word that the police were through. He was still not completely certain that he had disposed of all of the evidence of their operation.

Norma Jean was pretty smart. There was no telling what kind of information she had left behind or whom she had left it with. He'd been holding his breath, waiting for the other shoe to drop since her death. Griffin hoped she hadn't left anything behind that would link him to any impropriety. She seemed to have a good system in place for deflecting any involvement away from the participants, but it wouldn't have been hard for her to make a few well-placed entries that would lead them straight to him.

Though risky, it had been a stroke of genius to have a certified financial planner on staff to take the heat and catch any fallout that would occur if this thing erupted. Her plan of dating a police detective who she could easily manipulate in case things started to get hot for them was very bold as well. But Jean had told him on many occasions that Rob Hollingsworth was as malleable as Play Doh. He'd believe anything she told him. It was a gutsy move, but she got a rush from living on the edge.

Norma Jean was the sharpest woman he'd ever met. She was scheming, double-crossing and shrewd. His kind of woman. Unfortunately, he would no longer be able to use her talents. But it had been a thrilling ride while it lasted.

The doorbell interrupted his thoughts and the meeting. Griffin gave his guest an envelope and led him through the kitchen and out the back door. Rushing to the front of the house, he swung the door open so fast it left both he and Rob Hollingsworth startled, though for different reasons.

"I'm sorry to drop by unannounced Mr. Griffin. But a situation has arisen that needs your attention." Rob Hollingsworth didn't look like a pushover to Griffin. But then, of course, they were all guilty of succumbing to the beguiling Norma Jean Strange.

Griffin perspired slightly; his breath came in rapid cadence as his eyes darted around the detective, making sure that he was alone.

"I was just finishing up a call, Detective. Please, come in." Griffin led Rob into his study and offered him a chair. The detective declined. He stood before Griffin, tall and imposing, his hands behind his back.

"I won't take much of your time, Mr. Griffin. As you know, the investigation of the death of Norma Jean Strange is ongoing."

"So you haven't found the killer?" Griffin raised his eyebrows questioningly.

"Not yet. But we have discovered some irregularities in the Township's books."

"I thought you had new information Detective, we've already discussed that there was probable theft on Norma Jean's part."

Griffin shook his head mournfully, casting his gaze away from the detective's.

"It's a crying shame. It was I who recommended Jean for the Director position." He turned his mouth into a frown as he continued. "I'm deeply wounded by her betrayal of my trust and that she would jeopardize our position to obtain funding in the future. You try helping folks out and it gets you a kick in the pants every time."

"We've had an outside audit firm review the records," Hollingsworth said, ignoring Griffin's ploy for sympathy. "They've concluded that any movement of cash of the magnitude that they've found could not have happened without the involvement of other members of the Board of Directors and staff."

Griffin drew back in indignation.

"Detective Hollingsworth, are you accusing *me* of being involved in this?" He put his hand to his chest and hoped Hollingsworth couldn't hear his heart pounding like a kettledrum.

"I'm not accusing anyone of anything." Rob said evenly. "I came here tonight to see if I had covered all the bases. Is there any other member of your staff who you'd consider a likely candidate for this sort of criminal behavior?"

Griffin sat down in the chair he'd earlier offered to the detective. He looked down at his hands pensively, then up at Rob.

"Well, there was that woman who Norma Jean hired to assist with the filings. I always thought there was something unusual about that arrangement."

"Unusual?" Rob squinted his eyes, reading carefully what Griffin hoped he could hide from this human crime Geiger counter.

"Yes. Why would a person with Norma Jean's credentials need to hire someone to check over her work? When she came to us and requested a certified financial planner we posed the question to her. After all, we had just hired her based on her strength in her field.

When she said she needed help a few months after her arrival, we...the Board...questioned whether we'd made the right decision in hiring Ms. Strange. Norma Jean assured us that this happened all the time. It was a way of making sure there where enough eyes on everyone involved to insure that no one person maintained too much control over sensitive areas. She explained that in finance, there are specialized fields of study, much like medicine or law. She said it was a common practice to have a CPA or someone with similar education to discuss accounting theory with and make sure that general accounting practices were being followed."

"Sounds plausible." Rob asserted.

"Upon reconsideration, we thought so too." Griffin responded, then continued. "When she brought Audrey Wilson on board, we gave Norma Jean the responsibility of checking her background. I know it seems foolish now, but none of the rest of us really understands any of that number crunching stuff. We just left it up to them to do the right thing."

"So you think Audrey Wilson was involved in the embezzlement?"

"Well Detective, you said yourself that it was unlikely one person acted alone in this. That would certainly explain a few things."

"Like what?" Hollingsworth moved closer to Griffin, who began to relax sensing he had the detective's curiosity piqued. All that he needed to plant was a kernel of doubt. Suspicion was a mighty weed. He gleefully envisioned its tiny roots breaking soil and spreading like a brush fire.

"Audrey Wilson has been going around pumping Board members for information about any discussions they had with Norma Jean before her death. She was even discovered breaking into Norma Jean's old office last night."

"What? Was there a police report filed?"

"No sir, I just learned of this myself. But why would she be snooping around unless she was trying to hide something? Or find something and destroy it."

Hollingsworth seemed to seriously consider the information he'd received. He thanked Griffin and made his exit. Griffin rubbed his hands together with relish as he watched Rob Hollingsworth head for his vehicle. The stage was now set. Audrey Wilson was going down.

17

Marshall Fixx was walking on air. He was full from the wonderful meal he'd just eaten and from the company of the beautiful woman he'd spent the evening with. Thoughts of Audrey rattled around in his head like a mischievous poltergeist. He couldn't wait until the next time they met.

Remembering their late afternoon meeting, he tilted his head back and smiled. The woman was striking in appearance and sharp as a tack. Seeing her like that, in her element and so on her game, was such a turn on. Not to mention those big, long legs and high, firm ass. He felt something within him stir as he turned the wheel of the car into the driveway. He opened the garage door and rolled the car inside.

As he undressed, his mind traveled back to their dinner together and how she looked in the candlelight that evening. She talked almost non-stop and laughed heartily from the gut with a confidence most women don't show in the presence of men. She exuded a refreshing truth he rarely found in people.

He hated that they hadn't spent more time together. He tried to be cavalier when she mentioned her late night meeting. But the thought disturbed him. Who was this person she was meeting? Was she married or involved with someone? If she was, he hoped it wasn't anything serious. Determining that he would like to get to know her better, he wanted to make sure that the path was unobstructed. He didn't need any drama.

When she made the suggestion for their next "date", he was delighted. Finally, he thought, a woman who knows what she wants and is not afraid to ask for it. How could he tell her no?

Marshall brought his hand up to his face. Smelling her fragrance filled him with longing for her. When the phone rang he leaped for it, thinking that the power of suggestion had moved Audrey to call. But after he answered it he remembered he hadn't given her his home number.

"I saw you tonight!" The voice on the other end blared. "Who the hell was that cunt you were with?"

"Chloe, lose my number." No sooner did Marshall hang up the phone than it rang again.

"Look. I told you not to call me again." He hesitated, listening for a response before continuing. "Don't do this to yourself..."

"Uh, Marshall Fixx?"

Who the hell was this? It wasn't Chloe. Irritation nearly led to his hanging up the phone. Then sudden recognition warmed his face with embarrassment.

"It's Audrey. Sounds like this is a bad time."

"Audrey? Ah, no...I'm glad you called." Marsh sat down on the bed. This was a pleasant surprise. Her voice was like good music. He caught himself grinning like an idiot as he held the phone.

"I took the liberty of getting your home number from the fact sheet you completed when you were in my office. I thought I'd call before my appointment gets here and tell you again how much I enjoyed your company this evening."

"I'm glad to hear your voice." Damn! She'd caught him off guard. His heart pounded, anticipating her next word.

"I called to ask you something. How long do I have to keep my hand closed?"

"Are you still holding my kiss?" Remembering what he'd asked her, to hold his kiss, made him feel silly. It was an adolescent request, or maybe something some lame player would say, but she made him feel like a kid. And she had a crippling power over him.

"I'm still holding your kiss." Her breath wound through the words, fluttering flute soft. Enough to make a snake rise from a basket. He willed the lid down tight.

"Put your hand to your mouth. Open your hand slowly and kiss me back." Marshall wished she were there, in his arms. He felt the swell between his legs winning the battle of wills. "Are you kissing me Audrey?"

"Can't you feel me?" She cradled the receiver in her hand for a moment before hanging up. Marshall left the phone off the hook. He didn't want to hear it ring again that night. He didn't want another person's voice to interrupt his groove. He lay on the king-sized bed smiling, longing for her.

"Yes, I feel you, Audrey."

Audrey stood by the phone for a moment, smiling. The sound of his rich baritone was like mood-setting music. She couldn't wait until they could be together again. But for now she had to get ready for Rob's visit. She hoped he wouldn't have more bad news.

Pulling off her skirt and blouse, she replaced them with a sweat suit and a pair of footies. At the stroke of eight her doorbell rang. Rob Hollingsworth looked grim. Audrey knew then that she could forget about him having anything good to tell her.

"Come in and have a seat." She motioned in the direction of a chair.

"You want some coffee or juice? Or, I can get you something stronger..."

"No, I'm fine." He replied taking the chair. He was silent for only a moment. Audrey sat across from him, waiting. He turned towards her, his face serious.

"I'm going to be up front with you Audrey, and I need for you to be honest with me." Rob leaned over, his elbows rested on his knees. His fingers were threaded together. His serious brow furrowed in concern as he watched her waiting for him to continue.

"There's some serious shit going down. You're right in the middle of it." His aloofness was disconcerting. It seemed she didn't know him anymore.

"There has been embezzlement of federal, state and private funds from Rosemont Township. I'm talking millions."

Her eyes grew wide.

He continued.

"From all indications, you either knew what was going on and participated, or at the very least, looked the other way. I came here tonight because I wanted to give you the opportunity to tell your side of this mess." He leaned in; his eyes were cold, accusatory.

"I know that you haven't been up front with me and I don't know why." He stabbed a finger at her. She felt its sharpness from across the room. "You need to start talking and you need to do it now. There will be an investigation into your finances and business practices, most likely as soon as they can produce a subpoena." He continued. "And it won't take long."

Audrey sat there a moment, absorbing everything she had just heard. She could lose her business because of this shit? Damn that Norma Jean. How could she do this to her?

"As I've told you, Norma Jean called me shortly after she was hired by the Township. I didn't tell you how much she called though. It was ridiculous, Rob. She called about the slightest things. Things I knew she had to have known. I thought it was just new job jitters and I helped her at first. But then she began to be a real pain in the ass. She'd call at all hours. She was at my office waiting for me some mornings before we even opened." She searched his face. There was no hint of sympathy. Audrey swallowed a thickening lump of despair and continued.

"At times when I'd come back from lunch, she'd be there, waiting for me. It had become a major grind. I felt guilty because I thought we were friends. I finally put my foot down and told her that I couldn't afford to give her any more of my time unless I charged her.

"I gave her a rate that no sane person would have agreed to in an attempt to get her off my back. Not only did she agree to my terms, but she gave me a signing bonus to work with her indefinitely."

"How much was the bonus?"

"Thirty thousand dollars." Audrey snorted. "Enough to make me take her seriously."

Rob whistled. "Didn't you think that seemed a little strange?"

"I've heard of companies giving larger bonuses than that; until now, it's just never happened to me." She shrugged, searching his face for understanding. "You gotta understand that this was the first client I'd had that was paying me more than a few hundred dollars a month. I was in debt up to my eyeballs, facing foreclosure on my condo. I had borrowed from all of my funds to pay my share of the debts Emory had stuck me with during our marriage. I was under a lot of stress. I felt this would be an easy way for me to get out from under."

Audrey averted her gaze, glancing outside the window into the darkness. Her friend's betrayal brought forth so much emotion. She was not only troubled at Norma Jean's actions but also disappointed in herself for not just walking away from a situation that in hindsight had all the markings of a scam. Audrey had sold her soul for thirty thousand dollars. It was like she was her own Judas, betraying herself for thirty pieces of silver.

"So that's why there are all those payments to you."

"I asked for ten thousand dollars a month. She agreed to that, plus offered me weekly bonuses if I made myself available during off days and weekends. I really wasn't doing anything but answering her inane questions." Audrey shrugged again in response to his curious gaze. He didn't believe her.

"So you're telling me that you didn't have direct involvement with any transactions requiring movement of cash?" His suspicious eyes held hers.

"How could I?" She tried to control her tone. The decibel level of their conversation was several degrees higher than when he'd arrived. "I was a contractor. I didn't have the authority to sign on any of the accounts."

"Whether you were authorized is not the point here."

Audrey opened her mouth then closed it. What the hell was he trying to do to her? She thought Rob was her friend. But she'd also thought the same thing about Norma Jean.

"Rob, Norma Jean was paying me to do a job. I did what she asked me to do." Audrey jabbed an angry finger at him. She was yelling now. "You can try to twist our business relationship into whatever you want. I had nothing to gain by stealing, especially from a federally funded program. I would never be that stupid."

"Exactly. That's why you extorted the money from Norma Jean." He shot back. "Money to keep you quiet about what she'd been doing."

"Oh come on, Rob! You don't believe that, do you?"

They were standing now, eyeing each other. Faces pulled inward, angry slits for eyebrows, nostrils flaring, and lips jutting in defiance. The hunter backing the hunted to the wall. Rob was the first to blink.

"I don't want to believe it." He put his hands on her tight shoulders. His demeanor softened. "You still haven't convinced me that you weren't involved. If you can't convince me, you damn sure won't convince the suits when they bring you downtown."

It had been an exercise, a test. She hadn't scored very well. Sick to death of dealing with all of this stuff, Audrey plopped dejectedly onto the sofa and pondered his last statement. She was definitely tangled up in this mess. There was no denying that.

Norma Jean had wrapped her in the cocoon of deceit and illegal activity, which had no doubt lead to her death. If Rob wouldn't help her unravel this situation, she was doomed.

"I think I will have some coffee." The tension that was in the air began to ease with his request. Audrey rose from her place on the sofa and headed for the kitchen.

She dropped a cup of roasted beans into the grinder and turned it on. The deafening whir of the machine drew Rob to the kitchen to see what the ruckus was about. She clicked the button to the off position.

"What the hell are you doing?" He asked her.

"I don't have any beans ground."

"Skip the coffee. I only got one more thing to ask you."

Audrey felt deflated. She was sick of Rob's questions and wished he would leave. She put the coffee grinder and fixings away and they went back to the living room.

"You've been going around asking a lot of questions. You were seen at the Administration Building last night after hours. How did you get in there?"

Audrey went to her purse and produced the key she had lifted. She gave it to Rob.

"The only thing that I'm guilty of stealing is this. It's the key to Norma Jean's old office. The cleaning guy left the door propped open when he went to smoke a cigarette. That's how I got into the building. The night before Jean was killed, she called me and told me she had discovered that someone was stealing. She never told me who. She said she couldn't be completely sure but she'd created some reports to try to prove her suspicions. We were going to meet that Saturday morning to see if I concurred with her findings."

"Then what?"

"Then I don't know what. We never met. She didn't tell me any more than that she had a report proving the theft had occurred. I've been trying to get my hands on that report. At first I thought it might lead to her killer, but as more evidence seems to lead to my involvement, I wanted to find the report to prove I had nothing to do with this."

"Audrey, the records that we collected not only have you signing off on invoices and work requisitions, but there are letters on stationery from your office recommending vendors that have turned out to be completely bogus."

"That's not possible!"

"We've got everything at the station Audrey. You were either in this thing up to your neck, or Norma Jean Strange has involved you in one of the most airtight frame-ups I've ever seen."

* * *

After Rob left that night Audrey called her sister. She gave her the details of Rob's visit and told her to get some bail money ready.

"You think this thing will go that far?" Renita was incredulous.

"It's already gone that far. I'm in deep shit. I'll be lucky if my license isn't suspended while the investigation goes on. I still can't believe this is happening to me."

"It's going to be all right Audrey. Norma Jean obviously took a long time to put this plan together. But no plan is airtight. We'll just have to find the holes in this thing and chip away until we break through. I'll come over. We'll figure this out together."

"Thanks Ren, but it's late and I plan on getting an early start in the morning. I need to get things in order...just in case. Let's get together later tomorrow. I'm really exhausted and I just want to sleep."

They didn't hook up the next day, or at all that weekend. Audrey spent Saturday and most of Sunday, staring at the TV. She didn't even answer the telephone, letting her messages pile up on the answering machine. She was too depressed to talk to anyone. The only thing she could think of was how she had been betrayed by her friend just when her business seemed to be taking off. She would have cried but she was too hurt for tears.

18

Just as Rob had indicated, the sheriff was at Audrey's office at 10:00 Monday morning. They presented her with a search warrant and began to remove the computer and take all of the office files and load them into brown cardboard containers.

Carrey looked on in horror as they went through his meticulous filing system, pulling out anything related to the work Audrey did with Norma Jean.

One of the men directed the other three about which things to take and which were okay to leave. They worked swiftly, as detached as robots. The man who was in charge walked over to her and cast a deep blue stare that made her shiver.

"Ma'am, I'm afraid I'm going to have to ask you to come with us."

"Where are you taking me?"

"City Hall."

"Carrey! Call Marshall Fixx. Tell him to meet me at City Hall."

*   *   *

No one spoke to her on the ride downtown. This seemed too incredible, but it really was happening. The theme from the TV show COPS kept playing over and over in her head. If she hadn't been afraid they wouldn't think she took the whole thing seriously, she would have sang it out loud. Singing was her way of easing a troubled soul. Right now her soul was fine; it was the rest of her that needed help.

Audrey tried to ignore the smell of stale cigarettes, body odor and piss as she adjusted herself on the slick vinyl seats. They had not handcuffed her, but she felt fettered just the same. The male detective smelled like he'd run out of deodorant about a month ago and never bothered to replace it. The acrid smell stung her nose and made her eyes water. Her stomached flopped during the bumpy ride and she thought she might become ill. She was definitely feeling claustrophobic. The space seemed to become smaller with every mile.

She tried to focus on the abstract, to keep her heart from beating out of her chest and the sourness that was rising in her stomach from splattering onto the patrol car floor.

Audrey fixed her eyes on the wrinkled red neck of the man and the very manly looking woman who sat next to him. The scratchy voice of a female dispatcher frequently broke into the silence, describing criminal activity in codes that Audrey could not decipher.

What if they don't take me to the station? She thought as panic mixed with the pain and nausea that sat on her stomach like a bad meal. What if they took her somewhere and raped her or beat her and left her for dead? No, they wouldn't do that. Carrey knew that they had taken her and he had contacted Marshall Fixx by now. Thinking about Marshall made her relax a little. She knew little about him, other than what she'd seen on paper. But somehow, she knew he wouldn't let these people hurt her.

When the car stopped and the door was opened, she was tempted to brush past the detectives and run with all of her might. She'd run to the beat...*Bad Boys, Bad Boys, what you gonna do...*The cops would catch her, push her down prostrate and make her atone while they pressed their knees into her back and neck and doused her with pepper spray. Things were going badly enough as it was. She'd been battered mentally. She could certainly do without a physical beating. With that in mind, Audrey let them guide her from the back of the car and into the station.

Bright light flooded the room and Audrey blinked to adjust. A row of chairs and a long wooden bench straddled either side of a scarred gate, separating the detectives' area from the rest of the room. The chairs were empty. On one of the benches, there was a boy of about thirteen sitting next to woman with her face twisted in anger and humiliation who must have been his mother. The woman cast Audrey a quick glance as she and the officers walked by. She turned away quickly, but not before Audrey noted something familiar about her. The woman was a total stranger but possessed the proverbial despair of all mothers struggling to raise their children when the street has them in its grip.

Audrey was led to a small, windowless room were she sat alone at a battered, gray metal table for about ten minutes. The scent from Officer Body Odor clung to the thick, unmoving air, making her want to gag.

The door opened suddenly and Rob Hollingsworth and two other men entered the room. When she'd seen Hyram Phillips on television, he exuded an air of no nonsense. His cold, lifeless eyes never smiled. Looking at him now, Audrey shivered. He stood there with his arms behind his back, silent. Rob and the other man spoke to him in hushed tones. Without saying a word, Phillips exited, closing the door behind him.

"Miss Wilson." Rob was using his TV detective persona. Audrey decided to play along. "This is Detective Ed Blake of the criminal investigation bureau. He'll be asking you a few questions. Just answer truthfully and with as much detail as you can."

Detective Blake gave a friendly smile as he asked her the same questions she had already answered one hundred times. His manner gave her a comfort level that she hadn't expected. He was like a younger version of Peter Falk's *Columbo*. The thick, salt and pepper hair, which he repeatedly ran his hand through, was in need of a cut. He wore an ill-fitting, brown suit that could use a pressing. He cast a warm, trusting smile in Audrey's direction with teeth slightly stained from coffee and cigarettes.

"So you worked with Miss Strange for several months?" His warm eyes crinkled when he smiled at her.

"Yes." Audrey replied. "Officially from May until her death."

"When did you first learn that there were some irregularities with the books?" Audrey glanced over at Rob who nodded slightly.

"Norma Jean called me the morning before she was killed. She told me she had evidence that one of the Board members was stealing. There was a report or some records proving her suspicion. She wanted me to review her findings to see if I agreed. That was the last time I spoke with her."

Audrey felt her hands trembling and slid them underneath her rump. She felt hot. Sweat beaded her forehead like after an intense workout. But she couldn't stop shivering.

"You were at the crime scene the night Miss Strange was killed." Audrey looked over at Rob again, this time; he looked away, not meeting her eyes. Bastard.

"I heard about what happened to her on the news." She faltered.

"Are you in the habit of frequenting crime scenes?" Columbo didn't seem so nice anymore.

"I...she was my friend. I was in shock. I left my house and I went there without even thinking."

"Or maybe you went there because you *were* thinking." The detective countered.

"Excuse me?" Audrey whirled around, looking to Rob for help. Columbo was suddenly turning into Dirty Harry. Her "friend" Rob was non-responsive, standing behind Blake, supporting his co-worker and treating Audrey like a stranger.

"I believe you were thinking *very* clearly, Miss Wilson. You made it a point to talk to the detective on duty that night, making a blatant attempt to try to use a brief, prior association with him to garner information about the case."

"What? That's bullshit!" She looked again to Rob for support. "Rob, you know that's not what happened."

Rob Hollingsworth looked at Audrey with a coldness she had never seen. Tears sprang to her eyes. How could he betray her this way? She knew now that she had been wrong to trust him. She tried to quickly replay the conversations she'd had with him. Had she said anything that could be incriminating? He could likely take anything she had said and bend it like modeling clay, creating the backdrop for whatever scenario would achieve his goal. She knew now that Rob Hollingsworth would do whatever it took to close this case.

This must be a nightmare or she had stepped through the looking glass, or fallen through a crack and into the *Twilight Zone*. When she looked at Rob she could almost detect tiny horns protruding from his head. She could see that Blake was just getting warmed up. He looked at her like he was at a ball game and she was a hot dog. He couldn't wait to tear into her.

Just as Audrey felt all hope slipping away, there was a knock at the door. She'd never seen a man look as good as Marshall Fixx looked right then. He extended a business card and introduced himself.

"Is Miss Wilson under arrest?" It was as though Audrey were watching a play. Marshall Fixx entered, taking immediate control of the stage, pushing the two-bit supporting cast into the shadows.

"We have an order from the court." Blake glanced at the business card, tossed it onto the table and slapped at Marsh with the documents he was holding. "This is a formal interview to gather facts in a capital case. Your client is suspected of concealing information, which proved embezzlement of government funds and the murder of Norma Jean Strange. We have proof that she was receiving payments. With the other evidence we've gathered we can prove that she was responsible for orchestrating the entire operation." Detective Blake was nearly a foot shorter than Marsh. He craned his neck, pushing his smug nose towards Marsh's.

"She's not saying a word to either of you." He eyed Rob contemptuously. "Anything you've coerced from her in my absence is inadmissible."

"Coercion! Don't bring that bullshit in here, Fixx. Your client's guilty. There is really no point in her trying to be evasive. She is obligated to answer the questions that are put before her." Blake snapped and snarled at Marshall, who remained calm throughout the diatribe.

"My client will not utter another word to anyone here until we have a conference. If she is not under arrest, we will be leaving now." He turned away from Blake, touching Audrey's shoulder. "Any other conversation with Miss Wilson will be done though me or in my presence."

Marshall took Audrey's hand and led her out of the room.

19

The air outside was staggeringly sweet. She didn't know if her legs buckled from mental and physical exhaustion or from the high she felt at being free. Marsh's holding her hand seemed to be the only grip on reality for her.

"Miss Wilson?"

The woman before Audrey was much smaller than she looked on television. Tonya Elling's microphone vied for space with the cameraman's Panasonic in front of her face.

"Is it true that you are the center of an investigation of alleged misconduct that took place at City Hall?"

"We have no comment." Marshall pushed past the reporter from Channel Five who followed them across the street to the parking lot before giving up the attempt to get an interview. Marshall took her hand, helping to quicken her steps to the car. Audrey could hear Tonya talking to the camera

"Boston attorney Marshall Fixx has been brought in to handle the case. We're not sure at this time if the city has retained this high-profile attorney or if Miss Wilson..."

They hurried into the elevator, both of them catching their breaths as the car moved slowly to their floor. They exited the garage, safe behind the tinted windows of the shiny sedan.

Settling into the soft tan leather seat of his Mercedes and watching the scenery fly past them, Audrey felt safe for the first time that day as Marshall sped up the freeway. She let herself relax. The broken white lines on the highway punctuated the distance being put between her and the nightmare that her life had become.

She thought they were headed to the office but he did not turn off on the Plum Street exit, but continued south toward Northern

Kentucky. The car rolled smoothly over the Taylor Southgate Bridge, the murky water of the Ohio rippled below as traffic approached, then passed them as they sped across the bridge.

"Where are we going?"

"To my place."

Audrey should have been irritated by his presumptuousness, but instead felt glad to be going some place that she hadn't been before. To be somewhere where she could pretend the past few hours had not occurred was likely just what she needed.

His strong hands held the wheel effortlessly. Audrey wondered what it would be like for those hands to hold her. Her eyes roamed his body, liking the way he looked in his tailored suit. The pricey threads lay on him casually, as natural as a waterfall. He possessed a masculine beauty and strode in a manner that exuded his privileged past. His occasional attempts to use urban vernacular landed with a resounding thud. He was a part of that seldom spoke of black upper class, the select band of well to do Colored Folk of New England lore. In spite of this, he wasn't snobbish, just self-assured and relaxed. Audrey was curious to see the way that he lived.

The car turned off the expressway onto a quiet, tree-lined street that wound upwards into the blue Kentucky hills. Sprawling, manicured lawns sprinkled with large houses of stone and brick peeped from behind ten-foot high hedges and walls. They turned into a hidden stone driveway that wound forever before reaching a lovely English cottage tucked romantically behind rows of flowers and flanked by huge oaks.

"What a wonderful place." Audrey said as Marshall drove into the four-car garage. The only other vehicle there was a polished red and white antique Ford. The convertible top was drawn back, showing the slick cherry wood dash and white leather seats. The machine appeared to have the original wheels and accessories. Audrey looked at it and gasped in awe.

"This is gorgeous! Can I touch it?"

"Sure." Marshall said. "If you're a good girl, I'll even take you for a ride."

"Oh, will you Marshall?" Audrey asked in her best imitation of a little girl's voice.

"Yeah, but only on *one* condition." Marshall looked at her and smiled.

"You gotta call me Marsh. You gotta make yourself at home. You gotta get ready to do some serious work."

One condition. Right. The boy may be fine, but he needed some help with his math skills she thought as he ticked off all of the things he wanted her to do. He led her through a huge living room with polished wood floors and tall ceilings with exposed dark wood beams. A massive stone fireplace, made for cuddling up with someone, was the room's focal point. Vivid geometric patterned rugs hugged gleaming floors. Chunky oak tables and chairs were fitted with plush cushions that made Audrey want to curl up with Marsh and forget that the last few horrible hours had ever happened.

But he was strictly business. They continued through the living room into a spacious office. Its furnishings were comfortable, but not at the expense of functionality. The room was equipped with all of the latest technical devices imaginable, some of which Audrey hadn't a clue to their purpose. She sat down in the stiff looking chair he offered, surprised at the comfort it provided. Audrey waited for him to begin.

Marsh walked over to a bar in the corner of the room and started fixing coffee. As he worked, he recounted the events as they knew them and formulated a plan of action.

"From what we know so far, someone has gone to great lengths to enshroud you in an embezzlement scheme that could possibly lead to some serious time in a federal penitentiary. I'm warning you, I'm going to ask you details about everything. You're going to get tired of me and probably want to beat me up when we're finished."

He brought two steaming cups of coffee to the table and sat down across from her. The deep aroma of the strong brew filled the room. She took a sip and the jolt of caffeine was like a wakening slap.

Audrey felt a shiver, remembering the reason they were together today. She was already tired of this and didn't know where she would find the energy to rehash this thing one more time, let alone all night. As if reading her thoughts, feeling her fear, he put his hands on her shoulders and looked into her eyes.

"It's going to be okay. I'm going to fix everything."

She smiled. His reassurance relaxed her. "What is that, a slogan or something?"

"As a matter of fact..." he pulled out a business card and presented it to her.

MARSHALL FIXX

ATTORNEY at LAW

"Let Marshall Fixx Everything"

They both laughed.

"That is *so* weak." She was still laughing moments after he'd stopped.

"I think it's very catchy." He seemed a little embarrassed. "I was fresh out of law school when I first had them made up. I still carry them as a way of staying grounded." He was suddenly serious.

"Before I was lured by the excitement of corporate litigation, I was a public defender. I wanted to help people who couldn't afford good legal representation. The system is so one sided. If you're not a millionaire, you don't have a prayer of getting a fair trial in this country. I wanted to change that."

"Why did you stop? I mean, why are you now working for the establishment?"

"The work was overwhelming. There are so many people out there who need help." He shook his head. A sorrowful look washed over him. "I was so swamped I was becoming ineffective. Now I take only a case or two a year. I can really make a difference that way. I never want to forget that I went into this line of work to help people. I'm an advocate for my client. First. Last. Always." His eyes caught hers and held them.

"When I tell you I'm going to fix everything, I mean it."

Audrey believed that he would.

20

It was close to midnight when Marsh brought her home. He'd questioned her about everything from her favorite food to the types of games she and Norma Jean had played as children. The ordeal was as vigorous as a workout followed by an eight mile run. Audrey felt herself falling for him as he pulled out every detail. She imagined him in the courtroom, winding his way into the hearts and minds of judge and jury.

Too soon, they were sitting in the car in front of her brownstone. Soft jazz from the radio eased them into a comfort zone. Out of the blue the question came. Audrey didn't know what made her ask it, but she was disappointed at his answer.

"Why did you break-up with your wife Marsh?"

He was quiet for a moment. Reflective. She knew that what he was going to tell her would be the truth. She knew that he was weighing how she would view him after he spoke.

"My wife left me because I was unfaithful to her. I had an affair with a member of my staff in Boston. It was the stupidest thing I ever did." He looked away from her, out onto the street. "I tried to maintain a relationship with this woman after Marlena and I were officially divorced, but I began to resent her as though the loss of my family was her fault. It wasn't her fault at all. It was mine." He released a heavy sigh.

"She was vulnerable and I was lonely. I was putting in so many hours, trying to keep my practice going, that I was shutting Marlena and our son completely out of my life." He paused. Audrey reached for his hand but he pulled away. He drew closer to the window, looking out into the darkness. Audrey watched as his jaw constricted. The memory, it seemed, caused him physical pain.

"She had given up so much for me and I blew it." His knuckles tightened on the steering wheel. He was facing forward again.

"What exactly did she give up?" Audrey wanted to soothe him, but she didn't know how.

"When I met Marlena Procter she had just completed her studies abroad and was quite an accomplished painter, sculptor, and architect." With his Boston accent, her name came out Maw Leenah Prock Taw. "She was just beginning to make a name for herself in urban design when we met and fell in love. She put her career on hold because we both wanted children."

"Wait a minute." One eyebrow moved upward, her forehead wrinkled in disbelief. "You're telling me that you were married to Marlena Procter, the artist?"

"Oh, you're familiar with her work?"

"Familiar with it? My sister and I each have several pieces of her work. I have the sculpted piece 'Lindy Hop' on my mantle at home. Set me back a couple of house payments, but it was worth it."

"Marlena really is talented." Marsh smiled. Audrey could tell by the sound of his voice that he was somewhere else. "I was happy that she returned to her work after we broke up. I'm sorry to say that I never appreciated and respected her gifts until we split."

"What about your son?"

"Toots?" He beamed. His chest protruded the tiniest fraction.

"What?"

"Our son, Marshall, Jr. We call him Toots because since he was about three years old, he was always rolling up paper or using old tissue rolls for horns. When we couldn't get him to stop, we bought him a horn and when he was five, enrolled him into a music academy close to where we live. The kid really took to the horn. He's ten now and quite good." He spoke with the parental bias of a proud papa.

"Another Wynton Marsalis perhaps?" Audrey nudged him slightly.

"Shi...I wish! But who knows? He loves the trumpet and he's very good."

"I'd love to hear him play sometime when he's in town. Does he ever visit you here?"

"He's never been here. I go to Boston to see him once a month."

"It must be really hard spending so little time with him, especially at his age. Children need both parents."

As soon as the words were spoken the temperature in the vehicle dropped noticeably. She caught the glint of irritation that darkened his face, but he quickly recovered. He checked his watch.

"Look at the time." He cleared his throat, swallowing his discomfort. "We'd better call it a day. Let me help you with your things."

Marsh collected Audrey's handbag and jacket, his movements stiff as they walked together towards the door. The night was quiet and added to the tension that was wedged between them.

If she'd touched a soft spot, she didn't mean it. Since Audrey hadn't been able to have children of her own, it was hard for her to imagine having a child and not seeing him every day. Her brother Bobby had fathered a son years ago that he never saw. She was constantly trying to get him to talk about the little boy who lived in Atlanta. But Bobby refused to discuss him. Audrey pushed anyway, which led to big fights. She hated the thought of having a nephew so far away that she never got to see. Bobby's nonchalance angered her. It seemed this would forever be a point of contention between them.

Audrey looked at Marsh's face. It showed an emotion she could not name. He seemed vulnerable for the first time since she'd met him. This new side of Marshall Fixx was so attractive that she leaned over and kissed him on the cheek. She touched his hand softly, speaking low.

"Marsh, everybody makes mistakes. If you've talked to Marlena like you did to me tonight; she has most likely forgiven you. Stop beating yourself up about it."

He looked away. She caught the misty look in his eyes before he had time to avert them. The two of them stood on the top landing, neither knowing what to say next. Freedom pounced from out of nowhere, startling them both.

"This is Freedom." She tickled the cat underneath his chin.

"Freedom?"

"I'll have to tell you about *my* dissolved marriage the next time we meet."

Marsh pulled her to him and kissed her so sweetly that for a moment she felt like she was floating on a cloud. She broke away from him, giving him what he really needed. A hug. She held him. Consoled him. She was sorry that she'd dredged up his pain.

He whispered goodnight, galloped to his car, opened the door quickly and got in. Audrey opened her door and followed Freedom into the house. She could barely hear the soft purr of the Mercedes as it pulled away from the curb and down the street.

21

The wind had kicked up slightly, whooshing against the big steel machine as Marsh turned into his street thirty minutes later. He blinked back tears thinking about how much he still missed his family. How had they started talking about that stuff anyway? He'd never shared his thoughts with anyone like that, especially a woman. He thought back on how Chloe had begged, cajoled, poked, and prodded, trying to get an indication of what made him, at times, so sad. How could he tell Chloe that every time he looked at her he was reminded of how much he had hurt Marlena and ultimately himself, when he gave her no choice but to walk out of his life?

Once he realized that Marlena and Toots were gone, he no longer had the same feelings for Chloe. He tried to ease himself out of the relationship, but the situation had become messy and difficult, leading him to relocate to the small town near his mother's birthplace in Rosemont, Ohio.

What the hell was Chloe thinking about, moving to Rosemont? He had made it abundantly clear that there was no future for them and that he wanted what had happened between them to be forgotten. He felt like a dog. Like he had taken advantage of her at a vulnerable time in her life. But he had apologized; he was sorry. What more could he do? He was just not willing to drag out a situation that had no way of working.

Chloe had become controlling and possessive. He had dealt with her type before. As soon as he saw the all-too-familiar signs...the excessive calling, the questions about things that didn't concern her...he'd put up a wall that made the one in Berlin look like a picket fence.

He hadn't told her he was moving to Ohio, but somewhere in one of their early conversations, during a harmless bout of small talk, he had revealed where his mother was from. Apparently, she had used this as a starting point for her detective work and hit pay dirt.

He hoped she would not resort to any of her antics while she was here. Marsh prayed that she would somehow be struck by the futility of her mission, and would, in the words of the old James Brown lyric, "Give it up and turn it loose".

Though it was late, he didn't feel the need to sleep just yet. Marsh plugged in the large stainless steel Krups coffeemaker and put a couple of scoops of hazelnut coffee into the basket. He used to think a man had to be priggish to drink flavored coffees, until someone gave him a selection as a gift. Shortly after receiving them, he came down with a nasty cold and couldn't leave the house. He was out of his regular brand and brewed a pot full of a fruity beverage that tasted like no coffee he'd ever had. He developed an affinity for the hot flavored liquid, made more enticing by adding a dash of liqueur.

Though he'd tried to run from it, Marshall Fixx was a product of his upbringing. He truly was priggish in many ways and downright snobbish in others. It was strange that during his college days he'd struck up a curious, but very real, friendship with three of the hardest brothers on campus. Phil Davis and Joe Brinkman were from Chicago's Cabrini Green housing projects. Jasper Isaac Pace was from Biloxi. The three had been granted full academic scholarships to Harvard.

Initially the relationship was antagonistic. They knew of his privileged background. Hell, his family name adorned a study hall. They'd never met an African American of money and position. It was intimidating. The trio took every opportunity to challenge him. The fact that Marsh met or exceeded expectations in any physical or mental test put before him did little to warm them to him.

The tide turned when they found him at a Roxbury basketball court playing a fierce game with some brothers from the neighborhood. He handled the ball easily, generous to his teammates and brutal to the opposition. At the end of the session, the sweaty men congratulated each other on a good game.

Marsh grabbed the ball, dribbled it, and then nodded to Phil, Joe, and Ike to join him for one of the most intense games he'd ever played. They were as thick as thieves ever since.

Marsh thought they were all incredibly cool. He wanted to be like them. When he tried to be "down," they just laughed at him and told him to relax. Eventually, he did. It was through these guys, who'd become his best friends, that he learned the true meaning of manhood, self respect and respect for others.

The coffee was ready. Marsh poured the steamy, aromatic liquid into a huge black mug, adding a splash of crème de menthe. The morning paper lay in the foyer, untouched. He picked it up and snapped off the elastic that held the paper cylinder in place. Changing his mind, he popped the band back in place. Who was he kidding? Why try to trick his mind into dealing with local and global events when the war between his head and his heart raged within him? He was falling hard for Audrey Wilson. Why not just surrender to the power she had over him?

He replayed the conversations they'd had that evening. He thought about the intense set of her face when she spoke, the way she moved her hair back and pushed it behind her ear, like it prevented her from hearing his every word. He couldn't remember when he'd seen that level of concentration on anyone's face before. She was both captivating and captivated.

As much as he wanted to let his thoughts remain light, wondering what it would be like to be with her romantically, he had to stay mindful that this lady was in trouble. His intuition told him that she had nothing to do with the missing money and most certainly had no involvement with Norma Jean Strange's murder. But she was tangled up in a hell of a web. It would take some time to free her.

Marsh had been irritated by all of her questioning that evening. He wasn't in the habit of talking about his personal life. Especially with women. But there was something in her manner that put him at ease. It wasn't the same feeling that he'd had with Marlena; a long fought trust born after years of more error than trial until they could each relax and accept each other. His feelings for Audrey were almost familial. The closest he could match it to was the way he'd felt talking with his mother. He'd never mean to open his heart to his Mom, but next thing he knew, spilled beans would be flying everywhere.

Loneliness stabbed at him. He wished he were home, cloaked in the familiar warmth of his family and friends. Marsh sipped his coffee but found cold comfort in the brew. He snatched up the cordless phone and punched in the Chicago area code and digits that he knew by heart.

"Philly!"

"Fixx? What up man?" Phil Davis' voice was the answer to a prayer. "Guess who I got on the horn!" Phil shouted to his houseguest. Marsh was immediately beamed from his lonely space to Phil's messy living room full of junk food, beer cans and wayward husbands.

"Fixx, Ahma put you on speaker."

"Hey, bitch!" Joe Brinkman laughed loudly.

"Ho Brinkman!" Marsh shot back. He and Joe had been in constant competition during their college days to see who could get the most women. There really was no contest. Track star Joe Brinkman, with his tight athletic body, quick wit, and tawny good looks, had women chasing him like hounds at a foxhunt. He'd told Marsh that he was so good he could make Marsh his woman.

"You ain't nothin' but a ho." Marsh had replied. From that day forward they'd greeted each other as Marshall Bitch and Ho

Brinkman. The fact that they were two educated, professional men well into their forties didn't seem to diminish the pleasure they derived from the juvenile repartee.

"Hey, man! We was just talkin' about you. When you comin' back out?"

"I would hop a plane this weekend," Marsh explained. "But something's come up and I can't get away."

"Shit man, you stayin' in Dry Gulch, Ohio."

"My house is in Kentucky." Marsh corrected him.

"That's even worse. What the hell could be going on there that would keep you from coming here and gettin' some lovin' from a real man?" Joe teased. "You know you miss me."

"Bite me, Ho." Marsh laughed at the silly exchange in spite of himself. Nobody but Joe, Phil, and Ike got to see Marsh's silly side.

He loved these guys. Keeping in contact with them gave him a chance to get away from his stodgy roots and pressure-filled occupation and just be a guy. With them he was twenty years old living the carefree, easy life where responsibility was a four-letter word. He longed for their companionship but he didn't see how he could get away. After taking a few minutes to play catch-up, he invited them to his home for a weekend.

"I got a suite at Cinergy Field. You guys pick the weekend. We can catch a game or two and hang out." He felt like he was once again a standoffish youth using his new basketball to lure the popular kids out to play. But it worked. Not only would Phil and Joe fly in, but they would call Ike in Boston to round out the group. Before hanging up, Phil said, "The Black Pack is back!"

Marsh beamed like a kid after he hung up the phone. The exchange with his friends numbed the pain of his loneliness and temporarily doused his smoldering desire for Audrey Wilson.

22

Carrey had gone to run an errand, so it was pretty quiet in the office that Tuesday morning. Audrey didn't know how long she'd be free before Rob Hollingsworth and his crew would pick her up again. She'd been up for hours answering e-mail, sifting through bills and throwing out junk mail. It was just after ten a.m. Still feeling bad for him after last night, she thought about calling Marsh. She picked up the phone, and then put it down. She was sympathetic but not in the mood to coddle him. Audrey decided to take advantage of her freedom and, once again, see what kind of information she could wheedle out of the Township Administration.

She scribbled a note on a yellow sticky letting Carrey know she'd be out of the office the rest of the day. Audrey pulled the door shut and left the building. She got in her car and headed into town.

Sarah "Pit Bull" Collins had apparently been taken out by one of her masters for her morning constitutional. Audrey slipped through the open door and into Juanda Griffin's musty office.

Juanda didn't try to mask her irritation. She fumbled around the mess on her desk before locating the telephone. She buzzed the console and waited. When no response was forthcoming, she mumbled a curse word before looking up at Audrey.

"You shouldn't be in here."

"I came to talk to you about a discussion that I had with Norma Jean before her death." Audrey decided that the best route was the most direct one. A flicker of interest lit Juanda's eyes. In an attempt to hide her nerves, or conceal her guilt, she grabbed a familiar looking, colorful egg from her desk. A gift from Norma Jean. Her hands fumbled with the faux Faberge egg cigarette lighter in the nervous manner that Audrey recognized as that of a closet smoker. She knew that as soon as she left Juanda Griffin would light up and enjoy the dirty little secret that she shared with no one. Jean had obviously peeped her game and just happened to give her the perfect gift. Norma Jean. Such an insightful person; maybe Juanda had killed her.

"I don't have a lot of time. Sit down." She motioned to a stiff-looking leather chair, positioned to the left of the desk. "You can put that stuff on the floor." Audrey did as she was told, moving a mound of books and papers before depositing herself gingerly on the chair's edge, holding the gaze of the woman across the desk.

"Norma Jean called me the morning of the day she was killed and said that she had evidence that one of the administrative staff was embezzling funds from the City of Rosemont. She wasn't absolutely sure and wanted me to verify her findings."

Juanda released the lighter. Her face was snapshot still. She looked Audrey dead in the eye, her gaze unwavering as she spoke.

"It has been brought to my attention that the only persons who may have been involved in possible unlawful activities were Ms. Strange and yourself."

"Someone is trying to frame me, Mrs. Griffin. My only hope of getting to the truth is to find a report that Norma Jean was working on. I'm sure it will prove my innocence."

"Accounting and finance issues were handled by Norma Jean and you." She repeated. This time her voice was slightly elevated. "Even if I knew anything about this alleged report, I don't see how this document would exonerate you, Miss Wilson." Juanda replied briskly.

"You know full well that Norma Jean and I didn't operate autonomously. Everything had to be approved by Mr. Griffin" Audrey moved forward in her chair defensively. She wasn't about to roll over and let these people bury her in crap.

"I think you'd better leave." Juanda Griffin looked at the door nervously, like she expected someone to come to her aid.

"There's no company that I know of where the financial staff has complete control over expenditures and revenues." Audrey challenged, egged on by Juanda's discomfort.

"We're not talking about approving invoices for office supplies here. The federal government approved a sixty million dollar grant for the Rosemont Township construction project. There has to be meetings with the Executive Branch when those funds are deployed. There would be areas that would require the signatures of your husband and yourself or the bank would not let a dime out of the accounts."

"So what exactly are you implying?" It was Juanda's turn to play defense.

"Mrs. Griffin," Audrey could see the veil clouding the woman's eyes. She was losing this fight.

"I'm not accusing anyone of anything. Believe me. I'm just trying to find some way of getting to the truth." Audrey couldn't mask her exasperation. She slumped in the uncomfortable leather contraption that wouldn't let her relax. "Discussions with the police have led me to believe it was Norma Jean who was stealing from the city. She has me mixed up in this mess, intentionally or not, and I don't know what to do. I'm facing losing my livelihood at the very least. I could be facing a prison term at worst. Please, Mrs. Griffin, can you help me?"

"I'm afraid there is nothing I can do to help you." There seemed to be a softening in Juanda Griffin's manner. For the first time since the meeting began, she almost seemed human. But she offered no help.

"If you're innocent, surely the police will figure that out. It's their job. Now if you will excuse me, I do have a meeting to attend."

Audrey rose to leave. When she reached the doorway, she turned when Juanda Griffin called her name.

"Good luck."

*   *   *

"Mr. Alstead! Mr. Alstead!" Audrey spied the diminutive man getting into a white Lincoln as she left the government offices. Determined to get some information from one of these characters, Audrey flagged him down. She wasn't about to let the meeting with Juanda Griffin defeat her. She ran over to the car, reaching him just as he was getting ready to close the door. Sylvester Alstead smiled in recognition. He picked up where he'd left off at their last meeting. She could almost feel his eyes peeling away the layers of her clothing, her breasts exposed, nipples hardened by the cool autumn wind as he ogled her like a rabid dog. The thin camisole that completed the suit she'd chosen that morning suddenly seemed like a fashion don't. She pulled the jacket of her light brown boucle ensemble together with one hand, extending the other for him to shake.

"Just as I thought I could not be blessed by a more lovely day, I'm graced by a vision of sheer beauty!" He rubbed her hand then kissed the back of it. She struggled not to gag.

His high-pitched voice raised the hairs on the back of her neck. She hadn't slept well at all last night and felt she looked like warmed over crap. His reference to her "sheer beauty" most likely meant that he appreciated the peep show she provided him by wearing the wrong top. She ignored the comment, tightening her hold on the jacket and cursing herself for wearing the silky blouse underneath it.

His leering annoyed her, but she was certain that he was the type that did more wishing, hoping, and dreaming than taking any kind of action on the lewd fantasies that must be swirling around in his tiny head. Besides, Audrey was determined to get some answers.

"I'd like to know if I could have a minute of your time."

"I was on my way to one of my favorite spots in the city." His salacious grin turned her stomach. "Would you care to join me?"

"Where are we going?" Audrey said as he closed the passenger side of the car.

"Brumby Park. It's lovely there, especially this time of year with the foliage starting to turn. I get to work so early that I like to take lunch early as well. There aren't very many people there this time of day." He smiled proudly like he'd just imparted something of great importance that only he was privy to. "We could pick up a couple of sandwiches and some juice and watch the leaves change."

"How romantic, Mr. Cockroach," Audrey thought. Who better to spend time in the park with than a friggin' insect? But she was cool, smiled politely and said instead, "Yes, it is beautiful there."

The smell of the cheap pine tree air freshener was overwhelming. Warm air from the vents swirled near her feet, making them sweat. Light sounds from a classical radio station filled the car with soothing sounds that accompanied Audrey while Sylvester Alstead went into a deli to get their lunch. Her sleepiness started to get the better of her as the beautiful strings and the soft leather seats relaxed her.

Audrey didn't hear him come back. He was suddenly there, watching her lounging in the slightly reclined seat. She grabbed at the jacket again. Alstead got into the car and turned the heat on full blast.

"Would you mind turning your heater down?" The vents threw heat with a vengeance, making her hair stick to her face and neck.

"Oh, you seemed to be cold."

"No, I'm fine."

"But you're sitting there all bundled up. You're freezing."

"Please turn the heat off." It was more demand than request.

"Only if you promise to sit back and relax." The all-powerful Heatmaster said. "I won't bite you." He gave her a stubby, dull-toothed grin.

Audrey let her hands drop to her lap. The skirt she was wearing had ridden up when she sat down, exposing her entire thigh. If for some reason the big car was pulled over, they would have a hard time convincing the cops that she wasn't a hooker, and that he wasn't her mean little pimp.

She laughed to herself thinking of this meek character slapping around young hard-looking women asking for his money. Looking at him in the cheap polyester suit and discount store loafers, he better fit the role of the John. She wondered if he ever bought companionship.

Alstead pulled the car into a breathtakingly lovely place beneath a cluster of trees. He turned off the car and retrieved a bag from the back seat.

"There is a table right over there where we can eat our lunch or if you prefer, I have a blanket in the trunk."

"The table!" Audrey shouted like a contestant in a game show. "Uh, sorry. I mean, I don't think I'll be able to sit on the ground comfortably with this skirt on."

Alstead rubbed at the wooden tabletop and benches until the paper towels he held were gray from dirt. Then he took some napkins from the bag, unfolding them for her to sit upon. She moved toward the makeshift place setting. He was still holding his hand on the napkins.

"I don't want them to blow away before you sit down. It would be a shame to mess up that pretty brown suit."

Audrey inched onto the pile of napkins. Alstead put his hands on her shoulders and moved them up and down gingerly. He looked down into the scoop of her neckline. She fought the urge to stuff her cleavage with a napkin like she had at the restaurant. Maybe she should say something to him about his behavior, she thought. Perhaps he didn't realize he was being such a pig.

"I've been calling you, Audrey. Why haven't you returned my calls?" He whined, moving his hands down her shoulders. She stiffened and shifted away from his grip.

"I've been really busy. Why don't we have our sandwiches now, I'm starved."

Alstead brushed by her, moving around to the other side of the table. He extracted the contents of the bag, spreading them out on a paper tablecloth. He set a lovely table, complete with plastic wine flutes and clear plastic utensils. Audrey felt like she was playing house with Renita and Bobby. When she looked up from taking a bite of her sandwich and tasting the potato salad, Alstead was watching her like she was dessert.

"Mr. Alstead."

"Sy."

"What?"

"Sy. Call me Sy."

How fitting, Audrey thought, for such a boring little man.

"Sy, I need to get some information about Norma Jean Strange."

"Oh not this shit again!" He spat upon the ground. His eyes became angry slits. Audrey drew back in surprise. The unexpected outburst seemed uncharacteristic for the tiny, gentle man. That high voice, and the anger in his eyes, sent a tingle of fear through her.

"That bitch is dead! Why can't everybody just forget about her?" He hit the table with a big fist, jolting the plastic stemware. Audrey had always thought Alstead was a peculiar little man, but suddenly a red flag appeared warning her that this man might be dangerous. She was frightened beyond words. Here she was, alone, with a maniac. No one knew she was here. Had he killed Norma Jean?

"She didn't give a shit about nothing but herself." He was leaning closer to her so she could clearly see the madness in his eyes. "She used people. She lied, cheated, did anything to get what she wanted. Somebody got sick of her games and gave her what she'd been begging for for a long time. Yeah buddy! She got what she had coming."

Alstead finished his ranting and breathed deeply for a moment, in and out. He seemed distant suddenly like he was focused on some long ago thought. When his breathing normalized, he looked at Audrey and smiled with those little yellow teeth.

"I really enjoy your company Audrey." He started touching everything on the table, putting every item neatly in its own place. "Let's just have ourselves a nice little lunch. It's such a beautiful day. Don't you agree?"

She didn't know what to do or say. She cut her eyes beyond him, looking discretely for a rock or something to use for a weapon. Her purse and keys were in his car. The utensils they were using were plastic. She had nothing. Audrey bit into food that was as tasteless as sand trying to act normal.

They finished their sandwiches, salads and drinks in silence. When they were through, Alstead moved over to her bench and sat down beside her. Audrey thought of *'Little Miss Muffet'*. Along came a bug and groped at her jugs, and frightened Miss Audrey away.

"Mr. Alstead!" she tried to push him away, but he was incredibly powerful for such a small man. He was ripping at her shirt. One of his huge hands was inside her blouse. She winced in pain as the thin fabric of her brassiere cut into her flesh. Alstead pulled and twisted until Audrey heard it rip. Bile swelled inside her as she felt his hands pulling, pinching, his sweat and his drool touched her bare skin turning it cold. She tried to wiggle away from him and felt herself falling backward, onto the ground. Her head pounded from the fall. Through dizziness and pain she felt

Alstead on top of her. He was quick as a cat, using one massive hand to pull her legs apart, tearing at her shredded nylons and pulling at her panties.

Though Alstead was small, he possessed the strength of a madman. Audrey was still blinking away the cobwebs in her head that resulted from the fall. She lay there dazed, hardly aware of him taking liberties with her body. She tried to fight him off. He was much too powerful for her.

He moved away from her. She heard the sound of his zipper, and blinked her eyes again to focus. A wall of flesh sprang from his pants, the length and thickness like nothing she'd ever seen on a man. He positioned his knees onto her arms, effectively pinning her to the ground. Her stomach tightened with shock and disgust as he tried to force his huge penis into her mouth. She gagged at the sight and smell of his vein-swollen organ that reeked of his lust for her. She moved her head away, feeling powerless as he rubbed himself along her face and breasts.

He struggled to position himself to enter her. God help me, she prayed. Though the pain was still sharp, her head began to clear. Audrey started kicking. She managed to pull away from him. He pulled her back. His breathing was loud, like a huge panting dog. He murmured non-sensical words of desire to her, begging her to love him back.

She tried to kick him. He responded with a short, hard jab to her mouth. Audrey tasted the tart saltiness of her own blood. They tussled on the ground for several long minutes before she was able to free her right arm. With strength derived from fear producing adrenaline, she rammed her fist between his legs. Alstead howled like an animal.

"Nasty, crazy bastard!" Audrey said. She hobbled on one shoe, finding its mate near the place where she had struggled moments earlier. She put it on her foot and walked back to where Alstead lay writhing. She stood before him defiantly, grinding the heel of her pump into his side. He grimaced in pain, rolling into the fetal position to avoid the full force of her attack. She spat at him for good measure before running to the car.

She was relieved to find he'd left the keys in the Lincoln. Audrey jumped in, slamming the car door shut. The sound of the ignition drowned out Alstead's moaning. She resisted the urge to hit him as she rolled the car past him.

The drive back to the Administration Building was like the blur of a dream. She swung the big car into a space, grabbed her purse and keys and walked on wobbly legs to the Saab. She bent to open the door and was overwhelmed by the return of the headache pain and an upset stomach. Audrey vomited up everything she'd had for lunch in a messy pile near her feet. Beads of sweat dotted her head as she propped herself on the car to keep from passing out.

A minute or two passed before she felt steady enough to open the car door. She sat with her feet still on the ground until the trembling subsided. Audrey grabbed a handful of tissues and wiped her mouth and face. She swallowed back tears and the memory of the vivid nightmare that she had been a part of, murmuring a prayer of thanks that things hadn't been worse.

23

Theolonius Griffin was in the library of his home listening to his wife recount her meeting with Audrey Wilson. She'd left the office early so she could get a jump on her favorite pastime—drinking. It was now almost seven p.m. Juanda had been drinking for nearly four hours. Her facial features, her hair, her clothes, and her speech drooped from the weight of intoxication.

He watched her facial expressions carefully. Juanda wasn't exactly the brightest bulb in the lamp. He prayed she hadn't given anything away. His instructions to her had been plain, no more interviews of any kind. But according to her, Audrey Wilson had showed up unannounced, barged into her office and refused to leave until she was heard.

"Why didn't you just tell her to buzz off?" His faced wrinkled in annoyance. "Why do you feel you have to talk to people just because they want to talk?"

Juanda Griffin seemed to ponder the question put to her. Her head bobbed slightly as though it were too heavy for her neck to support it. He hated her when she drank.

Juanda was always impeccably dressed and coifed. But when she drank she didn't care what she looked like or what she said. Juanda would get what they used to call "pissy drunk", one minute cursing, the next crying, and then cursing again.

"Well, if your bitch had been doing her job and monitoring who comes into the offices, none of this would have happened." An auburn tinted lock from her upsweep plopped between her eyes.

"None of what?" His lip curled in disgust as his eyes followed a trickle of drool trailing down her chin. "Just what did you say to Audrey Wilson?"

"I told you, you fuckin' bastard, I ain't say nut'in to her." She burped loudly, then hiccuped, before adding, "And don't try to change the subjeck. You and that gray-headed bitch were fuckin' today, weren't you? That's why I couldn't—burp—find you."

"That's ridiculous, Juanda." Griffin grimaced as the stench of expelled gas from Juanda's belch whiffed towards him. "Honey, you know that's not true."

"You're lying!" Juanda stamped her foot angrily. "You hired her when I begged you not to. I asked you to let her go and here it is seven years later and she still workin' there." She stopped talking for a moment as a violent tremble quaked her. The next words rumbled forth on a sea of pain. "Now you spect me to believe ya'll ain't still fuckin'?"

Her face contorted into a mass of wet, broken sobs.

"Why you do this to me Theo? You know I love you. You treat me like sheee it!" Juanda slobbered all over her blue Donna Karan pin striped suit.

Pulling a handkerchief from his pocket, Theo approached her and lifted her face to wipe at the mascara that ran down her cheeks. He handed her the hanky and looked the other way as she blew loudly into the cloth.

"Honey, don't be mad at me. I need you baby." He pulled her to him and hugged her. "You know I don't care about anyone but you. This whole plan came into being so that we could live a better life. Don't you appreciate the things I've given you?"

Juanda shook her head. Theo held her face in his hands and kissed her. The sour taste and smell of bourbon made his stomach churn. He couldn't afford to have Juanda unhappy. She could make big trouble for him. If he wasn't careful, she could mess up everything. Who knew what she might do? He had to keep her illusion of his love for her strong.

Griffin ignored the disgust he felt as he continued kissing her. He waited until he felt her misery subside before moving his hands under her suit jacket and massaging her sagging ass. He unzipped the skirt and let it fall to the floor. His kisses traveled downward, stopping when his head reached the delicate white lace panties. Theo slid his tongue inside the edge of the fabric until he heard the submissive groan that meant she had forgotten why she was angry with him. He was once again in command. Not that he ever really doubted that he could control Juanda. She was so weak for him. She was such a fool.

He unzipped his pants and pounded her, all the while thinking about what he needed to do next to silence Audrey Wilson.

24

At 1:00 Audrey called Carrey from home and told him she would be out of the office the rest of the day and maybe the next as well. She gave him instructions on how to complete several projects he was working on. She hung up just as the doorbell rang. Renita blew in like a tornado when Audrey opened the door, talking a mile a minute.

"Oh my God! Look at what that bastard did to you." She touched the scratches on Audrey's face. "Your lips are swole up like mets."

"Just what I needed to hear." Audrey moved the ice-filled bag she was holding against her head to her mouth. She winced and put it back to her head.

"Are the reporters still out there?" Audrey positioned herself gingerly onto the couch. There were news crews swarming in front of her door when she'd reached her street. She would have turned the car around and gone to her office when she saw them, but she was just too tired. After the ordeal with Alstead the only thing on her mind had been getting home and washing the filth of him off of her. She ducked their questions and cameras until she was safe behind the door of her home. Now she would be certain to see her fat lipped, wild haired self, splashed all over the television and newspapers.

"I saw a couple of trucks but no one hovering near the door." Renita kicked off her shoes, slung her bag onto the couch, and plopped down so hard that the sofa slid back several inches. When Audrey called her earlier to tell her about her morning, she could scarcely get the incident in the park out of her mouth before her sister said she was on her way over. Audrey wished she had a cigarette.

"Girl, I thought you *had* to be lying! That fool Alstead tried to rape you?" Her intense gaze studied Audrey's face for the punch line to a bad joke.

"I wish I were lying." Thinking of Alstead caused her to tremble with anger. "If I hadn't been working out I may not have been able to get away from him like I did. He is such a creepy guy. I should have known better than to go anywhere with him."

"That's right." Renita wagged an accusatory finger at her. "You should have known better, but that doesn't excuse what he did. Bobby will be back in town..."

"Renita don't. Bobby would go stone crazy on that fool and mess around and get locked up. It's just not worth it."

"Well at least report his ass." Renita's cheeks huffed, full of angry air. "He needs to get his ass kicked by some of Rosemont's Finest, or better yet, send him over to Cincinnati. They'd beat his ass so bad he wouldn't even be able to feel his dick let alone try to force it in somebody. You did report him, didn't you?"

"If the police find out that I'm still snooping around about the theft and murder case, they're liable to beat *me* instead of Alstead."

"You can't just let him get away with what he did. What if he does it to someone else?" Renita's stern gaze was a cover for her worry. Audrey was afraid too, but she had to play the brave big sister. She fanned at the air with her hand like it was no big deal.

"I wouldn't be at all surprised if he had pulled a stunt like this before, or worse. In retrospect, I kind of got a glimpse of his temper during the early part of our so-called luncheon. But I didn't peg him for a rapist."

"What did he do?" Renita's studied her face, trying to hear every word.

"Do you know that when I brought up Norma Jean's name he went completely off? He called her a bitch and said that she was a user who would stop at nothing to get what she wanted. He said she messed with the wrong person and got iced."

"That's our girl all right." Renita shook her head and frowned. "So what do you think that was, a confession?"

"I don't know what to think anymore. When I talked to Alstead before today he told me they worked together to get the projects approved. Maybe he was afraid she would implicate him and he killed her."

"Or maybe they were fooling around and he beat her to death with that big ole dick."

They laughed.

"That shit was unreal. I'm not kidding you Renita; it was like something on Animal Kingdom. I've never seen a human male with a thing that big. We're talking Barnum and Bailey freak show action here." Audrey frowned in distaste. "I wouldn't ever want to fuck *anything* that big."

"Well, we can't have freaks like that running around loose in society. Either call the police or P.T. Barnum on his ass. Get him off the streets." Renita said.

The two of them laughed again and Audrey felt relaxed for the first time since Renita's visit began. The release of tension was cathartic. It was like they'd each carried the weight of what the day's occurrence meant to them both. They were suddenly just glad to be safe in each other's company.

Renita went over to the cupboard and took out two cups. She fished around in her sister's small liquor cabinet until she found an unopened bottle of Bailey's Irish Crème.

"All this talk about Barnum & Bailey and big penises is making me thirsty."

Audrey brewed a pot of coffee and filled two cups. They each added a dash of the creamy brown liqueur and sipped from their china cups as they debated the next course of action.

"Audrey, I think it's too dangerous for you to keep asking questions about this case. Look at what happened today. Alstead could have raped you, cut your body into a million pieces and fed them to the catfish in the Ohio River." Renita placed all of her fingers around the cup like her hands had suddenly grown cold. "He sounds dangerous to me. What if he gets your address and comes over here? I don't think he's going to let you get away with what you did to him. He sounds like a real nutball."

"I know." Audrey saw the fear that reflected in her sister's gaze. It mirrored her own. "I'll stay away from that fool and I promise to tell Rob Hollingsworth everything that happened. He's going to chew my ass though for even talking with any of those people." Audrey sipped the warm coffee, letting it comfort her before continuing.

"Speaking of *those people*—I met with Juanda Griffin this morning. She wouldn't help me, but I got a feeling I'll be hearing more from her. Towards the end of our meeting she seemed more sympathetic."

"You need to be careful of her, too." She lifted Audrey's hand and gave it a squeeze. "The killer could be a woman just like it could be a man."

Audrey shuddered, remembering another murder in Rosemont. The killer had in fact been a woman. Though it had crossed her mind earlier, Audrey tried to imagine the staid, Juanda Griffin beating up and killing the feisty Norma Jean Strange. No way. The killing had been too messy. Juanda wasn't trying to get dirty doing anything.

Renita rose. She slipped on her shoes and grabbed her purse.

"I've got to go in early this evening. Call me in the morning, okay?"

"I will." Audrey closed the door behind Renita, making sure all the doors and windows were locked tight. The house seemed too quiet after Renita left and took her strong opinions and robust laughter with her. She left behind a deafening silence and Audrey felt very much alone and undeniably, afraid.

25

Marsh left a message at Audrey's office for her to meet with him at eleven the next morning. He'd left several messages over the weekend, but she hadn't returned his calls. She must have forgotten about their brunch plans. He wished he could be so casual. Absence was working on his heart as the saying goes, and it was definitely growing fonder.

As he went through his day, it felt like he was walking on air. Every time he thought about her, his stomach fluttered. He looked forward to a relaxing evening at home that night with his fantasies of her and couldn't make the sedan speed fast enough to get him home.

He uncorked a bottle of Chardonnay and sipped between mouthfuls of the shrimp and clam sauce he had picked up from Castini's. Afterward, he made a fire and lost himself in his classic R&B music collection. He listened to the Dramatics, the Dells, and the Temps. He savored the sounds of Curtis Mayfield as he lead the Impressions in *I'm a Fool For You.*

"Don't need no Audrey, being mean to me..." he created his own lyrics, struggling to hit Curtis Mayfield's falsetto before giving up. He thumbed through row after row of the encased discs. When he came to an artist he hadn't heard in a while, he popped the case open and put the CD into a slot behind the others.

He continued to hum the rich harmonies as he washed the dishes and cleaned the kitchen. Looking outside, he watched the sun setting; leaving the sky a wash of muted colors. He enjoyed his house, the meticulous lawn and bold blooming flowers. But it wasn't a single man's house. This was a home. A place to be shared with a wife and kids. Marsh missed having his family with him. He found the hole in his heart being filled more and more by Audrey

Wilson. But he had conflicting feelings. His feelings for her were genuine, but he didn't want to lead her on. He couldn't deny that the plug that had been gouged from his heart resided in a home similar to this one in Cambridge. He missed his wife and son.

As if some kind of warped sign, the record changed to the old Jerry Butler tune *One Night Affair*. He didn't want to Hit-N-Run like the son-of a gun in the Ice Man's song. But he was scared to death of being hurt by another woman when the painful separation from his wife was still so fresh. Audrey deserved more than a casual roll in the sheets, but he was hesitant to make it anything more than that. If he approached it that way, he was sure she'd run from him. He couldn't blame her.

He wanted to move on with his life. He needed to. Marlena had. But he was afraid of getting too close to someone else. And a part of him still held the hope that Marlena would call him, tell him to come on home. But that was about as likely to happen as him finding a pot of gold at the end of a rainbow. He had stopped believing in fairytales long ago.

Besides, Audrey was a good woman. She possessed many of the qualities that Marlena did. She was bright, attractive, funny, outgoing. He could tell that she liked him but she didn't hover or try to rush things between them. He could see himself being in a long-term relationship with her.

Marsh pulled off his clothes, tossing them in a cloth hamper on his way to the bathroom. He opened the glass-enclosed shower stall and turned the dial to the red H. Water pulsed from three showerheads, heating in a matter of seconds. He stepped inside and let the water pound at his body, beating back conflicting thoughts about the women in his life. Beautiful Marlena. Sexy Audrey. Crazy-ass Chloe. Audrey was like a sweet river of sanity sandwiched between the banks of not a chance and no way in hell.

He screeched off the water and dried himself with a fluffy, spring fresh towel. Things were so easy with Audrey, he thought on his way to the living room. The music continued to play. When the familiar bass guitar beginning of Isaac Hayes' *Walk on By* rolled out like a dirge, Marsh rushed for the remote control.

"I don't need to hear that shit." He said to himself, clicking the remote past Ike and the oldies to Regina Carter's upbeat violin, which lifted his spirits immediately.

Audrey. No pressure. No conflict. She could be the missing link, the stabilizing force that his heart needed. Marsh pulled the oversized pillow from the sofa onto a sheet he'd spread onto the floor. He pulled a down comforter over his nude body and fell asleep in front of the fireplace. Visions of Audrey danced in his head.

26

It was ten fifty a.m. when Audrey opened Marsh's office door. The outer room was spacious and tastefully appointed. If the attorney had a receptionist or paralegal, they were nowhere in sight. He smiled at her from his office, rising to greet her.

"Is this a one man operation or are you so unbearable to work for you just can't keep good help?"

He put his hand on her arm and led her inside, looking at her curiously.

"What happened to you?"

She told him about her encounter with Alstead. He listened quietly, his eyes revealing nothing. He let her finish what she had to say before he exploded.

"What on earth were you thinking going off with some man you don't even know? He could have killed you."

"I know...I mean, I didn't think he was that kind of person. I'd talked to him before and he didn't seem like that big of a whacko."

"But he did seem kind of nutty and you went off with him anyway? Audrey, you're smarter than that." Marsh's chest rose and fell as he tried to level his emotion. He pulled her into his arms, hugging her in a way that made her feel he appreciated her being there.

"Are you all right?"

"I'm okay."

"What did the police say?"

"Well, I haven't exactly told them." She mumbled pulling away from him.

"Are you crazy?" He erupted once more. "I'm calling the police right now."

"But I have a doctor's appointment." Audrey put her hand on the back of her tender head.

"Well you're just going to have to be a little late for it. I'm taking you to police headquarters."

* * *

Luckily for her, Rob Hollingsworth was out in the field when she and Marsh arrived at the police station. Audrey filled out a form, before answering the questions posed to her by a mousy looking woman behind a desk.

"That's all we need Miss Wilson. Mr. Alstead will be served on his job and you'll be notified of the hearing date."

Marsh dropped Audrey to her car in plenty of time to make her doctor appointment.

On her way out of the Doctor's Building, a peculiar feeling shook her. She looked behind her but there was no one in sight. She opened the car door and slipped inside. Light pellets of rain pelted the windshield. She turned on the wipers.

Audrey breathed deeply, relaxing the knot that was forming in her shoulders, before starting up the car. She turned on the radio before pulling into the light traffic flow.

A car whizzed by her, causing her to swerve and just barely miss a guardrail. The darkening sky reduced visibility and she didn't get a license number or description. Who ever it was, was now gone.

Audrey trembled with fear. She pulled the car over and tried to relax and reconstruct what had happened. Concentrate as she might, she couldn't envision the make or model of car, let alone a description of the driver or other information that might track him down.

Though still shaken, she took a few deep breaths, composed herself and continued onward. Perhaps it was a coincidence.

People drove awfully crazy sometimes. Just because someone cuts you off doesn't mean they're trying to kill you. Nevertheless, relief settled her rattled nerves when she finally reached her street.

Audrey pulled the car into its normal spot in front of her brownstone. The rain had stopped but the sky was still gray. She stooped to retrieve a thick white envelope that was propped against her door. Freedom leaped onto the ledge, giving her all kinds of grief for being gone so long. She mixed the white package in with the pile of mail she collected from the ornate iron mailbox. Freedom almost made her drop the stack as he darted past her into the foyer.

"What's the matter boy, bad day in the jungle?" Freedom shook remnants from the leftover rain on his master, and then wound himself around her legs, crying loudly while she piled chicken liver into his dish.

"You're in a foul mood today, Free." The cat cast her a wicked yellow-eyed glare before attacking the contents in the bowl. Audrey grabbed an apple from the large arrangement of fruit on her dining room table and was preparing to go through the mail when the phone rang.

The caller hung up without responding to her hello. Audrey returned to her spot near the mail pile when the phone rang again.

"You'll be sorry, bitch!" The caller rasped.

"What? Who is this?" Her voice shook. An angry, annoyed frown wrinkled her face.

The phone went dead. Audrey shivered. The voice was not a familiar one. She couldn't even detect the gender of the caller. With everything that had been going on, it could have been anyone calling, or simply a wrong number. A check of the caller ID box showed an unlisted source. Great. She couldn't even call the fool back and give him a piece of her mind.

She could hear the whispered threat reverberate in her mind as she thought about recent attacks on her car. She was certain someone had been following her today, now this.

Glancing at the clock, she was disappointed that it was only a little past three. She hit the speed dial but there was no answer at Renita's.

Audrey turned her attention once again to the pile of mail. Sandwiched in with the usual grouping of bills, advertisements and other miscellaneous junk mail, was the mysterious white envelope. It was free of any markings. Knowing someone had dropped a package off at her home terrified her. She remembered Renita's warning about Alstead and shuddered.

That could have been him on the phone just now, not only angry with her about the incident in the park, but also about the warrant she'd filed with the police. He had some nerve! Hell, after all she'd been through lately, if anyone should be calling somebody making harassing calls it should be her.

She tried to deny the feelings of foreboding that washed over her every time she caught the unmarked package from the corner of her eye. She thought about letter bombs, poisonous powders, snakes, severed body parts and half a dozen other things that could be in the package. Audrey's stomach did a little flip as she opened the kitchen drawer. She pushed through a hodgepodge of note pads and pens, batteries, candles and small tools to retrieve the pearl handled letter opener.

Taking a deep breath she slit the top of the envelope and extracted its contents. There was a spiral bound report with a blank cover. A plain sheet of paper covered a thick pile of photocopied documents, held together by a large black metal clip. Audrey folded back the cover on the bound report, revealing several columns of information related to the construction projects for Rosemont Township.

The first column listed about twenty names of companies that were familiar to Audrey as those used for the renovation and construction. The next column listed the type of concern and the contact name. The last column displayed the estimated cost of the jobs.

Subsequent pages showed change orders detailing additional costs, which arose at various stages as the entire project neared completion. A flowchart diagrammed each vendor, and how it related to the others. Lines were drawn from major vendors linking them to all subcontractors that were used for different parts of the job.

The majority of the subcontracting was done through a company called GAS Construction, Ltd., which had not been included on the other documents. A series of estimates were included for work to be handled by GAS with costs ranging from fifty to one hundred thousand dollars per job. The problem was that most of the work contracted to GAS had already been performed by other PRICE Construction subcontractors.

GAS TECH had billed the Township for several million dollars in computer equipment and services that had already been handled by another company.

"I can't believe this." Audrey mumbled to herself. Jean had to have known about this. But that same argument could have been made against Audrey. Why hadn't she seen this before?

A quick mental calculation told Audrey that this company had been paid well over a million dollars for each job. Her eyes grew wide as she calculated the figures. It was immediately obvious that something was funny about the relationship with the Township and GAS Construction. No wonder Rob was looking at her like she was trying to play him for a sucker. Somebody had been played, but it wasn't Rob Hollingsworth.

"This must be the report Jean wanted to show me." Audrey thought. There was no information on GAS's officers or location. Audrey telephoned information.

"GAS Construction, please." Audrey doodled on a sheet of paper while she waited for the operator to locate the listing. The dull voice on the other end responded just as Audrey had expected.

"I show no listing for a GAS Construction."

"How about GAS, Limited?"

"Nothing for GAS, Limited."

"Would you try GAS TECH, please?"

"There's nothing listed for GAS TECH." The voice on the other end said after a brief delay. "Can I help you find anything else?"

"No. Thank you." Audrey hung up the receiver and finished looking at the rest of the documents. The last page included the names of the Rosemont Township Administrative staff and their titles. Her eyes were immediately drawn to her own name and the caption "Financial Counsel" listed directly below the familiar names of the Rosemont Board of Directors:

Theolonius Griffin	President and CEO
Sylvester Alstead	Head of City Planning
Norma Jean Strange	Director of Finance
Juanda Griffin	Treasurer
Laughton Glen	Chief Information Officer
Sarah Collins	Executive Administrative Assistant

Next, Audrey loosened the black clip and examined the group of papers that were segregated from the rest of the report.

"What on earth..." Audrey was surprised to see a copy of her office stationery. The gold embossed WILSON ASSOCIATES, emblazoned across the top of the page of some correspondence, was darkened by trips through the photocopier. There was a copy of a letter on her stationery making wonderful claims about GAS,

Ltd., followed by reports and letters showing Audrey Wilson d.b.a. WILSON ASSOCIATES signing off on squeaky clean audits.

There was only one problem. Until Audrey opened this package, she had never heard of GAS, Ltd. She had never seen this letter before and certainly had not signed it. She could feel the clutch of claustrophobia pushing her windpipe shut. Audrey took a few slow breaths and tried to calm herself before continuing.

There were copies of GAS invoices, which "Audrey" had signed-off on, and the familiar stamp on each from the Rosemont Township Accounting Department as they processed the invoices for payment.

There was a copy of a check register for Rosemont Township showing the payment history of GAS. Audrey checked the numbers twice and was astounded to find the total payments for the construction and computer equipment company totaled nearly ten million dollars.

Audrey felt sick to her stomach as she continued reviewing the pile of incriminating documents. If Rob Hollingsworth had seen all this, she could understand why he had suspected her involvement. She could feel the bile rise from her stomach like mercury up the shaft of a thermometer.

Running to the bathroom, Audrey wiped at the tears that streamed her face. Her stomach heaved up a few sour-tasting drops of liquid. She washed her face and patted it dry with a soft cloth. The person who looked back at her from the mirror with tired red eyes supported by dark bags was almost unrecognizable. This was serious. What if she couldn't prove that she had nothing to do with this stuff?

Audrey returned to the kitchen and put the clip back on the sheaf of papers. Instead of answering questions, the package had only added to her confusion. Who'd sent her the package? Was it someone she knew well? It was obviously someone who knew where she lived. She thought of Rob Hollingsworth, but quickly dismissed the idea. There's no way that he would take evidence in a pending case and share it with a civilian. She couldn't even be sure that this was the evidence that the police had.

She looked at the letters of recommendation once more. This couldn't be the report Jean had called Audrey about. This report obviously came from someone who knew that Norma Jean was involved in the theft. The questions were swirling around her head like flies at a picnic. Did the package come from the killer? Why on earth would the killer send her this information? How could she prove that the signatures on the invoices and the letters were forgeries? There was only one person who could have hung her up like this. Why would Norma Jean want to hurt her in this way?

She would have to talk to the police about this, but she thought about how dreadful her previous meetings had been and how, since she was already under suspicion, this would do little to shore up her already shaky standing in their eyes. She walked over to the phone and dialed Marshall Fixx.

27

Forty-five minutes later, Marsh sat in the same spot that Audrey had occupied, studying the information from the package. She didn't have to ask him what he thought. His facial expression, the wrinkled brow, and turned down mouth, summed up his feelings.

When he was finished, he questioned her extensively about her office controls and about Carrey. Who has access to your office supplies? How well do you know your office manager? Have you ever left Norma Jean in the office by herself? Could Carrey be involved in the frame-up as well? Of course not, Audrey had answered him. Carrey was just a kid doing a job. But to Marshall Fixx, everyone was a suspect. Audrey knew that Carrey had been just as hurt and shocked by all of this as she had. Norma Jean had been left alone there on occasion. She had most likely lured him away from his desk so she could have free reign of the office. Carrey was another victim in this. With no other clients and the possibility of Audrey losing her license, Carrey was going to be out of a job.

The more questions Marsh asked, the worse she felt. His questions were valid and the points were well taken. Somehow, her letterhead had gotten out of the office and been used by a con artist. Her signature was on documents that she'd never seen. As a person who had been involved in finance her entire life, she should not have been so careless about how her office was managed. Why didn't she have better controls in place? She had no idea where the stationery supply was kept; much less how much was on hand.

Norma Jean had constantly been to the office; sometimes she would be there when Audrey arrived in the morning. She had no doubt been there alone on occasion. Audrey trusted her and would have thought nothing of leaving her there while she ran an errand. She could have taken the stationery at any time. She could have practiced writing Audrey's name and gotten good enough that only a trained eye could tell the difference. At other times she had simply used Audrey's signature stamp.

"Why would she do this to me?" Audrey looked down at the incriminating documents. "I've got to find out who sent me this stuff. Whoever it is, knows the truth."

Marsh saw the pain and confusion and gathered her in his arms.

"Don't you worry, old girl. We're going to figure this thing out together. We're going to win. You know how I know?"

"How do you know?" She didn't like that "old girl" crap. Who was he, Cary Grant or somebody?

"Cause I'm Marshall Fixx, that's why. Eribody know I fixxes erithang." He made an exaggerated sign with his fingers. Audrey wasn't sure what that was supposed to mean.

She couldn't help but laugh at the Ivy Leaguer's lame attempt at Ebonics.

"Now go get out of those funky clothes. I'm going to draw you a warm bath, kiss your face and make sure that you get a good night's sleep. Now where's the dish soap?"

"What?"

"I heard you ghetto girls bathe in dish detergent."

Audrey laughed again. Maybe he was Cary Grant, in a "round the way" kind of way. Picking up a pillow from the sofa, she made a weak attempt to hit him with it. He patted her lightly on the butt and pushed her in the direction of the bedroom while he made his way to the bathroom.

She could hear him stirring around, deciding from the selection of bath salts on the cart near her tub. Soon she heard the water rumbling and smelled the gardenia scented bath oil as Marsh poured the thick gel into the cascade flowing from the bathtub faucet.

Audrey followed the sound of the roaring faucet. The water had foamed into a mountain of aromatic suds that shown like jewels in the glow of multicolored fragrant candles. He'd grouped them together throughout the bathroom, giving the room a soft romantic glow. He turned on the sound therapy machine, completing the mood.

When he saw her in the doorway wearing a soft pink silk kimono, she caught him trying to mask the excitement that flickered in his eyes. She felt incredibly sexy. Every part of her wanted him and she knew he wanted her.

He kissed her softly on the lips, pushing at the thin fabric until fell to the floor. He guided her to the steamy tub and she stepped into what felt like heaven. He tilted her head upward and kissed her forehead.

"I'll let myself out."

Audrey opened her eyes and watched him walk away. She thought he was joking. How could he leave all this? The warm water teased her. The scented suds tickled her everywhere she wanted him to.

Audrey sighed, leaning her head back onto a rolled towel that Marshall had propped for her. Lulled into a peaceful state by violins, French horns, and waves crashing against rocks, she heard the door close gently behind him as he left her in the heavenly place he'd helped create.

28

Across town, Theo Griffin sat next to his wife on the sofa sipping champagne in front of a roaring fire. Classical music wafted clear and sweet in the air, transporting them to a far away time in their lives when they'd attended concerts at Music Hall. Eric Kunzel conducted the orchestra, playing it seemed for only Theo and Juanda Griffin.

"You shoulda seen the look on J.C. Norton's face when I told him Audrey Wilson was working for us as a contractor and she had been stealing us blind." Theo Griffin's laughter rolled up from the base of his stomach until tears sprang to his eyes.

"He believed you?" Juanda smiled at her husband. Theo saw nothing but undying devotion for him registered on her face.

"Did he believe me? Shit, Juanda, he wanted to know if he could help the police in the investigation." Griffin smiled; a self-satisfied twinkle lit his eyes. "When I told him they suspected her involvement in Norma Jean's murder, I thought he was going to round up a posse and track her down and hang her."

Griffin took a deep swallow from his glass.

"He thinks she was trying to make Norton Group her next conquest. Now the bastard wants to get even." Griffin rubbed his hands together, his eyes danced wickedly. "Norton's also dumping Fixx as an associate."

"Isn't he afraid of being sued?" Juanda said over the rim of her glass.

"Naw. He'll simply buy Fixx's contract out. I'm sure it's peanuts for a company the size of Norton Group. Norton says that by the time he's finished nobody will touch Fixx or that Wilson woman with a ten foot pole."

They laughed at the possibility of reaching closure feeling relieved to have gotten through it unscathed.

"Surely the police have everything that they need to arrest that nosey broad. There's enough evidence to ensure that she will be indicted for the theft. It won't be that much of a stretch to put the murder on her as well. And that, my wife," he touched her nose playfully, "will be the end of Audrey Wilson."

"You don't really think they will put that murder on her, do you? That's quite a stretch." Doubt clouded her eyes as they searched her husband's face for reassurance.

"No, it's really not. A person involved in that level of criminal activity could very easily commit murder."

"I don't think the police will buy it." Juanda was still uncertain.

"I sure as hell hope they do." He snorted, taking another gulp from the glass in his hand. "Otherwise, we're fucked."

"But she didn't have anything to do with that."

"Who gives a shit if she's involved or not." He turned up the glass, and then frowned at its emptiness. "That bitch is a troublemaker. I say the faster they stick her with this thing, the better for the rest of us." He rose and walked over to the bar. Bored with the champagne, he selected a decanter of whiskey.

"Speaking of 'the rest of us', what about Sy and Laughton?" Juanda left the sofa and stood near her husband.

Griffin shrugged. "What about them?"

"How much do they really know? Do you think they'll be a problem?"

"Sy and me go way back." The whiskey spilled over the rim of the tumbler. He tossed a handful of cocktail napkins at the spill. "He may suspect something, but he's the kind of guy that's not going to raise a stink as long as he gets his." Griffin bent over the glass, taking the top off his drink. "Once I promoted him to Head of City Planning and gave him that fat raise, he was as right as rain. As far as Laughton's concerned, he's just waiting for retirement. He's hardly in his office long enough to know what's going on, or care for that matter."

Griffin grabbed the bottle from the bucket and topped off Juanda's drink. He raised his glass and gazed into his wife's eyes.

"To better days."

Their glasses clinked and they turned them up. Griffin didn't speak again until they were finished drinking.

"Tomorrow I'll check with Hollingsworth on how the investigation is going. Either way it goes, we're going to put an end to Audrey Wilson once and for all."

29

Audrey spent the following day trying to figure out when Norma Jean could have accessed her files and supplies and how she could rectify some of the damage that was being done to her reputation. It troubled her that she didn't know who had sent the package and that there was some nut out there following her, attacking her car and making threatening phone calls. Were all these events related? None of this stuff started happening until Norma Jean was killed.

Norma Jean. Every time she thought about her she got mad all over again. It's bad when you're stabbed in the back, but when it's done by someone you consider a friend, the wound is twice as deep, and hurts ten times as much.

"You're just not yourself today." Carrey eyed his boss with concern.

She couldn't remember the last time she'd had a good night's sleep. Her dull eyes were puffy and shadowed.

"The cops released you so they must know how ridiculous they were to suspect you would ever do anything illegal." He assured her. "Why in the world did they come here, Audrey?"

"They have a lot of incriminating evidence, that's why. Carrey, do you remember ever seeing Norma Jean go through our files?"

"What? Of course not. Why would you ask a question like that?"

Audrey had kept Carrey in the dark about this situation but knew that the time was ripe for a little enlightenment.

"Listen, Carrey. I'm involved in a police investigation regarding money which was taken from Rosemont Township." She ignored the bug-eyed stare her assistant gave her and continued.

"That's why they came in here last week rummaging through our files. It seems our good friend Jean took some of our stationery and forged my signature so it would look like I was involved. If I don't find out the truth soon I could be put *out* of business and put *in* jail."

Carrey closed his mouth and started throwing his hands up in the air like he was at a revival meeting.

"You mean we might be shut down?"

"It's a possibility."

"But I need this job to support my Mama." Carrey was distraught. She knew he wouldn't take the news very well. Her heart ached for him, but what could she do?

"Carrey, calm down. I'm going to get to the bottom of this." She hoped she sounded stronger than she felt. "The first thing I need to do is find out how Jean accessed our office supplies and what all she did with them."

"Audrey honey, I'm so sorry. Jean came here several times while you were out of the office." He clucked and waved his hands expressively. His blond hair made him look like a chicken. "She relieved me a couple of times when I needed to get my hair done and when I had to pick up some medicine to take to my Mama. I had complete trust in her and never thought she would do anything to jeopardize your friendship." He looked at her with eyes full to overflowing. "I'm sorry, Audrey."

"Don't worry about it C." Audrey shook her head in dismay. "If she hadn't used you she would have figured out another way to get what she wanted. I've discovered so much about her since her death. I never really knew her at all."

A weary sigh escaped her lips as she headed for her office, her shoulders rounded by the weight of recent events. Carrey grabbed a handful of pink slips and trotted after her.

"Oh, Audrey, here are your messages. The people from Graves Editing finally returned your call to say they'd decided against using our services. Ditto for Hadley Papers." Carrey knew she would be disappointed to learn that the potential accounts had decided to exercise other options. He hesitated before dropping the biggest bombshell. "There's a message in there from Mr. Norton's office."

"Great. I've been waiting for that one. I'll be inside making calls, Carrey."

Audrey tried to remain optimistic as she dialed J.C. Norton's office. When his secretary intercepted the call, not putting her directly through, she expected the worst.

"Miss Wilson, Mr. Norton wishes to express his pleasure in meeting with you the other day, but he has decided to go with another firm."

Audrey hung up the phone, the rejection echoing in her head as she slumped in her chair. What else is going to happen? She was really counting on the Norton job. She didn't realize until now just how much. Beginning to feel like she was in a bad dream, Audrey left the remaining stack of messages on the desk. She drifted through the rest of the day, trying to work around the negative cloud that seemed to lurk overhead. Audrey hadn't been able to concentrate all day. It was now after five o'clock so she shut her PC down. She could hear Carrey outside her door making the quick bustling sounds of a worker who's glad to see another day end. Today she beat him to the punch. He stopped fidgeting with items on his desk and turned when she opened her office door.

"I'm out of here, Carrey. I'll see you in the morning." She told him on her way out of the office.

* * *

It was nearly six o'clock when Audrey parked the car in front of the brownstone. An eerie stillness surrounded her as she jogged up the steps to her front door. Freedom usually pounced on her like someone had propelled him from a slingshot. But he was nowhere in sight. He must still be out hunting she thought, closing the door behind her.

When Audrey walked into the living room she almost cried. Her house had been completely ransacked. There was broken glass and debris everywhere. They'd smashed in her TV set. A tire iron lay on the floor next to the set like a petrified snake. CD's and old LP's were out of their containers and strewn everywhere.

The kitchen was far worse than the living room. There were broken eggs on the floor and flour had been shaken about. All the cookware had been taken out of its place in the cabinet and littered throughout the house. The bedding had been shredded. The pillows were slashed. Dirt from the plants was strewn about the bed and the bedroom carpeting.

A quick inventory proved that nothing was missing. If they had been looking for the package, she had it with her. That meant they would be back.

A slight scratching at the door made her heart flutter. She opened it a cautious crack to let Freedom in. She scooped up the cat and gave him a hug. She had feared the worst when he didn't greet her at the door as usual.

"I wish you could tell me who did this Free." She hugged the cat, who twisted his head around and looked at her curiously before struggling out of her arms and onto the floor.

She called Marshall Fixx first. Audrey held the receiver to her pounding chest for a moment, and then called 911. Rob Hollingsworth was ringing her doorbell ten minutes later.

"How did I know *you* would answer the call?" His sudden appearance irritated her and she wasn't sure why.

Hollingsworth ignored her and instead asked a lot of scripted questions from the police academy handbook. He was looking around at the mess and taking notes when Marsh arrived.

Rob checked out the newcomer suspiciously before recognition set in. He turned away and continued writing.

"Good day to you too, Detective."

Rob mumbled something that sounded like either you too, or fuck you, closed his notepad and addressed the couple.

"Well, since nothing is missing and there are no witnesses to the break-in, there's not a whole lot else I can do for you. If you need a formal police report for your insurance company, you can pick it up downtown."

He tipped his hat like the cowboys do in the movies and moseyed on off into the sunset.

"That guy is weird." Marsh looked after him, shaking his head.

"I used to think he was a nice guy, but this case has changed him. Can you keep a secret?"

"Sure."

"He was dating Norma Jean Strange." Audrey whispered. "Nobody knows about it at the precinct."

"He could get in all kinds of hot water for holding back information about personal involvement on a case. If he's giving you a hard time I could..."

"No, please." She raised a hand in protest. "Forget about him. He's going through a grieving process and he can't even talk to the people he's the closest to about it. He'll bounce back." Audrey pulled the white envelope from her valise.

"I have a feeling that this is what the burglar was looking for."

"Who else would know that you've got that?"

"Hell, I don't even know who sent it. I had planned on telling Rob about it but I wanted to discuss the whole thing with you first." She cast a sly glance in his direction. "We kind of got a little side tracked last night."

"You were beat and I didn't think anything else that needed to be said or done couldn't wait until another time." Marsh said and smiled.

"It's a good thing that I got that brief moment of pleasure in my cute little house." Tears brimmed and spilled onto her cheeks. She wiped her face, and then mumbled. "Look at it now."

It wasn't until this moment that Audrey really began to absorb what had happened to her. She felt violated, angry, and afraid. It was as though the whole world had it in for her. Every day it was something new and at this point she was beyond weary.

"Look, why don't you stay in my guest house until all of this stuff is over. It's in back of the main house. It has a bath, kitchen, and nice sized bedroom. You'd have plenty of privacy and no one would know you were there."

"What about Freedom?" The cat's ears pricked to attention at the mention of his name.

"Bring him with you." Marsh replied. "He'll love it there with all the wildlife. There are plenty of snakes, frogs and birds for him to kill."

"Hey, watch it." Audrey rolled her eyes feigning indignation. "My cat is no killer. He just does what he has to do to survive."

"Whatever. Just go get your stuff."

Audrey's first inclination was to decline. But as she looked around her she realized that she couldn't stay here. She would have called her sister, but Renita's place was small. She had a spare room that doubled as a studio with a let out couch. Bobby was out of town. If she went to his place she'd have it all to herself. But his house was so nasty she'd just as soon stay in her own place if she were going to be faced with cleaning up a mess.

She could always get a hotel room, but business hadn't been great before her work with the Township. Those big government checks were just beginning to correct a shaky situation before everything went haywire. Who knew how long it would be before this thing ran its course? She could scarcely afford to make some hotel chain richer.

"Well, maybe for a few days." She conceded.

Marsh smiled and said, "You got a pet carrier, right? Grab the kitty and some of your things. I want you to feel free to stay as long as you need to."

Audrey sighed deeply, giving him an appreciative nod. He pulled her into a warm embrace.

"Try not to worry, Audrey. Everything will be fine."

30

It had been a beautiful bright fall day. Remnants of the setting sun swirled subdued colors across the sky. The trees stood like proud burlesque queens, flashing their autumn wardrobes haughtily while the wind whipped away pieces of their costumes, tossing them onto the ground.

Audrey leaned back in the spacious car. It felt good to let Marsh take command. She was tired from everything that had been going on and decided to turn everything worldly over to Marsh and her spirit over to God.

She looked at him, the sun reflecting off his cocoa brown face. She'd checked him out on the sly when they were at her place. He looked so good she'd almost forgot about the break-in, the reason for his visit.

Her eyes caressed his tall, dark beauty, feeling a pang of longing for him. As he reviewed every piece of the damage, she surveyed every inch of him. The white sweater with tan accents woven throughout covered his strong arms and back. The jeans that he wore flattered the curve of his butt and accentuated his muscular thighs. The tan ostrich skin boots he wore exaggerated the slight bow of his long legs. Audrey wanted to slip her hand inside that gap and drive her hand up the long road of his legs until it was stopped by the hardness at its fork.

"You okay?" Marsh grimaced in concern.

"It's just been a long, hellish day." She shook the fantasy away.

"What else could have happened that was worse than getting your place trashed?"

"All of my potential clients are turning tail on me. Even Norton." Audrey's eyes grew moist and she tried to deny the growing feeling of self-pity. She looked over her right shoulder out the window.

"That's funny, I got a bit of bad news from Norton myself." Marsh shrugged, unconcerned. "The difference is, I don't need him, he needs me."

"I wish that were the case for me." She was quiet for a moment before turning towards him and touching his arm softly.

"I can't tell you how much I appreciate your being there for me these past few days." Audrey said.

"Aw, shucks ma'am. It's my pleasure." He drawled.

"You know you need to quit. That Southwestern Bostonian accent just ain't working."

"Wanna hear my John Wayne?"

"Please, spare me." Audrey replied. "I don't even want to hear John Wayne's John Wayne."

He slapped her thigh playfully, and then gave it a squeeze. The fire of his touch branded her thigh. She could almost hear it sizzle.

"Don't worry, old girl. It's going to be rough sailing for awhile but all of this will blow over and you'll get back on track."

She would have told him to cut the old girl bit, but she wanted him so badly at that moment he could have called her anything. When he removed his hand, the heat of it lingered, traveling up her thigh, touching every part of her. Each time he moved in her direction, his fragrance whipped at her senses. She knew that she was ready to surrender to him. The ache of her passion was overwhelming, tingling hot throughout her body. Audrey felt flush. She fanned herself with her hand.

"Is it okay if I open the window?"

"Sure. Go head."

She cracked the window on her side of the car and said a silent prayer of thanks as the autumn air rushed in, cooling her skin and her intentions.

When they arrived at Marsh's house he started removing her things from the car. There was still enough sunlight remaining for her to get a better appreciation of the property than she had on her previous visit. The grounds were beautiful, everything Marsh had said and more. Audrey took Freedom from the back seat, opening the door to the carrier. He peeped out from the opened door tentatively before darting out of the container and up a tree after a plump gray squirrel.

"I hope he remembers to come back."

"He'll be back." Marsh said, "After that squirrel kicks his ass." Audrey shook her head and they both laughed as Marsh led her down the stone path to the guesthouse.

With red embers smoldering in the fireplace, the room was warm and cozy. There were polished hardwood floors throughout, a wood-burning fireplace in the center of the main room and a wonderful old bentwood rocker in front of it. The Shaker style furniture fit the cabin to perfection. A beautiful spray of wildflowers decorated the table.

"This is really nice," Audrey exclaimed.

The open floor plan allowed for flexibility. Careful placement of the furnishings made the entire space feel warm and comfortable.

"Let me show you the bedroom." Marsh said, moving quickly to put her bags down next to a massive king-size bed that overpowered the right side of the room. There was no real "bedroom." The sleeping area was dressed for a country picnic with an airy gingham pattern on the pillows, curtains, and tablecloth. A beautiful duvet in a variation of the same design accessorized the comforter. There were fresh flowers throughout.

The only room that was enclosed was the bathroom. There was a sofa, a TV and small stereo to the left of the front door. The entire space was *Better Homes & Gardens* pretty.

"I really like this, Marsh." Audrey looked around the room approvingly. "If I didn't know any better, I'd think you were expecting company."

"I'm always expecting company. A brother's gotta stay ready." Marsh stoked the fire, adding a log. Audrey watched him stir the fire, not knowing if the heat she felt was from the fireplace or from somewhere within. He looked at her and smiled as if he knew what she was feeling.

She loved his cockiness. Her heart had surrendered itself to him, even though her mind wanted to resist. She could see them holed up in this lovely cabin together forever. But she wasn't ready to let her guard down completely. How much of what she was feeling had to do with her need to be protected? Letting her genitalia do her thinking was definitely not the way to go. No matter how fine he was and regardless what cozy little trappings were put in her path, this was about business. She would make a few calls, get herself back on track, get to the bottom of this frame-up mess, and get her place back. Then she could think rationally about Marshall Fixx.

* * *

Marsh pulled the door to the cabin shut and walked fifty yards to the main house. He was sorry that he'd gotten rid of the horses that came with the property. This would be an excellent day for a ride.

He still wasn't sure how long he'd be staying in Kentucky and he wanted his time there to be as hassle free as possible. Animals require a lot of care. He didn't want to keep the horses and then neglect them or pay a small fortune for caretakers.

He'd come to the Rosemont area to set up the midwestern branch of his business. Things were going very well. As a matter of fact, he'd been swamped with business from practically the first day there. It was time to select the attorneys who would man the site full-time and let them start preparing for their staffing and other needs.

In the meantime, Marsh was playing with fire. Her name was Audrey Wilson. He had purposely put on the jeans and boots when she called him. There wasn't a woman alive who could resist ole Marsh in this getup. He knew that she wanted him. He'd caught her a couple of times checking him out and when she started fanning herself and rolled the window down, it was all he could do to keep from laughing out loud.

He liked her a lot, and it took all that was in him to practice restraint. And restrain himself he must. He was treading on dangerous ground getting involved with a client. Once Audrey was completely exonerated of all suspicions, he would take his time and get to know her better.

He was lonely and she seemed like the perfect kind of woman to ease his lonesome heart. But he had to be careful that it didn't become anything too heavy. Kentucky was nice but he was a Yankee through and through. He'd be moving back to Massachusetts soon, or at the very least, flying between the two states.

In the meantime, why be alone when he could be with Audrey?

* * *

"Where the hell are you?" Renita had been worried sick and Audrey was sorry for not calling her sooner. Audrey listened as Renita told her she'd called repeatedly and gone by her house because she'd had a strange feeling that something wasn't right. Audrey told her about the break-in and that she was staying at Marsh's guesthouse.

"You couldn't turn on your cell phone?"

"I guess I just forgot." Audrey traced a pattern in the bedspread. "He came over so quickly, swooped me and Freedom up and brought us over to Newport."

"Well, isn't that cozy."

"Actually, it really is." Audrey lie across the soft, quilt covered bed talking to Renita on a yellow cordless phone that matched the décor of the bedroom. "He's not bothering me or anything. This house has all of the comforts of home without all the headaches. But I don't want to stay here but a few days at most. Can you put me up in your spare room till I get my place cleaned up?"

"I don't know why you didn't call me in the first place. I *am* your sister, Audrey."

"That's why I didn't call you. Somebody is trying to spook me. I don't know how dangerous they are and I didn't want to involve you."

"I'm already involved." Renita said. "You just let them try some shit up in here."

Audrey imagined her petite sister, craning her neck trying to make herself look more formidable.

"I'll get everything ready and you let me know when you want to come. You said you got your cell phone with you?" Renita asked.

"Yeah."

"I left you half a dozen messages." Renita shrieked in irritation.

"Sorry. I'll keep it on as long as I'm out here." Audrey assured her.

"Bobby's will be flying in tomorrow. Why don't you and Marsh join us at the Rack?"

"That sounds good. I'll mention it to him."

"I love you, Auddie."

"I love you back, Ren."

31

Theo Griffin put the receiver back in its cradle. He mumbled a curse when he learned from his source that they had not found the report. Having Audrey Wilson's house bugged had been a smart move that had paid off already. Griffin was able to keep tabs on her without her knowledge. He had initially thought about surveillance, but that was costly and he would always have the worry of the person being made. The Wilson woman was completely unaware of the bug.

Thanks to the recording device, he knew that she had received a packaged recently. Someone had sent her information documenting how money was funneled into a dummy corporation making it easy to siphon a substantial amount of the government grants received for Township construction. Griffin had an idea who sent the package. He'd deal with that later.

His goal was to get the information from Audrey Wilson before she turned it over to the authorities. He now realized that she was keeping the package with her and that she would be spending a few days with her lawyer, Marshall Fixx. That narrowed his chances of getting the information back. Trying to break into the attorney's house was a risk Griffin wasn't willing to take. Especially if he planned on continuing to use the services of the two undesirables he had in his employ.

Griffin was appalled when he learned that all the static he'd heard on the tape prior to Miss Wilson coming home was the sound of the house being ransacked. He told those idiots to look for the package. He'd said to make sure they left everything like they'd found it. Instead, these crack heads go in and trash the place. The fools should have known that to make it look like a burglary, you had to take something. Junkies! He knew he was taking a risk when he hired them. Maybe they'd left the door open and someone else had trashed it. Carelessness was carelessness. They would be penalized for their lack of diligence. If the police started snooping around and discovered the bug, there could be problems. How stupid could they be? He'd deal with them later too.

His main concern was still Audrey Wilson and what he needed to do to stop her from doing any more nosing around. Her strongest ally was her lawyer. Perhaps he could set up a meeting with the attorney and plant some seeds of doubt that would cause a rift between them.

Griffin smiled at the thought of turning the man against her. When he was finished with her she would not only be facing jail time but she wouldn't be able to pay someone to be a client of her firm. She'd be completely ruined.

32

Audrey woke to the sound of a telephone ringing. Her eyes cracked opened—sleepy slits and then wide as she looked around at the unfamiliar surroundings. Now she remembered. She was in Marshall's guesthouse. Her place had been ransacked.

The phone stopped ringing and Audrey looked at the clock. Six fifteen. No wonder she felt like shit. The phone started ringing again. She answered it.

"You up yet?" Marsh sounded entirely too bubbly for her. She started to hang up the phone, but *she* was a guest in *his* home. Be nice.

"Good morning, Marsh." The words were scratchy and thick with morning cobwebs.

"I hope you slept well. I made breakfast." Perhaps it was a caffeine high. Listening to his chipper greetings put her in the mind of those old fashioned percolators. "You could either join me over here or I could bring it there." Mr. Perky bubbled.

"I'm not exactly fit for company. I..."

"That settles it then. I'll be there in ten minutes." The phone went dead.

"Great." She mumbled, hanging up the phone. He was cute, but before seven a.m. nothing looked better to Audrey than her pillow. She scowled at the fluffy rectangle, envious that it could remain on the big soft bed as long as it liked.

On legs wobbly with sleepiness, she stumbled to the bathroom. The woman staring back at her from the full-length mirror was a scary sight to see. Her hair was all over her head and there were bags beneath her red eyes. She'd slept in her bra and panties. Creases from the sheets left her tummy looking gushy. Her legs, once slender and a bit shapelier, had grown slightly puffy from the weight she'd gained while sitting at home before business picked up. They reminded her of two overcooked fish sticks. It was like she'd gone to bed one night, carefree and light of spirit and form when a thief had come (sent by her ex-husband, no doubt) and taken her slender, curvaceous legs leaving her with slightly chunky logs. Renita told her she was trippin'. Maybe she was.

She was brushing her teeth when the ancient buzzer rang throughout the small cottage. Feeling no need to rush, she finished washing then rummaged through her bag for her cotton pajamas and pulled them on before padding on the cool wood floor to the door.

Marsh stood in the doorway, showered, shaved, and dressed in black slacks and a tan polo shirt that accentuated his buff chest and the ripples of his stomach. The shirt was unbuttoned at the neck, displaying a spray of curly, salt and pepper chest hair.

"You going to let me in or what?"

Audrey stepped aside so he could enter. When he brushed by her, squiggley bolts of heat shot between them. Audrey held her breath as he passed by.

The aroma of cooked bacon and biscuits tailed him into the room. Her eyes followed his hard, muscular back, his butt, and his thighs as he moved to put the tray on the table. He busied himself laying out the meal. Audrey watched him in silence. The urge to run her hands over his cute butt nearly overwhelmed her. He went about his tasks as if she weren't there. When he was through he turned to her.

"Want some?"

Do I? She thought, imagining running her hands over his smooth brownness. It wasn't her stomach growling for food, but the wild cat between her legs longing to lick his sweet, chocolate colored skin and feel him moving inside her.

"Huh?" She scolded herself for lapsing into the naughty daydream. She quickly replaced the clothes she had stripped away from him with her eyes; her face was hot with lust.

"Do you want some breakfast?" Blinding bright sunlight streamed through the windows. No match for the dazzling smile Marsh cast in her direction. He held out his hand. Audrey glided to him on the thin, lithe thighs of more than a decade ago. Pulling her to him, he twirled her around like a ballerina before brushing her lips with his own. Her head swam from the dance, from his presence, from wanting him.

"Are you hungry yet?" He nibbled her ear, nuzzled into her neck, and spun her around and back to him. His lips moved onto hers, a soft kiss. Audrey was ready to give in to him completely. She leaned forward, anticipating more. But instead, he walked her to the table and held out a chair. Deflated, she sat in the chair and watched him scooped bacon and eggs, potatoes, and fruit onto plates for each of them. He sat opposite her and grabbed a biscuit so tender it fell apart before it reached his plate. Marsh bowed his head in silence for a moment before attacking his plate voraciously. Audrey watched him for a moment before speaking.

"What was all that about?"

"I always bless the food when I cook so nobody will die after eating my cooking."

"Very funny. That's not what I'm talking about and you know it."

"What was what about?"

"That kiss." She said, annoyed.

"Oh." He worked a mouthful of food before continuing. "I've found that the best way to deal with a tense situation is to confront it. If I hadn't kissed you, I wouldn't be able to concentrate on anything today. I feel pretty good now." He bit into his biscuit.

"That's about as selfish a move as I've ever experienced." His touch left her tingling. Her body throbbed for more attention. When it was obvious that none was forthcoming, she became angry. "I'll have you know I won't be toyed with." She pushed her lips down into a frown.

"Shut up and eat before I really give you something to cry about."

"Oh, so you gon' have me cryin'?"

"Hell, you 'bout ready to cry now." He kept eating like he hadn't just rocked her world. "Look at you." He smiled and shook his head. "Eat up. We got work to do."

Audrey bent her head over her plate, moving the food around with the fork. She didn't know whether she was more irritated or titillated. She didn't appreciate him taking such liberties with her and would make it a point to have a serious conversation with him about his behavior...as soon as the hotness that coursed through her subsided.

33

"What do you mean you didn't trash her place? I heard her conversation with the police. The house was turned upside down." Griffin leaned closer to the two men; his eyes darted from one to the other.

"Well, we didn't do it." The young men shifted in their seats. Seven a.m. was too early for most folks to be visiting on a Friday morning, but the duo's addiction woke them early every day. They hadn't expected to be grilled like this by Griffin. They just wanted to get their money and step.

"Yu-yu-you told us to make sh sure to place everything back where we found it." Ronnie Steele, the loquacious one, stuttered. The impediment surfaced only when his Jones came down on him. The other man cowered behind him, bug-eyed and sweaty, shaking his head in agreement.

"When we left that house, it looked the same way it did when we came in. Suh, suh, somebody else broke into that place and wrecked it." He swallowed. Sweat beads rolled from his hairline to the end of his pockmarked face. "C-c-can we get our money now?"

"I'll give you your money." Griffin spat contemptuously. I can't believe it's come to this, he thought, as he peeled off a few bills and gave them to the one who did all the talking. The other one looked at the money hard enough to make the eagle fly.

"Just remember our agreement. Not one word about this or the two of you will be back in prison so quick you won't know what hit you."

The two men drove off in a battered Nova, no doubt to the nearest crack house. Griffin continued looking out of the window as if he half expected them to come back. He let the mixture of apprehension and disdain wash through him until he felt sure that they were gone. This should be the end of his relationship with them. He had dealt with their type before and doubted they would try to extort him. They didn't have the confidence. With the fifty he'd given them, there was always the chance that the junkies would ingest a fatal quantity of their favorite narcotic and he'd be rid of them for good.

Griffin was pleased with the way his plan to implicate Audrey Wilson was unfolding. Rob Hollingsworth didn't believe a word she said and rumor had it that her client list was dwindling to nothing. Outside assistance was falling like manna from heaven. The assistance of J.C. Norton, for example, had been an unexpected bonus.

He was pleased with the way the evidence was mounting against her, but there was one last area of uncertainty in this for him. She still had the package and she still had the support of her lawyer.

Griffin would place a call to Marshall Fixx later that morning. He was sure that if he could drive a wedge between them, it would provide additional insurance that could help seal her fate.

34

Marsh frowned as he listened to the man on the other end of the phone. In his line of work it was common to receive calls from those on the periphery of the case, so he was not surprised when Theo Griffin called him. He wanted to set up a meeting but Marsh resisted. He claimed he had information that would help prove Audrey's innocence.

"I'm just as anxious to put this behind us as you are, Mr. Fixx. This whole scandal has been a black eye on our city government. The murder is still being investigated. If we could at least get some closure on the embezzlement that occurred it would put us in a better light."

Marsh didn't trust Griffin in the least. The man was as oily as an auto mechanic's rag. Marsh didn't want to get none on him.

"Mr. Griffin, I've read your statement to the police regarding this matter. I'm well aware of your position and how you feel about Miss Wilson."

"I'm afraid you've got me all wrong. I admire Miss Wilson quite a bit and I'd like to see all of these issues resolved as expeditiously as possible."

Marsh let the statement hang where Griffin left it. Instincts told him Griffin was up to something.

"I was able to access an audio tape which might help your client. I have to turn it over to the police but I thought you might be interested in getting a copy of this information as well."

Marsh knew he was dealing with a snake but he had nothing to lose by getting the information. It was up to him to determine its value. He agreed to the meeting.

"I must tell you up front that I cannot divulge the origin of the tape, so please don't ask. I can assure you, it is authentic."

"How about we meet in your office in thirty minutes?" Marsh said before hanging up the phone.

* * *

Theolonius Griffin worked hard not to let his pleasure show on his face. He examined the troubled brow of Marshall Fixx, listening to the tape. Had he been honest about the tape's content over the phone, Fixx may not have agreed to meet with him, but no lawyer could resist getting a leg up on his opponent. Competitiveness and greed was the driving force with many lawyers. Marshall Fixx was at his door twenty-five minutes after the call to him ended. Griffin offered him a seat.

"I don't have a lot of time, Griffin. Let me see what you have."

Griffin shrugged and pushed the play button on the small recorder on his desk. Judging by the range of emotions that washed over Fixx's face within the first few minutes that he listened to the tape, he knew that he had him.

What he wouldn't give to have a picture of that look. Now he'd think that everything his client had told him about her work with the Township was a lie. The look on his face as he listened to Norma Jean Strange and Audrey Wilson go into detail about how they could steal the Township's money and not be discovered was priceless.

"Do you mind if I take this with me?" Marshall Fixx asked after a long reflective silence.

"Go right ahead, it's a copy."

* * *

Marshall Fixx felt as though he had taken a hard kick to the stomach. Considering how his feelings for Audrey were developing, the kick would have been more strategically placed just above his gut, or maybe directly below it.

He'd listened to the tape more than a dozen times after leaving Griffin's office. There was the unfamiliar voice that Griffin identified as Norma Jean Strange, and the other that he knew all too well, Audrey Wilson Kimborough.

They had made plans when he dropped her at her office door this morning. She had kissed him lightly as they said goodbye and his heart felt like it would burst clear through his chest. The tingling had passed from his lips and throughout his body, energizing him in his work. The call from Theo Griffin was like being doused with a bucket of ice water.

That Griffin was bad news. Marsh wouldn't put it past him to have fabricated the tape. But he still had to talk to Audrey and it wasn't something that he looked forward to doing.

35

Although the Spice Rack had a light crowd that evening, it was a lively group nonetheless. The piped in jazz could barely be heard over the din. Audrey saw Renita's hand waving when she and Marsh entered the club. Bobby stood when they approached the table.

Their friends Syd Lawson and Carmen Bausa were there in matching shiny red halter-tops and jeans. Both slim and shapely, they could have passed for middle-aged cover girls.

"Hey big sister." Bobby bent his six foot eight inch frame to give Audrey a kiss and hug that she accepted before turning to Marsh. She pointed to everyone at the table, speaking their names in turn.

"Everybody, this is Marshall Fixx." Audrey opened her hand in Marsh's direction.

"Call me Marsh." He said. "How's everybody doing?"

He shook Bobby's hand and waved to everyone else. They each acknowledged Marsh and made room around the table for the newcomers.

Marsh was preoccupied. During the ride over he was so quiet and as Audrey watched him making small talk with everyone, it was as though some alien presence had taken over his body. He definitely was not himself.

A waitress approached the table. Bobby ordered seconds for he and Renita. Syd and Carmen sipped from brown bottles of DOS XX. Marsh ordered a SKYY martini, and Audrey requested her favorite brand of gin and tonic.

"Man, I thought you looked familiar." Marsh was talking to Bobby now. It was like the women were no longer there as the men began a lively discussion on basketball.

Audrey waited to see if Marsh would hide his feelings about Bobby's abilities as player and his negative affect on the Cleveland Cavaliers.

"Man I remember back in '84, when you were drafted from OSU. You were something special to watch. Then I saw you and the Cavs a couple of years ago in Atlanta. I think that was one of the few games Atlanta won that year. What happened to you man?" Audrey admired Marsh's honesty and it was obvious from Bobby's response that he was finally more comfortable with his life after the game.

"The same thing that happens to everybody, man. Time and injuries, injuries and time. It's hard to realize that you can't do the things you used to take for granted." Bobby lifted his beer from the table and took a deep swallow.

Marsh nodded sympathetically, thinking about how his son teases him when he misses a shot that he just knew was going in. It's rough when your ten year old thinks you're a washed up senior citizen.

"I can't complain though," Bobby continued. "I had a lotta good years doing something that I love. Not everybody can say that."

"What are you doing now?" Marsh asked.

"After years preaching to me and much head butting, Audrey talked me into counseling young pro athletes. I started doing that recently and it machinated into many different things because we began to see that these young people had so many needs. A lot of these kids have nothing but dreams and raw talent. It's scary as hell when one day you're lucky if you can borrow some money to take your girl to a dollar movie and the next people are throwing more money at you than you can count. Girls who never would have given you the time of day are suddenly all over you, stripping butt naked, barking like a dog and doing anything else to get your attention." Bobby shook his head, his mind running through all the women who'd made themselves human sacrifices for him.

"Our goal is to develop life enhancing skills in our clients and keep them grounded so they will have something to show for their short lived fame and glory."

Bobby gestured with his big hands as he spoke. Audrey was proud that he had taken so well to this new part of his professional life.

"I hooked up with a couple of other ex-players and we're expanding the program to include money management, substance abuse, and family services." Bobby concluded.

"Man, that's really impressive. Are you looking for volunteers?"

"Always. No matter what your field or level of expertise, we would be happy to have anything that you could contribute. What field are you in if you don't mind my asking?"

"I'm an attorney." He nodded in Audrey's direction. "That's how we met. I worked for over a dozen years as a criminal lawyer before getting involved with corporations, working specifically in the area of employer-employee rights, international law and every area of litigation. But as the world's landscape has changed, so has the scope of my corporation."

"What do you mean?" Bobby was so engrossed in Marsh's conversation he'd stop sipping his beer.

"Technology, man. As the world becomes more technologically savvy, companies have to make sure that they are not setting themselves up for lawsuits by infringing on employees rights and vice versa. There is this gray area that exists. How does one divvy up the proceeds when technology is created using ideas from a company's talent but the idea could never have been developed without using materials and time that the company has provided?"

Bobby shook his head, his full attention focused on Marsh.

"Sounds complicated."

"It can be. I love it though." Marsh accepted the drinks they'd ordered from the waitress, throwing a few of bills on her tray and waving away her query to return his change. "I employ a staff of a dozen or so in my East Coast office. I'm in the process of growing that area of my business and expanding on a national, then global, scale."

Bobby looked across the table at Audrey. She, Syd, Carmen and Renita had their heads together, laughing and whispering in private conversation.

"Audrey, you need to marry this guy." Her brother said.

Marsh's expression darkened. It was as though Bobby had leveled a personal assault. Marshall's eyes bore into Audrey like he was trying to look inside her, read her mind. She felt a coldness from him that was unnerving.

"Why don't you get us something to eat?" Audrey said to Bobby. Marsh was really starting to get on her nerves. What was up with him? He seemed okay as long as he talked to anyone but her. She wished she had not agreed to stay at his place. There would be no getting around it; they would have to talk tonight. But the upside was she had already made arrangements with Renita. Audrey would move to her spare room on Monday. When this theft thing was proven to be a set-up, she would go on with her life and forget about Marshall Fixx.

36

Bobby had gone to the bar to put in their food orders. From out of nowhere it seemed, a woman approached the table and shoved the chair Bobby had vacated so hard it almost hit the floor. Everyone at the table looked at the stranger, wondering what was going on.

"So this is where you like to bring your whore." Chloe's eyes pierced Marshall's. She pushed her way over to where he was seated. She wore a revealing dress with obviously nothing underneath it but a heavy rose perfume that clung to her slight frame with the sheer fabric. She stood in front of Marshall; her get-up and wide-legged pose leaving little to the imagination. They all looked at the newcomer like she was a homeless person who just crashed their exclusive soiree.

"Chloe, what the hell are you doing here?"

"Remember this dress? I got it fixed." She moved her hand suggestively over the front of her body. "No one can tell where you ripped it off me."

"You don't belong here Chloe. It's a private party and you're not on the list." Audrey had never seen Marsh angry before.

"That's cute." Chloe snarled at him.

"Why do you do this to yourself? I told you, I don't want to have anything else to do with you. You need to leave before this gets ugly."

"Ugly? You ain't seen ugly, pal." She was getting louder. A lively piano riff from the DJ's booth punctuated her ranting comically. The DJ and the Rack's patrons had stopped to see what the commotion was about. People at nearby tables focused on them, waiting to see just how "ugly" the scene that seemed destined to erupt would be.

"Let's not do this." Marsh begged her. He was standing in front of her now. Trying to get her to calm down.

She pressed up against him, looking over her shoulder at Audrey. "She can't give you what I can. I've seen where she lives; she's got nothing. I know she can't make you feel like I can." Chloe moved her hands over his ass.

"Come on home. I miss that big black cock and the way you used to...AHHH! You black son of a bitch!"

Marsh had grabbed a pitcher of water from the table and threw it into Chloe's face. The party sat and stared while expletives streamed from Chloe to Marsh. She shrieked like a wild chicken as pieces of ice and droplets of water rolled from her golden head to her tiny expensive sandals on her feet.

A husky man with a bright yellow complexion whose job is was to throw out the bad was at their table in a flash. He had one massive hand around Chloe's arm, guiding her to the door. At the same moment, Bobby returned to the table followed by a waitress who carried a platter filled with the food they'd ordered.

He gave the diminutive woman being dragged away from their table an approving once over, casting her the smile that had given him entree to romp in countless secret gardens. He gave the big yellow brother a smile.

"I got this man." He handed the bouncer a rolled up bill and Big Man was gone.

"Hello, pretty lady. I'm Bobby Wilson. And you are?"

Chloe seemed to forget the reason she was there. She tried to rearrange her wet locks before throwing her hands up in exasperation and leaving the room.

Renita started laughing, more to break the thick silence that shrouded the once gay table than anything else.

"Shit Ren, how long has the Rack been doing the wet tee-shirt thing?" Bobby said, tossing down his drink. "She was fine as hell!"

The waitress sat the food on the table. Bobby paid her and headed in the direction of the wet interloper.

"I'll be right back." He said, making his way towards the exit.

"Marsh would you take me home please?" By now Audrey's blood was boiling. She had a history of becoming attracted to men with crazy-ass women in the closet. At that moment, she wanted to get as far away from him as possible. She wished that the repairs had been completed at her house. She needed desperately to go to her own place, away from Marsh and all of this confusion.

The partiers scattered like balls on a pool table after the first break. Audrey and Marsh walked to the car in silence, each seeming like they wanted to be any place but here, like this. The roomy car felt tight and smothering inside even though the couple maintained a distance wide enough to sandwich another person between them.

Audrey hated to be the one to bridge the gap that she felt was all his doing. He had been acting weird all evening and the appearance of his little friend did nothing to help matters.

"That was Chloe?" Audrey saw no reason to drag this thing out. He wasn't going to broach the subject and she'd be damned if she was going to pretend everything was okay. Regardless of the outcome of this discussion, she had made up her mind to get away from him. She would get her things together and move out as soon as they reached the house.

"That was Chloe." He shot the words at her like tiny pellets.

There he was again with that fucking attitude. I'm the one who should be pissed, Audrey thought. Obviously, he and that woman were still dealing on some level. Audrey felt like he was trying to play her for a fool.

"What did she mean by 'I've seen where she lives, she's got nothing'? How would she know anything about me unless you told her?"

"I don't know what that crazy muthafucka is talkin' about, Audrey. I told you the chick was loopy and I left the relationship when I left Boston. I don't give a damn if you believe me or not."

"What the hell is wrong with you? You've been acting weird since we left the Plum Building. I'm going through a lot right now and the last thing I need is you pulling me into some sophomoric games. You just take me to get my shit and we'll call it a fuckin' day."

"Not a problem!"

They rode the rest of what seemed like the longest ride since the start of modern times, in silence. When they reached the cottage, Audrey jumped out of the car before it was in park good, and stormed down the path to the guesthouse.

It seemed to her that he was taking his own sweet time to find his way to the door and let her in. He hesitated before unlocking the door. She brushed by him angrily, headed for the closet and started pulling out her things.

Audrey folded her belongings haphazardly and flung them into the large Louis Vuitton duffel. She felt him before she saw him. When he spun her around she tried to slap him as hard as she could but the touch of his hands holding her arms still at her sides and the warmth of his mouth on hers was like chloroform. She felt herself drifting and then being swept up by a feeling that could only be love.

He planted hot kisses on her mouth. Traveling downward, his lips burned tiny stars of desire everywhere they touched. Every part of her wanted him. She forgot about her anger, about his past, and about hers. The only thing that mattered was now.

He whispered her name and she felt red-hot lava erupting like a volcano of desire as she moaned his name in reply.

They pulled at everything between them until they lay on the large quilted bed wearing only the glistening passion their wanting had produced. Each one held, touched, and explored the other, drinking in each other's dark beauty.

Marsh pulled her arms over her head and nibbled at her breasts gently, then more hungrily as she called his name and begged him to stop the ache of her longing for him.

Her head told her to make him stop, but when she tried to verbalize the command the words got stuck in her throat. Her body couldn't tell the lie that her head felt it should have. His mouth moved over her, hot and determined. He traveled downward leaving the glistening, hard nipples pointing upward as if in prayer. The prayer was answered when he massaged them expertly with his large hands until she cried out.

He combed the bushy hair between her legs with his teeth; working his tongue in and around her juicy folds until she nearly fainted in anticipation of the greater pleasure that was to come.

It was like slipping in and out of a surreal, sexual coma. She suddenly felt his hands pull her legs apart and when he entered her she shuddered a half dozen times before she felt his quickening heartbeat and the throbbing that said he could hold back no longer. They joined hands in united climax.

"Do you still want to leave?" He asked huskily. Heavy-lidded eyes looked down on her, daring her to look away, daring her to refuse him anything he desired.

"Was that your way of getting me to stay?" She whispered.

"Did it work?" Marsh traced her lips with his finger, and then kissed her deeply.

"You don't see me going anywhere do you?"

37

Marsh looked down at Audrey and kissed her head lightly as she lay in the crook of his arm. He didn't know what had come over him. He had every intention of bringing her to the house to get her things and taking her to her sister's place. He wasn't ready for a relationship. Not ready for another situation where that person is your first and last thought of the day. Especially if that person could be taken away. What if she was guilty?

He felt he should know from past experience not to let his good judgment be clouded by matters of the heart. But as he'd watched her practically run from the car, he knew that it was too late. He was already in love with her. He didn't want her to leave. Doing a quick evaluation of the day's events, he had concluded that he was not being fair to her. Why had he been so quick to take Griffin's side based on the evidence he had revealed?

He had never given her a chance to review the information. That just wasn't right. Griffin obviously was no fan of hers. Marsh was taking what Griffin had given him at face value and treated Audrey as though she were guilty.

As far as Chloe was concerned, he was used to her crazy stunts, but to someone who was exposed to her for the first time, it might seem like they were still involved. Who knew what that crack meant about her seeing where Audrey lived? She had stalked Marsh in the past; perhaps she was reverting to her old forms of recreation.

When Marsh reached the door to the guesthouse and saw Audrey standing there so determined and so angry, yet confused, he knew he couldn't let her leave. He'd gone over to the bed where she was packing to talk to her, but God she smelled so good! He could feel the heat of anger radiating from her. There's such a thin line between the passion of anger and the passion of love. His instincts pushed his lips upon hers. He fully expected her to slap his face but she responded to his kiss. Marsh thought his heart would leap through his chest.

He wished that they could remain holed up this way for eternity. His feelings for her were so strong that it pained him to switch gears now. But there was no more putting it off. The time had come for them to deal with the tape.

Griffin had most likely already forwarded a copy to the police. It was just a matter of time before they would be bringing her in for questioning. They had to be ready.

He shook her out of the place of peace where she had drifted. They took turns showering and taking peeks at each other while they dressed. They walked arm in arm to the main house where Marsh put on a kettle for tea.

"Audrey. I met with Theolonius Griffin this morning. He gave me a tape and I need you to listen to it."

Marsh went out to the car and came back with a small cassette player. He put it on the coffee table. He inserted an audiotape and the two of them listened to a few seconds of static before the conversation began.

"Audrey, I'm afraid I can't do this anymore. You said two months and it's going on a year. I'm getting out!"

"Look you idiot, we got a good thing going on here. Nobody is going to find out anything as long as we play it cool. These people don't know jack about accounting and don't want to know. I'm making sure that everything is in order for the auditors so why are you trippin?"

"But what if we get caught? We could go to jail! I never should have let you talk me into this"

There was suddenly a loud clapping noise followed by the sound of crying.

"You'll do as I say, do you hear me? Miss one payment and you're dead. Is that clear?"

Audrey recognized Norma Jean's voice. The voice was true, but not the characterization. It was a lousy acting job. Anyone who knew Norma Jean Strange would never mistake her for a victim.

Audrey couldn't determine who was playing the part of "Audrey". She replayed the tape several times. The voice was vaguely familiar. Who could it be?

"You know, the more I listen to that thing, it almost sounds like a man trying to sound like a woman."

"You don't think Griffin staged the whole thing with Norma Jean do you?" Marsh looked at her lovely face clouded with concern.

"I don't know who it could be. I just know who it's not—*me*." Audrey started pacing from one end of the room to the other. "There should be a way that a voice analysis can be done to prove this is not me on this tape."

"I've got a friend back East." Marsh said. "He owes me a couple of major favors. I'll call him and see if he can get right on it."

Suddenly there was a knock on the door. They searched each other's face questioningly before Marsh went to open it. There stood two uniformed officers and a plain-clothes detective.

"Audrey Kimborough?" How on earth did they know she was here?

"I'm divorced. It's Audrey Wilson." She felt dumb. They were obviously there to arrest her, and the only thing she could say was, 'Get my name right.'

"We'll need you to come down to the Rosemont Division and answer a few questions in the murder investigation of Norma Jean Strange."

"I'm Miss Wilson's attorney, Marshall Fixx. I'll come with you."

"Suit yourself." The officer said.

Audrey couldn't remember any time in her life that she felt this afraid. Someone was trying to set her up for murder. And so far, they were doing a damned good job.

38

Hyram Phillips was imposing in stature as well as demeanor. The entire room seemed to darken when he entered it. He said nothing as he sat during Audrey's interrogation, the sleeves of his rumpled blue shirt were rolled up showing thick hairy arms folded over his massive chest. He evaluated Audrey with a killer stare from his seat near the door.

Apparently, Rob Hollingsworth and the man who'd entered the room with him had been assigned to do the dirty work. Rob seemed to take great relish in his assignment. Audrey's calm and collected exterior was a flimsy binding for the bundle of nerves that rattled within her.

The questioning was intense. Marsh made most of the responses. At one point during the grueling process, Audrey jumped when she heard the creak screech as Phillips rose from his chair and left the room. She didn't know how to analyze his departure. Did it mean he'd heard enough and was going back to his office to start making her noose?

The tiny bit of stale air that was in the room left with him. Audrey had difficulty breathing. If she'd thought things were tense with Phillips in the room, she was not prepared for the intensity that came with his departure. Perhaps his leaving was some sort of police code, an indication to those in his command that the pace needed to quicken.

For what seemed like the millionth time, she watched Rob push the button on the recorder. The whispered voices of two conspirators, one of which was supposed to be her, filled the room.

That dirty bastard Griffin had given the police a different tape than he had given them. There was an entire series of tapes. If one believed what one heard on the tapes, it looked like the only reason she had come to work for Rosemont City Government was to steal. She and Marsh were completely unprepared for what they heard today. The recording had been created using portions of actual conversations between Audrey and Norma Jean.

Norma Jean had gone to great lengths to ask her specific questions. She had been taping all interactions with Audrey since the beginning of their business dealings.

"How could Jean stab me in the back this way?" She thought. A painful lump moved into her chest as she waited for the static to stop, to listen again to the sounds of deceit.

Norma Jean: *What if we get caught Audrey? You may not care since you're just a contractor. But if I get caught, they'll seal my coffin with this thing. I'll never work again.*

Audrey: *There are so many ways to hide something like this. I'll only give the auditors what they ask for, nothing more.*

Norma Jean: *I don't know Audrey; maybe you should do this without me. What if they find out?*

Audrey: *There's no way they'll think to even check, not unless you give them a reason to. I'm not going to let that happen. They trust and respect you. They'll never suspect a thing. Stop worrying.*

Norma Jean: *I can't help but worry. What we're doing is illegal.*

Audrey: *You need to relax. They'll never find out unless you tell them.*

Norma Jean: *I just might do that. I'm tired of all the lying...*

Audrey: *What are you, crazy? That's stupid. If you tell I'll kill you.*

"But we were talking about something totally different. Norma Jean had confided in me that..." Marsh put his hand on her wrist, silencing her.

"This is the first time we've heard this information. I need a minute with my client before we say anything further."

"Ten minutes" Rob said.

The room cleared. Marsh looked at her like he wanted to scream.

"What the hell was all that?"

"More of the same Marsh. These are all conversations taken out of context. The subjects varied." She could tell by the puzzled look on his face that he wasn't following her. "For example, Norma Jean told me that she had lied about her graduate degree. She'd never completed her studies but lied about it during her interview. Apparently, they never checked. She got the job and was a nervous wreck that she would be found out.

"I told her that even if they found out, they probably wouldn't care. If it was that important to her, she should take classes until she got her master's degree. I thought it was stupid of her to alert them to this without giving herself a chance to complete her education." Her eyes searched his for understanding.

"Since she already had the job, it made no sense for her to broadcast her shortcomings. She kept going on and on about that. I was sick of talking about it. I told her that if she went to them, I'd kill her."

They looked at the cassette player like it was a viper about to strike.

"I was only kidding."

"Her educational background should be easy enough to verify."

"She may have been lying, Marsh, just using this to get me to say the right thing."

"What do you mean?"

"I think Norma Jean really did have her Masters Degree. She only said that she didn't to get me to say the things that she needed to use later."

Marsh shook his head knowingly.

"What about the other stuff? She mentioned an audit..."

"Norma Jean had told me she didn't have time to go back and review everything for the years that were to be audited. I told her to get a sampling from them of what they needed and I'd only give them what they asked for." Audrey pointed an angry finger like Norma Jean was there to see it. "In the tapes she makes it sound like I was trying to cover up something."

"I'll request copies of the tapes and send them to my source on the coast. He should be able to detect which of the tapes are fabrications. We can explain the ones that aren't." Marsh looked into her eyes.

"Are you okay?" He asked.

"I'm okay. I'll be even better when we get out of here."

Rob Hollingsworth and another detective returned to the room. Marsh asked if they had checked the authenticity of the recordings. Rob told him they were waiting on verification from their lab in Virginia.

"Well, if it's all the same to you, my client should be released until you confirm the validity of the tapes. In the meantime, I'd like copies of these recordings as well." He looked from one to the other. "If there's nothing else, I'll take Miss Wilson home now."

"Not so fast. Miss Wilson's alibi for that Friday evening doesn't check out." Rob said with a smirk when he saw the surprised look on their faces.

"We talked to Dennis Franklin, the man you claimed to have had dinner with that night. He said that you left the restaurant at eight." He pointed an accusatory finger in her direction. "That leaves several hours where you could have gone to the Administration Building and murdered Ms. Strange."

"I told you I was working at my office." Audrey shuddered. She'd never seen Rob so ruthless.

"Yeah, well you don't have any witnesses to that, do you?" He waited for an answer that didn't come. "Your call to your sister was after the murder had been committed. You had plenty of time to come back to your office and make that call. Between the tapes and the reports, we feel we have enough evidence to hold Ms. Wilson. We'll see that you get copies of the tapes." Rob said to Marsh.

The other cop, who had been silent until now, read Audrey her rights. She looked at Marsh in disbelief. She could contain herself no longer and collapsed into tears. The other detective read rights that ricocheted in her head like a surreal '60's TV show. Rob Hollingsworth led her from the room followed by the other detective, without saying another word.

They turned her over to two uniformed officers who led her down a long hall and a flight of narrow stairs. The roar of conversation, ringing telephones, and sounds she could not identify, echoed off the yellow cinder block walls in the brightly lit room that she entered. They stopped in front of a Plexiglas enclosed desk. A gray-haired man of average height and build, gazed in her direction. He opened a square chute, almost hitting her in the process.

"Deposit all personal items." He said.

Audrey pushed her purse, watch, and ring into the opening. The clerk grabbed a huge yellow envelope with a square bottom. He opened her purse, reading the contents as he wrote a description of everything he extracted on the outside of the envelope with a black marker. Once he'd finished, he looked over his shoulder and hollered to someone in the back of the room.

"Max, here's another one for you."

An attractive woman with light brown, pockmarked skin and flaming red hair surfaced. A white shirt pulled tightly over her sparse breasts. Her narrow hips were encased in black skin-tight trousers. A salacious eye roamed Audrey's face before she opened the door to let her enter the enclosed space. She was led to a doorless room the size of a small closet.

"She's a looker all right, Joe. That's for sure." She hollered to her partner at the desk while patting Audrey down. Humiliation heated her face. The woman cracked on a wad of gum as she checked every fold, fullness and crease of Audrey's body. Fear sealed her lips. An angry tear rolled down her face as the woman finished her job and lead Audrey to a four-foot high shelf where she was fingerprinted, then photographed. She was allowed to wash her hands before being led to a large holding cell. Some of the inhabitants were asleep. The few who were awake looked at her with varying degrees of interest. Sliding gates were opened for her entry, and then shut behind her. She was one of them now.

Too afraid to speak, too angry to cry, Audrey moved to a corner of the room and let the hurt and confusion wash over her until her senses shut down. A protective wall erected itself around her. For now, that would be her only friend. That and God.

39

Griffin hung up the telephone and rubbed his hands together with glee. Audrey Wilson was arrested the previous night for grand theft, deception, and murder. With the evidence that he had supplied the police, she would no doubt be convicted. Soon he'd be free to begin his new life—a life that did not include his current wife, Juanda.

After so many years of his dodging her, Sarah would no longer be denied. Lord knows she had put up with enough of his shit to have left long ago. But she hadn't. When she told him she'd booked a trip to Hawaii, how could he tell her no? She'd always wanted to go there and he had always put her off. There was finality in her demand this time.

How could he explain a trip like that to Juanda? They had spent their honeymoon there and she'd always wanted to return. He couldn't think of a reason to be away from home for an extended period of time. She knew all of the Township's business, so he couldn't use work as an excuse. He figured he would just say he needed some time alone and wouldn't tell her where he was going. He was a dog but not a damned dog.

But it didn't matter anyway. He had finally made a commitment to Sarah. He loved her and was too old to keep fooling around. If he didn't grab her soon she would surely come to her senses and leave him and that, he couldn't bear.

Through his marriage to Juanda, countless affairs, and just being an admitted son of a gun, she had stood by him. Juanda tried to be there for him, but she was so self-absorbed she only remained in the marriage because of the shame a divorce would cause.

He should have left her long ago, but he had grown accustomed to the wealth she had provided from her family's businesses. Having drained that well, Griffin had to find a method of keeping his lifestyle at a level he'd grown accustomed to. He had showered his mistress with luxuries throughout the course of their relationship. She would settle for nothing less. This had been the impetus for his and Sarah's descent into a life of crime.

They had siphoned a few thousand here and there, nothing of any significance. It wasn't until their partnership with Norma Jean Strange that they realized they were swiping penny candy. Norma Jean was out for the entire store.

The woman was a bitch on wheels, but she had a brilliant mind. She had immediately detected what he and Sarah were doing. She approached them about a partnership.

Griffin had never met anyone who was able to completely get inside of a person's mind the way that Norma Jean Strange could. She knew how to get the maximum benefit from every person that she met. She was the least sentimental person he'd ever known. Griffin had not been surprised when she ended up dead. That's the only way someone like Norma Jean could end up.

Pity. She was young, very beautiful, and sharp as a whip. She could be a real pill, but Griffin had gotten used to her ways. He had even forgiven her for practically biting his lower lip in half when he tried to kiss her once. That had served him right. She was a lot of things, but she wasn't a tramp. Griffin had just laughed as he dabbed at the blood that spurted from the wound. He took no umbrage with her. As his father once told him, everybody's not going to be a fan.

He was pouring himself a scotch when Juanda entered the room.

"Have you heard the latest, dear?"

"What's up?" Juanda, for the first time in quite a long while, was stone cold sober. Theo took this as a good sign. Maybe she'd get herself together and move on with her life after he left her. Perhaps this wouldn't be as bad as he'd thought. He'd just have to find the right time. He looked at his wife's bright clear eyes and smiled. Her face showed a sense of peace and confidence that Theo hadn't seen in years.

"Audrey Wilson has been arrested for embezzlement and murder."

"What?" Juanda blinked curiously. "I can understand the link to the theft, but murder? That's quite a leap. She couldn't have been involved. They really think she killed Norma Jean?"

"Apparently they've got enough evidence to put her away forever." He reported gleefully. "She's going to get exactly what she deserves."

Juanda glared at her husband with a raised eyebrow. She suddenly rose from the sofa and headed for the door. "I need to go and pick up a few things. I'll be back a little later."

Griffin watched curiously as she stepped to the car with the determined march of a just-released prisoner of war. There was something different in her. He could sense a change and for some reason, he found her demeanor disturbing. He tried to ignore the tickle of the warning hairs that rose on the back of his neck.

40

It was the beginning of the third day. Every minute pulled at Audrey, taunting her as she sat in the large holding cell. She never dreamed when they brought her there days before that she would still be here.

The dingy space was crowded with women being held for all sorts of offenses. She tried not to be judgmental, but when she looked at them, she found it difficult not to size them up and look down her nose at them. She had never been in a situation like this before. All of the stereotypes flooded her mind. There were several prostitutes, a few junkies, petty thieves, and women being held for assault. How on earth did I end up here, she thought, and where the hell was Marsh? She was angry and frightened.

Though she'd screwed herself out of telephone privileges by getting their answering machines, Audrey was sure Bobby and Renita must know where she was by now. Why hadn't they come to see her? She hadn't heard from Carrey either. Her assistant was usually the one constant in a sometimes-crazy world. Maybe things were becoming too crazy for even him.

A scary thought suddenly covered her rational mind like a cellophane bag, cutting off her air. What if no one came? What if she just stayed there until she was tried and convicted? Audrey realized that she had to start putting together a defense. She had to fight, do everything that she could to free herself.

She was certain that the answer to this whole thing was somewhere in the documentation she had received anonymously. The person who sent it was, no doubt, the weak link in the organized theft ring. Perhaps it was even the murderer tempting fate. Whoever it was, Audrey was more determined than ever to get to the bottom of this thing.

She summoned the surly woman who guarded the pit she had been thrown into, and requested a pen and paper. The woman gave a look like "Sure, I'll run right out and get it," and then kept right on reading her paper.

Audrey wasn't going to sit around waiting for the screw to decide whether she wanted to assist. She began to plot in her head specific areas to review with Marsh whenever he decided to bring his ass down there. She also had very specific questions that needed to be asked of all parties involved. Perhaps it was just as well that she was not able to approach them again. She knew they were as tired of looking at her as she was them. She'd been as thorough in her questioning of Juanda Griffin and Sylvester Alstead as she could. She could forget about getting any additional information from them now. Sarah Collins wouldn't speak to her at all and Leighton Glen had never returned her calls. She should have gone to Rob in the beginning. Now everyone thought she was guilty and they seemed to have abandoned her.

Suddenly the outer door opened and an officer entered. He walked over and whispered something to the uniformed woman reading the paper. She released an irritated sigh, put down her paper and sauntered over to the cell, looking Audrey in the eye.

"You, Lillian Hellman. Get your stuff, let's go."

41

Earlier that morning Marsh had sat in the tiny room waiting for Audrey. He paced from one end to the other; excitement at seeing her wouldn't let him sit. He had missed her fiercely and was happy that he had exciting news to share with her.

He had to catch himself to keep the gasp from escaping when he first saw her. He'd dealt with all kinds of people throughout his life. Some of the most docile types, the meek, when thrust into a life-threatening situation, would tap some hidden reserve, uncovering an inner strength that would help them through. On the other hand, there was the stalwart, the stoic. People who moved through life's situations like a rock, deflecting or seeming to not feel life's arrows when they penetrated their armor. When they found themselves in this situation, they would crumble. Unfortunately, Audrey Wilson fit into the later group.

She looked a mess. Her dark skin, which was always clear and smooth, appeared drawn and bore a sallow cast. Several eruptions of acne and alternate jaundiced blotches checkered her face. Her usual sleek bob was matted with lint and debris. Her clothes were rumpled and stained. Marsh had left his poker face at home.

Audrey looked at him. Her eyebrows were drawn together in an angry frown.

"What did you think I'd look like after you left me in here to rot." He ignored her comment and her appearance.

"I've got some good news." He waited until she sat down before continuing. He took the seat on the other side of the table and fumbled with the locks on his briefcase.

"You'll never believe who came to see me." Her grabbed her hand and gave it a little squeeze.

"I give." Misery weighted her voice. "Who?"

"Juanda Griffin. She and I had a long talk. She presented me with some reports that I think you'll want to look at." He detected a distant light in her eyes and let out a relieved sigh that he was reaching her. It lightened his heart to see her coming out of her funk.

"She's got taped conversations of her husband, Norma Jean Strange and Sarah Collins discussing the embezzlement scheme. These tapes are so incriminating it's almost beyond belief. She's making a statement to the police right now, exonerating you of all charges."

Audrey became completely hysterical, releasing what felt like years of restrained emotion. Marsh handed her a handkerchief and held her until she was able to speak.

She cleared her throat before looking down at the papers in front of her, trying to focus. She began sifting through the pages as Marsh removed them from his briefcase.

"How did she come across this stuff? And why is she coming forward now?" Audrey gulped the air, replacing depression-sapped energy. "There is certainly no love lost between the two of us. She was totally uncooperative when I tried to talk to her." Audrey continued combing through the mound of paper.

"I don't think she's doing this to help you. She's trying to bring Griffin down. The problem is that in doing so she slits her own wrist."

"How so?" Audrey asked without looking up.

"While Juanda was looking for proof of Griffin's infidelity, she found out that he was stealing. She didn't disclose this to the police, so that makes her just as guilty as him. I don't doubt that her attorney is trying to swap a reduced sentence in exchange to her testimony."

Audrey shook her head in understanding.

"She must have felt that she was living with a stranger."

"I guess." Marsh replied. "Though it was common knowledge that Griffin was a philanderer, the straw that broke Juanda's back was his ongoing affair with his secretary and his continuos lying about it. She'd caught them together years ago. Griffin claimed it was a one-time thing that he'd ended. But then Sarah Collins got a job in City Government working for one of the other executives. Juanda accused him of helping her get the job but he denied it. Juanda suspected her husband was lying but she was so afraid he'd leave her that she tried to ignore the voice that told her he was betraying her. She stood by for years letting them make a fool of her until she got tired. She decided to prove once and for all that they were carrying on this affair right under her nose."

"I see." Audrey injected thoughtfully.

"With this evidence as a weapon in divorce proceedings, Juanda Griffin would be in a better bargaining position."

"Or she could black mail him into a pretty hefty share of all the money they had taken over the years." Audrey surmised.

"That's exactly why she's got to be careful what she says to the D.A. She began recording Griffin's activities a long time ago in search of fodder for a possible divorce. She was shocked when instead of getting evidence of his philandering on tape; she learned he had been stealing from the City of Rosemont for many years. Somehow he learned of her discovery and tried to cut her in. But Juanda knew how much they had taken and was insulted by his offer. But she played along with him, all the while documenting what she could to use against him later.

"Through a recording device she had planted at Ms. Collin's desk, Juanda learned of their plan to make you take the fall for their wrong-doing and that they planned to pin Norma Jean's murder on you. They would then leave town until the whole thing blew over. Griffin would ask Juanda for a divorce and marry his mistress. That's when Juanda knew she had to put a stop to them. She wasn't about to stand by and let them do that to her."

"Lucky for me." Audrey said, still looking at the papers.

"Lucky for you is right. Your friend really had you wrapped up and ready to float down the river."

"Whoa!" Audrey hit her forehead with the heel of her hand. "GAS—Griffin, Alstead, and Strange. I was too busy looking to see what was staring me right in the face. Stupid! The three of them created the phony construction company to move money into their own accounts."

"That's right. The secretary, who Juanda suspected of screwing her husband, made all of the bank transactions. They used the stolen funds to purchase hundreds of thousands in municipal bonds and several bank accounts have been discovered in the names of Griffin and Collins. The two of them were able to compile a nice little nest egg."

"What about Alstead?" Audrey still had nightmares about the ordeal in the park. She hoped her attacker had been picked up and locked safely away.

"Alstead hasn't been seen or heard from in over a week. He's wanted for questioning in the theft and murder, not to mention the warrant that you filed on him. They'll catch that bastard."

"Did he kill Norma Jean?"

"It hasn't been proven as far as I know. I also don't know if he was able to pilfer some of the embezzled funds. If he did, he was so slick with it that even the principals in the crime didn't know about it. They called themselves using him to help set up the operation. It remains to be seen if he played a more significant part in this or not. There is apparently some money that the Feds haven't been able to locate. Alstead may have outsmarted everyone."

"I never would have thought that meek little man could be such a monster." Audrey said pensively then asked, "How long had they been stealing?"

"Juanda didn't know that. She also wasn't sure who's idea it was to implicate you, but it's obvious that the sole purpose of hiring you was to have a scapegoat firmly in place should this thing start to fall apart."

Audrey's mood visibly saddened as her mind flooded with memories of growing up with Norma Jean. She was a constant companion on the playground, at their dinner table and as they matured, at blue-light dances where pubescent boys got too close. Audrey had been like a sister to the skinny girl who used their home as a safe haven from an abusive stepfather.

At what point had Norma Jean's love for Audrey and her family turned into something that would make betrayal so seamless? Audrey cast aside her pain, and thought of another old friend and the wedge this whole thing had driven between them.

"What about Rob Hollingsworth? Was she using him too?"

"Perhaps, though I'm not sure why. It never hurts a criminal to have a cop on their side." Marsh surmised. "Maybe they used Hollingsworth to keep the police at bay." He started returning the reports to the briefcase.

"Or maybe she really liked Rob." They looked at each other and shrugged.

"Maybe. I've already spoken to Chief Phillips. Mrs. Griffin was speaking with him when I was on my way in here. They should have the paperwork for your release completed soon."

He was happy to watch Audrey's face brighten. She smiled for the first time since he'd gotten there.

42

The doorbell rang twice before Griffin reached it. He greeted Detective Rob Hollingsworth with a smile and he waved him inside.

"Detective Hollingsworth, what can I do for you this lovely day?" They probably needed further testimony to nail the coffin of that Wilson bitch shut.

"Theolonius Griffin?"

It seemed the two uniformed officers appeared from nowhere. Griffin's mood grew dark as he looked from one member of the trio to the other.

"What's going on?" Griffin didn't like this at all. It was almost as though...

"Read him his rights." Rob Hollingsworth said. The uniformed officers wasted no time. One of the men turned Griffin around, quickly binding his wrists with nylon restraints. He cursed and scuffled with them as they practically dragged him to the waiting patrol car.

*   *   *

Fresh air and freedom, what a blessing, Audrey thought as she headed for Marsh's shiny black sedan. She didn't even care that she was a mess and Tonya Elling and her news crew were all over she and Marsh like a cheap suit. Marsh shielded her from the camera as best he could and pulled her in the direction of the car.

It had been nearly eight hours since he'd given her the news she'd be released. As she sat in the holding cell waiting for his return, she had prayed that nothing else would go wrong. When the woman who'd earlier refused to give her paper called her name, relief strengthened her weary legs, helping her make each step.

Marsh told her that her house cleaning had finally been completed. The only remnant of the break-in was the mess that had been made of the walls. The painters had just finished up that afternoon. Audrey would stay at Marsh's place that evening while the new paint dried.

The drive was like a blur. Audrey remembered none of it. Before she knew it, the car pulled in front of his large country styled home. Marsh pressed the remote that opened the garage before leaning over to kiss her.

"I missed you, old girl."

"I missed you, too." She felt a tingle spreading through her as he guided the car into the garage. She didn't even care that he called her old girl.

"You know the most shocking thing about this whole situation?" He held her at arms length.

"What's that?"

"I never thought a lady as fine as you could look and smell so bad. Get in there and get cleaned up."

"Go to hell, Marsh. It's your fault. You shouldn't have let me stay there that long." She pouted.

"My fault? I worked like a Mississippi slave to get you out of there. You owe me big time."

"And what do you require for your services, sir?"

"Oh I think you know. And if you don't..." He leaned down to kiss her but stopped and pinched his nose shut with his fingers before putting his lips to hers. She nudged him in his ribs.

"Oh it's like that, huh? You gon' be beggin' to smell my stankin' ass before this night is over." She stepped out of the car and closed the door.

"In your dreams." Marsh teased her as he turned off the engine. They laughed when Freedom hurriedly entered before the garage door closed. He circled his mistress's legs until she picked him up and gave him a hug.

"This is what you call unconditional love, Mr. Fixx. Freedom loves me bad breath and all."

"See how quickly he runs after you feed him."

"You know you wrong Marsh."

It felt so good to be free and even better to be here with Marsh.

43

When Audrey stepped out of the shower, she could hear music in the other room. India Aria's strong, soul funk spoke of her lover's brown skin. Audrey thought about Marsh's milk chocolate sweetness and closed her eyes and smiled. She smoothed lotion over her own moist skin as the record beat to its end. She wrapped a towel around her freshly shampooed hair and pulled on the thick blue robe that Marsh had laid out for her.

The record had changed. The mellow, sexy strains of Natalie Cole crooning *'Say You Love Me'* drew her to Marsh. He sat in the cozy living room before a roaring fire in the big stone fireplace. A bottle of wine was chilled in an ice-filled bucket, but everything else was warm.

When she looked into his handsome face, smiling at her, waiting for her, she let the robe drop to the floor and she came to him.

Their lovemaking was tender and sweet. Marsh lay behind her, his hard body spooned against hers, holding her safe and easy. She couldn't believe that they were here like this. That she was happy at last. Audrey turned discreetly so that he wouldn't see the tear that pooled and rolled down her face. But he moved her face towards his and dabbed the wetness away. He looked into her eyes and whispered, "I love you too."

*   *   *

"Marsh."

"Marsh, someone's at the door." Audrey shook him until he began to stir. She and Marsh had fallen asleep in front of the fire. He picked up his watch and blinked until his vision focused and the lighted dial became clear.

"Oh, shit! It's nine o'clock." He sprang from the floor, dumping her off the makeshift bed.

"Owww!" Audrey poked her lip out and rubbed her elbow.

"Sorry, babe. Get dressed! Hurry up."

"What's going on?" He ignored her questions, pushing her to the bedroom where she was surprised to find a variety of under and outerwear from her closet at home. She wondered when he had gone to her place to get her stuff. She was also curious about who'd be coming to his home this evening, their first night together since she'd been freed. She took her time showering, dressing and combing her hair. Audrey suddenly felt a nervous wave wash over her. If it was that crazy-ass Chloe, Audrey would leave this time for good. She just wasn't in the mood for any more drama.

An eerie silence met Audrey as she left the bedroom and headed down the long hall to the main room. She'd heard the doorbell, but hadn't heard voices. Had Marsh left with the visitor? Had something happened to him? In light of everything that had been happening, Audrey was a little leery of walking into the living room. The tall wooden doors were drawn shut. Sealed like a tomb. The room was still. Too quiet. They knew who the thieves were, but what about the killer?

"Marsh?" she called tentatively. She put her hand on the hard wood of the door and listened. Silence. If he were in there he would have answered her. Unless something had happened to him.

"Marsh, where are you?" her heart beat rapidly.

She went to the office where they had worked long into the night her first time visiting the house. Marsh was not there. She returned to the hallway and moved back toward the living room. She was about to slide open the floor to ceiling wooden doors that led into the expansive area when she heard something behind her. Audrey whirled around in the direction of the sound.

"SURPRISE!"

There stood Renita, Lloyd, Bobby, Syd and Carmen. They all smiled at her, extending their arms in a warm inviting hug. Audrey looked from one to the other with teary eyes.

"What is this?" She put her hand to her rapidly beating heart. "You scared me half to death. Which one of you...Whose idea was this?"

Like a kid in kindergarten, Bobby pointed to Marsh.

"It was his idea." Bobby was six years old again, telling their mother on them.

"We tried to tell Marsh that you don't like surprises but he insisted. He figured you would like to spend your first night out the lock up with people who love you." Renita rushed to her, kissed her cheek and gave her a big hug.

"We were so worried about you." Syd added after hugging her.

"We tried to visit you but those assholes wouldn't let us see you in there." Carmen's accent was always weighted in terms of her degree of passion about a given situation. Hot words of Spanish profanity followed the statement made in English. The people at the jail had really pissed her off.

"Thanks for being here, guys." Audrey hugged Carmen and patted her back to calm her down. "The important thing is that I'm here now. I didn't realize how much I really cherished and appreciated you all being a part of my life until I thought I'd never see you again." She looked from one to the other through eyes brimming with tears. "I love you all so much."

The water started to flow as they hugged one another.

"Ah, how touching." Marsh laughed, swallowing the lump that was forming in his throat. The doorbell was ringing and he was glad for the distraction. "Open the doors and go on into the living room while I get that."

Bobby unlatched the thick pocket doors and shoved them into the walls. The living room was decorated for a party with streamers, balloons and candles. Platters of spicy chicken wings and cold shrimp for dipping in tangy cocktail sauce beckoned. There was also an array of vegetables and various sauces attractively displayed on a silver platter. They dove into the food and munched while they alternated between quips and praise for Audrey and the ordeal she had made it through.

Somebody turned on the stereo and the guitar strains of Johnny Cash's "*Folsom Prison*" blared throughout the house.

"Oh, I can see where this is going." Audrey said, as the talking and laughter made it seem as though the party was much larger than it was. They looked up when Marsh re-entered with Rob Hollingsworth in tow.

"There's been a report of a disturbance in the area. I stopped by to check it out." Everybody laughed. Rob smiled; grabbing Audrey, he hugged her quickly before moving back and looking into her eyes.

"Happy Release Party, Audrey. I'm so sorry for the pain I caused during this thing. I was *really* trippin'. Forgive me?"

"Without question." She placed a friendly peck on his cheek. "You *were* trippin'" If I didn't love you, I'd be mad as hell." She searched his face for the lines of sadness and worry that had creased it when this whole thing started. Rob's face was smooth and handsome as always. "You okay now?"

"I'm okay." Relief and appreciation that their friendship remained intact was behind his smile. "But I think everybody's going to want to sit down for what I'm about to say."

The small group sat around the semi-circular leather sectional waiting for Rob to continue.

"Theo Griffin was arrested today." Whoops of delight and high five's went around the room.

"When we started telling him the kind of time he was facing, he started singing like a member of the Harlem Boy's Choir. You're not going to believe this Audrey, but your assistant, Carrey Pensky is currently being sought for questioning in the murder of Norma Jean Strange."

A hush went through the room as the group absorbed the information that Rob had just given them.

"There's no way." Audrey sat there stunned, her forehead wrinkled in confusion. The very thought that her trusted employee could be involved, sucked the wind out of her. She looked at Rob teary-eyed. Syd Lawson sprang to her feet, searching Rob's face for clarification.

"What is this, some kind of joke?"

"It's hardly a joke, Syd." He moved past her and sat next to Audrey and pulled her hand into his own. "Griffin claims that Pensky found out about the money that was being taken from the Township. He wanted in. They worked out an elaborate scheme that would increase what they had already been taking ten-fold. They were all pleased—thick as thieves. Except Norma Jean. It pissed her off that he'd found out about the scheme. It made her angrier still when he wanted in and he was bringing his expansion plans along with him. Pensky's inclusion into the clan was a constant source of irritation for her according to Griffin. The two of them were constantly trading insults. While Pensky looked at Norma Jean as some sort of idol, always seeking her approval, Jean hated the sight of him. She was constantly being mean to him. One day she went too far."

Rob rose and stood before them like he needed to make room for everything that he was about to say.

"Pensky apparently came to Griffin's home after he committed the murder. He needed money. He was going to cash in his chips so to speak and get out of town." Rob rammed his hands into his pockets, rocking back and forth as he continued.

"If you believe what Griffin says, the night of the murder, Norma Jean apparently said some rather unflattering things about Pensky's appearance and sexual preference and who knows what all else. The argument turned physical and he killed her."

"That's ridiculous!" Audrey said. "He killed her because she said mean stuff to him? I don't believe it. His skin isn't that thin. Carrey's not that kind of person."

Audrey was standing now too. She walked over to Rob like being closer to him would change what she was hearing.

"We're all that kind of person, given the right set of circumstances." He replied looking down at her. "I guess he suspected it would be just a matter of time before Griffin's larceny would be uncovered. He knew the man would do anything to pull his own ass out of the fire. Carrey has not been at work. He's moved out of his apartment and his mother hasn't seen him. An APB has been issued. We'll track him down."

"I'm so sorry, Audrey." Syd said.

"It's not your fault, Sweetie." Carmen soothed, her Puerto Rican roots flavoring her words. She brushed the wild red hair away from Syd's face before putting her arms around her.

Audrey plopped back on the sofa in stunned silence. She truly liked Carrey but as she sat and thought, their relationship had not been one of substance. She really didn't know him very well at all. What she had most admired about him was his skill as an accountant. But in the end, it was his acumen in accountancy that led to his downfall.

Marsh saw the hurt and confusion on Audrey's face and wanted to lighten her mood.

"Hey, I thought this was supposed to be a party!" He stood with his glass held high.

"That's what I heard." Rob walked over and slapped Marsh on the back. "I'm off duty and I'm ready to throw down. What a brother got to do to get a drank up in here?"

Lloyd moved behind the bar and started taking drink orders. Renita headed for the kitchen while the rest of the happy crowd helped themselves to their favorite libation. The coffee table was filled with packages. Audrey was surprised that they had gotten her presents.

She became suspicious when her sister returned from the kitchen carrying a large square cake covered with swirls of white icing. A metal file protruded from one side and a stick of dynamite sprouted from the other. They all laughed when Audrey read the inscription out loud.

"*By any means necessary.*"

"We were going to bring these things to the courthouse since we didn't know if you would be getting out anytime soon." Renita placed the cake on the table near the packages that Audrey began to open one by one.

Marsh gave her a wink when she opened a box and pulled out his gift; a pair of convict striped, crotch-less pajamas. Bobby gave her a harmonica, a lesson book and a CD titled '*Songs from* the *Chain Gang*'. Audrey gave her brother a nudge.

"Where'd you get this?"

"These are original songs put together by some of the fellas from the old team. Mo Pritchard played harmonica while Paul and I sang. It's destined to be a classic."

"I can't wait to hear it." She said less than enthusiastically, tossing the disk aside. "I'm just kidding. We'll listen to it as soon as I'm done opening the rest of my presents."

She opened Renita's gift next. It was a bar of soap that was shaped like a gun. Rob's gift was a small pick and shovel and tiny bags to carry the dirt away as she tunneled to freedom. Everybody laughed and joked about Audrey bustin' out of the Big House.

There was a huge, rectangular shaped box from Syd and Carmen that contained a collection of movies. Audrey howled as she read the titles: *Penitentiary I, II, and III, The Shawshank Redemption, Birdman of Alcatraz, Women in Cages, I Want to Live.*

"You guys are bad. I should make you all stay here and watch every one back to back."

"They had '*Hurricane*' in that box but I had to keep that one for myself." Renita said.

"If I get locked up, I'd want it to be with Denzel!"

"You and Denzel. That's the only way he would give you some play...if he was on lockdown." Bobby said, ducking when his sister hurled a pretzel at him.

"Why don't we pop some corn and let Audrey tell us stories about how many guards she had to shank." Bobby said as he went over to the bar. "Did you have to fight off any big-breasted women who wanted to make you their girlfriend?"

"You did fight them off, didn't you babe?" Marsh couldn't resist getting involved in the fun.

"I'm going to pretend I didn't hear that." Audrey rolled her eyes at them. "If you really want to know how it is, try it for yourself sometime. Now, what movie are we going to watch?"

Women in Cages won out over the other flicks. They howled with laughter as Pam Grier gave 'em hell. It was still as bad a movie as they'd all remembered. Luckily, it was still as short.

Audrey put in '*I Want To Live*' and welled up as Susan Hayward spouted her innocence in the role of Barbara Graham. The guys all hissed and booed until she let them watch '*Penitentiary*'.

"Now if they'd had some fine brothers like Leon Isaac Kennedy in that cell with Audrey, she would have confessed to all that shit." Renita reached over and her sister gave her five.

"I would have had to do that time, girl." She quipped as Marsh pulled her down to where he was sitting on the floor.

"Oh, yeah? Well, we're going to reenact the shower scene tonight little missy. You better be ready."

"You the one better be ready." Audrey replied. "Tonight I'm going to make you *my* girlfriend."

"Just don't let her disrespect you man." Rob told Marsh. He pounded his chest a couple of times with his fist in a gesture of male solidarity. "Be strong!"

"The minute she calls you bitch, you got to leave her man 'cause the abuse just escalates from there." Bobby added.

"Thanks, guys. You know I don't want to go out like no punk." They laughed as they connected knuckles.

"True dat." Bobby swallowed down the remnants of his drink then uncapped a Michelob and guzzled it from the bottle.

"So when is your place going to be ready, Audrey?" Rob took a swig of beer.

"Tomorrow." She replied. "Did the police ever find out who was responsible for the break-in?"

"Oh man! I knew there was something I meant to tell ya'll." Bobby came from behind the bar. "You remember when we were at the Rack that night and that hot little mama that was giving Marsh such grief?"

They nodded remembering how Chloe had made such a fool of herself.

"I caught up with that little honey on her way out the door and we started talking."

"No, you didn't!" Audrey couldn't believe he would want to deal with that chick after the way she acted.

"Shoot—that girl is fine! Wasn't no women in the club that night. Syd and Carmen was there lookin' all luscious and just as gay as they wanna be."

Carmen licked her tongue at him suggestively and everyone laughed at the disgusted look on Bobby's face. He looked at them and shook his head. He took a swig of beer like he was trying to wash away a bad taste before raising his eyebrows and casting a glance in Marsh's direction trying to ignore Carmen.

"Anyway...Marsh was through with her and I didn't see no point in lettin' all that go to waste. I had to check it out." He gulped from the bottle and stifled a belch before continuing.

"Girl is nutty as hell. We was kicking it one night and started talking about old relationships. She told me all about you and her in Beantown, Marsh. She said she had to quit you cause you were just too possessive."

Everybody broke up at that.

"She said you ran down here to try to get over your hurt after she rejected you for the last time. She said you was calling her begging every night until she moved here."

"No, she didn't." Marsh shook his head in disbelief.

"If I'm lyin' I'm flyin'." Bobby said. "Anyway, she said you couldn't run away from your feelings for her and was mad when she didn't follow you."

Marsh just laughed and said, "I told you the woman is trippin'."

"You ain't lyin'. She told me you came here and hooked up with some black chick. It made her mad that she came all this way after you begged her to be with you and to find you had another woman. Anyway, she decides to start putting pressure on the rival hoping that will make her leave Marsh alone. I really wasn't paying too much attention to what she was saying at first. I wasn't trying to get to know her, I was just trying to get some."

He grinned before gulping some beer.

"Anyway, she said she followed this woman a couple of times and tried to run her off the road once. When she said something about trashing a house—I said wait a minute, what's the address? When she told me, I cussed that crazy bitch out."

Everybody fell out laughing.

"So that's the fool that committed felony feng shui at your place." Renita chimed in. "Nice work."

"How did she get into my house?" Audrey puzzled.

"Shit if I know." Bobby replied, shaking his head. "Crazy people can figure out everything except how to get some damn help."

"Ain't that the truth?" Lloyd quipped, raising his drink in agreement.

"Audrey, you should press charges against this woman." Syd said. Her face was wrinkled with concern. She still felt bad about Carrey and all the trouble he'd caused her.

"I agree." Rob said. "With a statement from Bobby, she would most likely get some time in jail." Rob was on a mission. He wanted to lock up somebody.

"You could also recover damages in a civil action." Carmen added.

"You better watch out man. Chloe won't take too kindly to you ratting her out. She's a stalker." Marsh told Bobby. "Once she gets her hooks in you, she don't want to let go."

Bobby smacked his full lips and waved an unconcerned hand.

"Marsh, I ain't even goin' there. I told that mutha fucka if I ever see her again or if she even think about bothering ya'll, she'd be pullin' one of these size sixteen's out her ass." He kicked the air with a long, wide alligator skin enclosed foot. "She just acting crazy. I told her crazy and me on a first name basis. She won't be stalking *nobody* else."

Everybody roared. Audrey and Renita knew their brother and knew he wasn't lying.

"So Bobby, how many times you bust that ass before she opened up her heart and told you her whole life story?" Rob had sidled up to him, trying to whisper, but everybody heard him.

"Who cares?" Audrey injected. "What about all the other stuff that was happening to me? The damage to my car, being followed, and run off the road, the phone calls. That nut did all that?"

"I suspect Griffin's hired thugs took care of some of the more unsavory aspects of trying to get you to cease and desist." Rob said between chomps on a chicken wing before continuing.

"Two crack-heads were picked up for snatching a woman's purse. One of them started singing about Theo Griffin when his rap sheet and history of small crimes made it apparent that he was looking at doing some hard time.

"Mr. Griffin is in so deep, he'll need a miracle to see the light of day within the next twenty years. As for the calls, that was your illustrious office manager, Mr. Pensky. He was also the actress who portrayed Audrey Wilson on some of the fabricated tapes."

"I still can't believe Carrey would stab me in the back like that." Audrey said.

"I'm sorry that I referred him to you." Syd was still feeling guilty that she had recommended a killer to work for her good friend.

"Don't worry about it, Syd—really. There's no way you could have known he would do that to me. I did a background check when he was hired and it came back clean." She threw her hands up in exasperation. "I trusted him completely."

"You shouldn't be such a puck." Renita told her.

"Just because I like to see the good in people doesn't mean I'm a dummy."

"You're right, honey." Marsh said condescendingly, kissing her forehead.

"Well, it doesn't." she said, rolling her eyes, resenting his patronizing tone.

"What about Griffin's wife?" Renita asked.

"If the court is lenient, she'll get off with probation. She knew that Griffin was stealing and she only spilled the beans when it was way past obvious that the marriage was over. Considering all the mental abuse heaped on her by Griffin, a slick lawyer will most likely get her to walk with little trouble."

"There's also that bastard Sylvester Alstead. He was just as involved as Griffin wasn't he?" Audrey was still smarting from the memory of that day in the park.

"Fortunately for him, there is no evidence to incriminate him. He's still at large for his attack on you." Rob said.

"He'll surface." Marsh gave her a reassuring hug. "They always do."

"But when?" Renita asked. "If you ask me, he's just as dangerous as Carrey."

"I wouldn't worry about him." Rob replied. "He middle aged, professional and has no record so I doubt he's a real threat. Guys like that committing crimes are rare."

"Maybe he and Chloe will meet and cancel each other out. Syd said with a smirk.

"That would serve his ass right." Renita clinked glasses with Syd and everybody laughed.

They partied into the night. It felt good for Audrey to be in the company of those who really loved her. Warmth blanketed her, making the torture of the last few months fade into the distance. She felt truly blessed and her heart felt tremendously full.

44

For what seemed like the dozenth time, the first CD dropped into place. Audrey had loaded three disks into the player, and then drove her car to Chillicothe without hearing a single note. She'd thought music would put her in a better frame of mind, transporting her to a time when things were perfect. But things had not been perfect. A good part of her life had been a lie.

It wasn't until she turned off the exit that she started to focus on the music that she'd turned down earlier to make room for the flood of thoughts that battered her brain like an abusive mate. She felt like she'd lost the ability to trust at a level that she'd never experienced before. She didn't know if she'd ever get over the pain.

Jill Scott's *Getting' In The Way* beat through the speakers and Audrey turned the knob letting the song fill the space. She remembered the first time she'd heard the song. It was last year. She and Norma Jean laughed about the part in the song when Jill talks about Queens shouldn't swing, but she was considering throwing down anyhow. If Audrey had known then what she knew now, she would have given Norma Jean an old-fashioned ghetto ass kickin'. But that was a long time ago. Norma Jean was dead.

It had been more than six months since the trial. To Audrey the whole thing seemed like a bizarre dream; a stage play starring everyone that she knew, portraying characters she didn't know at all.

She looked out on the expanse of corn and wheat, reaching up to shake hands with the setting sun. Talk about being in the middle of nowhere, this was surely the place. Since it was only a three and a half hour ride by car, she had decided to drive up to the prison. It hadn't occurred to Audrey that the roads along the way would be so desolate.

She swallowed the lump that formed in her throat, hoping she hadn't made another wrong turn. Each long road, every field of grain, looked exactly like the last. She would now have to get a room once she reached town. There were no lights on these country roads and there was no way she would be driving back at night. It made her start to second-guess her decision not to tell anyone that she was making this trip.

Renita and Bobby would have told her she was crazy and seeing her determination, would have come with her. Marsh wouldn't have wanted to hear it...period. He would have chained himself to her car or had his new friend, Rob Hollingsworth, put a boot on the wheel to keep her from driving it. But this was something that she had to do. She had to do it alone.

Audrey had been calling the prison for months but her calls had been refused. When he'd finally agreed to talk to her, it had caught her off guard after so many rejections. She had just about resigned herself to the fact that she never would know the truth.

A huge structure came into view. Before it, row upon row of some unrecognizable plant sprouted green and leggy inside miles of barbed wire fencing. Audrey turned off the main road onto the long blacktopped driveway that led to the cold gray prison. She parked in the area designated for visitors and headed for the entrance.

"Miss. Walk over to the telephone booth and pick up the receiver." A voice boomed as she headed for the entranceway. Audrey looked around and then up. There was movement in the lightly tinted glass on top of a watchtower.

Audrey looked around and saw no one else he could be talking to. A telephone booth stood to the right of the door leading into the building. She stepped inside and placed her hand on the instrument and put it to her ear.

She was asked a series of questions about whom she was visiting, and whether she had any concealed weapons, by the guard in the tower overhead. After responding, she was permitted entrance into the massive stone building.

She walked through a metal detector and was led to a small waiting room. It was less than five minutes before a guard in a tan uniform took her into one of the private meeting rooms.

A glass wall separated the chair upon which she sat from the seat on the other side of the table. She waited so long that she wished she had thought to bring something to read.

When the door was finally opened, the man who entered looked nothing like the way Audrey remembered. The familiar blond do was replaced by a dark brown crew cut. His face was washed clean of the heavy make-up that did an excellent job of hiding the scars, blotches and pockmarks that were prevalent on his slender face.

He sat across the pane from Audrey, pushed a cigarette between his down turned lips, waiting for the guard to light it. He inhaled deeply before looking into her eyes.

"Go ahead. Ask your questions, Audrey."

"What happened, Carrey? I thought we were friends." She looked into cold, unblinking cyan eyes set in the emotionless face of a stranger.

"Well that's what you get for thinking." He blew smoke in the direction of her face. It ricocheted from the glass back to him.

"Why are you mad at me?" Audrey was completely nonplused. She threw her hands up in frustration before slamming them onto the table. "If you didn't want to talk to me, you should have let me know and I would have kept my black ass where I was."

"All right girlfriend, don't get your panties in a knot." The man was schizophrenic. The old Carrey was back. The drag attire was gone, but the persona was there, hidden beneath the mottled skin.

"That bitch Norma Jean fucked up everything."

"What are you talking about Carrey?"

"I'm talking about The Operation. They had a good little set-up. When I found out about it, I wanted to be a part of it. I told them they were drinking the foam and leaving the beer. I told them if they got with me we could enjoy a good beer, leave the suds, and no one would ever know. They all hated me. But their greed got the best of them."

Carrey's face contorted in a self-satisfied smirk.

"They were a collection, let me tell you." He took another drag and exhaled smoke. "That wimpy-assed Griffin would have gone along with anything not to make waves. He hated me. Because I'm gay and because I'm smart. I don't know of which he had the greater phobia." He pulled on the cigarette, squinting as the white smoke irritated his eyes. He held the white stick, pulling it away from his face and frowning at the opaque cloud it left behind.

"Sarah Collins is possibly the iciest bitch that ever walked the earth. She resisted at first. But when I convinced them how I could widen their little net of larceny, greed won out over whatever ill feelings the ice queen had toward me. Sy Alstead is like the stupidest motherfucker that ever slid out of a bitch's slimy cunt." Carrey took another drag enjoying each nicotine rush more than the last. "To this day he doesn't know what he was involved in. He was used to procure legitimate contracts. We made the phony ones mirror these companies with the exception of a lower or upper case letter, or some characteristic that could by-pass their computerized accounting systems. The vendors are huge. They have no idea we were double billing them. If they're ever audited—look out!" He laughed until he coughed. Then he pulled on the cigarette again.

"Wait a minute." Audrey interrupted. "The money was taken from the Federal Grants to Rosemont."

"Oh we took the grant money, but we tested the process on commercial vendors first." He laughed again, this time until he coughed up phlegm. Audrey couldn't believe his gall. He spoke as cavalierly as if he were reading a script. He didn't care that he had nearly ruined her life. She watched the redness in his face lighten as the coughing subsided.

"Where was I? Oh yeah, Laughton Glen knew nothing about the plan. He's just a lazy bastard who doesn't care about anything but playing golf as a guest at country clubs that won't let him be a member."

Carrey stopped and rolled his eyes at the stupidity of this man that he obviously didn't think too highly of.

"He never looked into updating the hardware or programs with something that had better controls. He just didn't care."

He sucked on the cigarette. The paper went from red to gray as it burned and thickened the air with smoke.

"The systems that Rosemont uses are so antiquated we had a field day processing phony invoices. The imitators were GAS subs. GAS of course, was the creation of Norma Jean Strange."

"What tipped you off to what they were doing?"

"Oh, Norma Jean did. Not intentionally, though. She used to come by the office when you weren't there. We'd do the girlfriend, chitchat thing. She just pretended to be my friend. But I really liked her back then. She was beautiful, had a wonderful sense of style. I made no secret of the fact that I tried to emulate her in little ways at the office. During the gigs with the band, I would really let my hair down. What performances those were!" His eyes held a faraway, glassy look.

"When I was on that stage, I *was* Norma Jean Strange. I was so good. Anyone who knows Jean said I had her dead to rights. A mutual acquaintance caught the show and told her about it. Anyone else would have been flattered, but not Miss Thang. Oh no." He held up his hand like he was testifying in court. "Her ass was all up on her back about it. Whenever she'd get "Strange" with me, I would put on my Norma Jean bit and it would drive her up the wall."

Carrey laughed until he wheezed. He took another drag of the cigarette. Hazy blue smoke filtered from his lips and rose above his head.

"Anyway, I had gone to get my highlights done. I'd forgotten to bring a picture that I wanted to show Evan, my stylist, so I came back upstairs.

"I opened the door to the office and there's Jean, rummaging through my desk like a rat at a cracker factory. She came up with some lame-ass excuse when I fronted her. I acted like everything was cool. As soon as she left I checked the stationery and other supplies. I'd thought that you had taken some of my stash when I noticed them low before. I should have known something was up because you have me do all of your correspondence. I made a mental note to ask you about it when you came in. I logged onto your PC and started checking into some of the files that Jean had left with you. It didn't take long to figure out what they were doing."

"I never suspected Norma Jean of a thing."

"You never paid any attention to Jean." He waved a dismissive hand. "She was a pain in your ass and that's exactly what she was trying to be. She always gave you some inane bullshit to work on so you wouldn't take her seriously. She didn't want you to delve into what was really going on with Rosemont's books. She just wanted your name placed strategically enough so that when the shit hit the fan, it would splatter all over you and not her." He waved the cigarette like Bette Davis. "Don't you just love her?"

Carrey stamped out the remains of the cigarette and looked over at the guard and gave him a salacious wink.

"Hey handsome, how about giving me something sweet to suck on?"

The guard tossed him the pack and the matches like he was afraid of catching something. Carrey blew the man a kiss before lighting up and inhaling like he hadn't just finished a cigarette a minute before.

"I called Theo Griffin and told him that he was to set up a meeting with all the principals or I'd go straight to the police. The chicken shit bastard tried to play hardball with me until I gave him detailed entries into the primitive ledgers that Norma Jean had set up and how quickly I could prove to the authorities what they were doing. I gave him my number and told him if I didn't hear from him by nine o'clock that night, I'd be talking to the cops by nine a.m. the next day."

"You never thought about coming to me with this information, Carrey?"

"What for? You had every opportunity to see what to me was so obvious it was ridiculous. You let the annoyance that you felt for this woman overshadow your professionalism. I must say girlfriend, as sharp as you are, I was surprised that you let this happen to you. You let Jean use you so easily. Why shouldn't I take advantage of an opportunity to become rich before I'm even thirty years old?"

Though what he said was true, Audrey couldn't get over his nerve. He spoke to her with such disdain. Had he possessed these feelings for her all along?

"You made those calls to me, didn't you?"

"Guilty as charged." He flicked a wicked hand upward as quick as a serpent's tongue and laughed. "That was just to shake you up. I knew that you had to be moving closer to figuring out what we were doing. I thought I could help scare you into leaving this thing alone, but you just kept on pokin' around. Griffin wanted to have you killed."

Audrey thought about the vicious phone calls she'd received and the day she was nearly run-over and shuddered. She snapped back to the present as Carrey continued his story.

"Griffin called me that night, nine o'clock on the dot. We met an hour later, Griffin, Sarah Collins, Jean and me. I told them that I needed to look at the accounting software that they used. If the system had the flaws that I surmised, I had a plan that could take what they were currently doing and multiply it many times over.

"They were all ears as I explained my theory on how we could beat the system. As I said, the imitators were my idea. I told them that I could produce letters recommending them as worthy vendors and sign your name. Everybody was excited, their greed pushing me to continue, telling them how they could expand their wealth. Everybody but Norma Jean. Jean saw this as a demotion of sorts, a step down, if you will from her lofty position as the go to girl, the person with all of the answers.

"But the others quickly adopted my proposal, moving Jean to a subordinate role in our little organization. She took every opportunity to diss me. She was mean and bitchy. It hurt because I really loved her. I never understood why she was so mean to me. People have messed with me my whole life, called me names. Sure it hurt, but they meant nothing to me. I thought she was different. She acted like she liked me at first and I was so glad. I idolized her. I would have done anything for her."

"What happened that Friday?"

Carrey looked at Audrey like he had forgotten she was in the room. A long gray cylinder of ash had formed on the end of the cigarette. Carrey tapped it and the ashes tumbled to the floor. He took another drag before continuing.

"She and I were supposed to meet that evening. I'd found out that Jean was trying to undercut me. She should have known that she couldn't get anything by me. But she always tried. She had some flimsy document that implemented me and you as partners in a theft ring. I laughed when I saw what she'd put together."

"I tried to tell her to relax, that everything was fine the way that it was. She told me to get out of her office. She didn't want to talk to me anymore that night but I forced the issue. I told that her that she needed to let go of this jealousy that she had for me before she ruined everything.

"She laughed at me. I can still hear her...still see her. She touched my hair that I'd just had done, and laughed. It looked just like hers. She used to wear that little upsweep in back with tiny-feathered crimps around her face. It was so chic. I'd gotten a wig that I had cut in that style. I wore it during my gigs while letting my hair grow out enough so that Evan, that's my stylist, could fix mine just like hers. I'd just left the salon and rushed over so Jean could see my hair. It was laid, girl. It was exactly like hers, only platinum.

"I thought she would have been flattered. But she was pissed. She must have taken a double dose of her bitch pills that day. Not only did she say a lot of ugly things to me, she laughed at my do and said I'd never have the right equipment to be her no matter what I did. Then she hauled off and hocked the biggest Louie you've ever seen, right into my hair. Before I knew it, I decked the bitch. She stood there for a minute and looked at me like I had lost my mind. Maybe I had. She snapped out of it pretty quickly though and it was on."

Carrey patted his bristle stiff hair like he'd just left Evan's chair.

"I spent all morning and eighty-five bucks getting my hair done and she messed it up. Jealous bitch! I was so upset, I couldn't do nothing but cry." He put the cigarette to his lips. It had burned down to a stub.

"She laughed at me." He stabbed out the cigarette with so much force the table shook. He looked at Audrey with cold hate filled eyes that brimmed with the redness of the painful memory and cigarette smoke.

"I could think of only one way to hurt her. You know those trashy, heavy ass faux Faberge eggs that she liked to give people?"

Audrey nodded.

"I took the big one, her favorite, and put it inside this long sleeved tee shirt I had wrapped around my waist. That got her! She was pissed and started trying to snatch the egg from me. I hit her with it and it felt like a good fuckin' high." He was smiling now, remembering the pleasure he felt at having the last laugh.

"She was dazed but when her head cleared, she hit me back. The bitch had some power too." Carrey laughed. "If it had been someone else she was hitting instead of me, I would have been impressed."

Carrey's eyes were glazed over. A strange, silly little laugh escaped his lips.

"Honey, we were going at it, just punching each other like two men. I don't mind telling you, she was more man than me in that department." Carrey felt around in the cigarette pack but it was empty. He crumpled it and let it fall to the floor.

"I grabbed my little makeshift weapon and just started flailing on her ass. She fell and hit her head on the desk. Her head split open and she lay there not blinking. I knew she was dead but I didn't give a shit. The way I figured it, I was doing the world a favor."

Carrey looked at Audrey with an evil glint in his eye. A wicked laugh bubbled up and slipped out. It was the sick, scary, uncontrollable laughter of a madman. Audrey was terrified that she had spent so much time with this dangerous man and had never known him at all.

Their visit was over. Audrey heaved a sigh of relief that Carrey Pensky was locked away and would remain that way for a long, long time.

* * *

Audrey woke early the next morning and was checking out of her room at the Days Inn in Chillocothe. The haggard woman behind the desk had the small black and white tuned to the news. Audrey froze as a flash of the familiar face stopped her cold. There had been a fire in one of the cells at the prison last night. Carrey Pensky was found on the charred mattress with severe burns over most of his body. He died of asphyxiation from the fumes.

"Something's always going on out at that prison. They say that boy started the fire on purpose. He cooked up some kind of gasoline and doused it all over himself. Set hisself on fire." The woman shook her head as she processed Audrey's bill. "Seems kind of stupid to give those people matches don't' you think?

Audrey just nodded.

"What would make somebody take they self out like that?" The woman drawled. "Musta been crazy. Or just plain bad."

"I guess you're right about that." Audrey wiped at a tear as she took the receipt from the clerk and left the building.

The day was warm and so bright that she had to blink several times before she could focus. She pushed a pair of dark sunglasses in front of her wet lashes and took a deep ragged breath. The air smelled of dew and freshly mown grass. Birds danced and sang in the morning sun that shown as bright as any new day's promise. Audrey inhaled the newness, letting its splendor wash away the grief of lost friendships and loves that never were.

About the Author

C.M. Miller is an Ohio native currently residing with her family in Georgia.

ACCRUAL WAY TO DIE is the second installment in the Audrey Wilson Mystery Series. *Taxes, Death, & Trouble* is available through iUniverse.com. Look for *What She Left* Behind in 2002. E-mail feedback to www.Pageturner.net/coramiller

0-595-19165-7